Make a Stand

Make a Stand

AGNEW SMITH

Make a Stand

This is a work of fiction. All of the characters, names, incidents, organizations, and dialogue in this novel are either the products of the author's imagination or are used fictitiously.

iUniverse books may be ordered through booksellers or by contacting:

iUniverse
1663 Liberty Drive
Bloomington, IN 47403
www.iuniverse.com
1-800-Authors (1-800-288-4677)

ISBN: 978-1-4917-4300-3 (sc)

Library of Congress Control Number: 2014913964

Printed in the United States of America.

iUniverse rev. date: 02/09/2015

To my wonderful mother, Bernice
Your love and devotion is like a flame that can never be extinguished

To my loving sister, Teresa
Your kindness and motivation inspires me to be the best that I can be

To my special daughter, Ashley
You bring continuous happiness into my life
I love you with all my heart

To my father and hero, James
You were called home to glory, but you will never be forgotten
Your strength, courage and love lives on within me

To my family and friends
Thank you for your prayers and encouragement

And to God for blessing me with His eternal love

Chapter 1

The Atlanta Convention Center was packed as celebrities from every entertainment field frantically searched for available seats for the start of the annual music awards program. Screaming fans were pushing and shoving from the lobby to the balcony, trying to get a glimpse of their favorite stars. Terry Freeman was sitting in the second row, excited that he and his band, Infinite Noise, were one of a select few nominated for the music artist of the year award. The other nominees sitting around them glanced their way, perhaps anticipating that Infinite Noise would be taking home the prestigious award this year. The room brightened and music blared loudly as last year's winner, Lorene Jennings, walked to the center of the stage. As she reached the center stage podium, she took a moment to wave at her many fans that were showering her with applause. Moments later, she was handed a sealed envelope. She opened it and began to smile as she announced the winner. "Ladies and gentlemen, the music artist of the year award goes to . . . ." A loud noise goes off and Terry is awakened in his bed. "Damn," he said to himself as the sound of his alarm clock shattered his dream. He hit the snooze button and rolled over hoping to finish his dream, but he knew he needed to get up now if he was going to make it to church on time. Terry was asked by his uncle to play the guitar for the church choir and he didn't want to be late, especially since his uncle was the pastor of the church. He glanced at the clock on his night stand and convinced himself that he had enough time to take a quick shower, get dressed, and drive to his uncle's church in College Park. Forty minutes later, he was driving into the parking lot of Keep the Faith Baptist Church. He quickly looked into the rearview mirror to make sure his tie was on correctly, noticing the stubbles of hair on his unshaven face. As he sprinted to the church, he noticed the large banner attached to the side door leading to the choir room, which read, "Fifteen Year

Anniversary." Fifteen years ago, his uncle, Pastor Henry Freeman, started a small, Baptist church with a modest congregation of around thirty members. Today, the church had grown to around 250 members. With a lot of hard work from the congregation and generous donations, Terry's uncle was able to build an addition to the church to accommodate the growing members. As Terry entered the church, he noticed Deacon Pedigrue and the rest of the choir lining up and preparing to enter the sanctuary.

"Has anyone seen Terrence?" Deacon Pedigrue asked.

"I'm right here," Terry said, rushing into the room.

"I'm so glad you made it," Deacon Pedigrue said, shaking Terry's hand.

"Sorry, I'm a little late."

"You're not late, you're right on time. Have you heard from Reginald?" Deacon Pedigrue asked, handing Terry his choir robe.

"No, I tried to call him on his cell phone before I got here, but he never answered."

"Nobody's been able to reach him. Where could he be?" Deacon Pedigrue asked, sounding concerned.

"Maybe he's running a little late," Terry said, trying to sound optimistic.

Knowing his cousin, Reggie, he was probably still in bed with a hangover or exhausted from partying all night. The rich, vibrant sound of a pipe organ began playing and the members of the church choir started walking into the sanctuary.

"Is everybody else here?" Terry asked.

"Yes. I'm sure you hear Sister Jenkins out there playing the organ. Deacon Young is already on stage making sure all the instruments are hooked up. We're just missing our drummer."

"Don't worry. If Reggie doesn't make it, you can take his place."

"Me?" Deacon Pedigrue responded, with a surprised look on his face. "Terry, I don't think I can do this. I'm way out of my league," he said, looking nervous. "Sister Jenkins teaches music at Spelman College. Deacon Young has been playing the bass guitar for over twenty years. You've been playing the guitar for several years in your band. Everyone is more experienced than I am. I'm just a beginner on the drums."

Terry walked over and put his hand on Deacon Pedigrue's shoulder.

"Listen to me. I've heard you play before. You're a better drummer than you think you are."

"I appreciate that, but you shouldn't lie in church," he said, smiling.

"Just relax and you'll do just fine. I believe in you. You know what our pastor always says."

"Yeah, I know, I know. Keep the faith."

"Come on, let's go out there and raise the roof off this church," Terry said, patting Deacon Pedigrue on his back for some much needed encouragement.

As the two walked toward the main sanctuary, they could hear Sister Jenkins playing the final version of her song, signaling the start of church service. As Terry and Deacon Pedigrue entered the side door leading to the stage, Deacon Young greeted them with a smile.

"Good morning, Terrence. I already made sure your guitar is tuned and ready to go," Deacon Young whispered to Terry.

"Thank you," Terry whispered back. As he sat down with the other members of the choir, his uncle, Pastor Henry Freeman, walked up to the podium to address the congregation.

"Good morning, church. The Lord has blessed us with another beautiful day. Please give Sister Jenkins a round of applause for her beautiful playing. She has been the church organist for twelve years and we are so blessed to have her play for us each Sunday." The church began to applaud, with shouts of "amen" throughout the sanctuary. "I'm so glad you could all be here this morning for Keep the Faith Baptist Church's fifteen-year anniversary. We've come a long way and we're going to keep on keeping on!" The church erupted with loud cheers and applause. "We have a special treat for everyone. The youth and adult choirs will be performing together. They have been working extremely hard and I know we're going to be blessed with a glorious performance."

As Terry put the strap of his guitar around his neck, he looked up and noticed his uncle smiling at him.

"Before our choir performs, I would like to acknowledge my nephew, Terrence Freeman, for being part of our anniversary celebration. Terrence was a member of our very first youth choir and now he's here this morning as part of our adult choir. Now that he's performing with the adult choir, I guess I need to start calling him, Terry." The congregation laughed in unison as Terry smiled and waved to his uncle. "Amen!" Pastor Freeman shouted into the microphone. "I believe Terry's mother is here this morning," he said, looking around at the seated worshipers. "There she is. Please stand up, Cora."

Terry's mother stood up as the congregation applauded loudly. Terry looked over at his mother who was wearing a beautiful pink dress with a matching hat. His mother looked over at Terry and waved at him, with a big smile, as he blew her a kiss in return. Pastor Freeman glanced at Sister Jenkins seated at the organ. She nodded to him, indicating that the choir was ready to perform. "And now, the Keep the Faith Baptist Church choir will perform for us." Pastor Freeman walked over to his chair on the stage and sat down while Sister Jenkins raised her hand to direct the choir. The choir began singing, "There's A Bright Side," an uplifting gospel song that had the entire church clapping their hands and stomping their feet. Terry smiled as he watched Deacon Pedigrue playing the drums. The deacon started off playing a little nervously, but shortly afterward, he was bobbing his head and tapping his feet to the rhythm of the song. It became very obvious that Deacon Pedigrue was definitely "caught up in the holy spirit." When his uncle asked him to play for the church's fifteen-year anniversary, Terry was somewhat reluctant. Performing in his uncle's church brought back so many fond memories, but also the sad memories. However, it was the church's anniversary and he wasn't going to let his uncle down. After the choir finished their last song, the congregation jumped to their feet in loud applause. Pastor Freeman walked up to the podium, clapping his hands.

"Thank you, choir! Let me hear the church say, amen!" he shouted into the microphone.

"Amen!" the church responded.

After the congregation settled down, Pastor Freeman began to preach. His sermon for the day was about patience and forgiveness. As Terry listened to the sermon, he couldn't help but wonder if the message was somehow directed to his cousin, Reggie. Even though

Reggie was seven years younger than Terry, they had always been very close cousins. Terry's younger brother, Warren, was about the same age as Reggie and they were more like brothers than cousins. Around the age of sixteen, Reggie began to go through a dramatic personality change. He started getting into a lot of fights at school, his grades started to decline, and he started hanging around the wrong crowd. When Reggie turned eighteen, he would constantly hang out in the clubs and party almost every night. Terry always assumed it was because Reggie was trying to prove to everyone that he wasn't soft or weak because he was the son of a preacher. Terry's thoughts were broken by the loud sound of his uncle's voice, preaching a sermon that had the congregation standing and shouting their approval. After Pastor Freeman finished his sermon, he said a prayer and ended the church service.

"Thank you all for worshipping with us on our fifteen year anniversary. Please join us downstairs in the dining room. We have a wonderful anniversary meal prepared by many of our talented church members. God bless you all and I'll see you in the dining room." Sister Jenkins began playing the organ, signaling the end of church service. Terry walked over to Sister Jenkins and gently patted her on the back.

"You were making that organ sing, Sister Jenkins."

"Thank you, Terrence," she said, reaching out to shake his hand while still playing the organ with the other. "Maybe one day you can teach me how to play that electric guitar."

"No problem. You just let me know when you're ready," he said, waving good-bye to her. As the congregation began to slowly leave the church, Terry began to dismantle and help pack up the church's musical instruments.

"I think we sounded pretty good," Deacon Pedigrue said, tapping his drumsticks on the wooden chair beside Terry.

"Pretty good? The way you were playing those drums, we sounded great."

"I was okay," he said, modestly. "I started off a little slow, but I think I played better halfway through the song. Anyway, I just want to thank you for all your words of encouragement. You are a very talented musician and you've motivated me to become a better drummer. Your father would be very proud of you."

"I appreciate that, Deacon Pedigrue," Terry said, shaking Pedigrue's hand.

"Terrence, you and the choir sounded just wonderful," a voice said from behind. Terry turned around and received a warm hug by Mrs. Paula Dalton, vice-president of the church committee.

"Thank you, Mrs. Dalton," he said, giving her a hug.

"I hope we'll see more of you in church. We need strong, dedicated men like you in our church."

"Yes, ma'am. Take care, Mrs. Dalton."

"Hello, Terrence. It's so good to see you in the choir again," another church member said, patting him on the back.

"Thank you, Mr. Wilson."

For the next fifteen minutes, Terry is hugged, kissed and his hand shaken by what seemed like every member of the church. As Terry slowly walked through the crowded church, he looked up and saw his mother talking to his uncle. Seeing them standing together, reminded Terry of the times his mother and father were smiling and laughing after church service. As Terry walked over to talk to his mother and uncle, he felt someone patting him on the back. He turned around and saw Mrs. Darlene Braxton, the church's oldest member. Everyone affectionately called her Mother Braxton and even though she was in her early nineties, she was a very energetic lady who would talk your ear off if you gave her the chance.

"Terrence Freeman. It's a blessing to see you in church today," she said, giving him a hug.

"How are you, Mother Braxton?"

"I guess I'm doing okay. I woke up this morning and my feet were swollen. Then, as I was leaving my house, my arthritis started flaring up in my joints," she said, rubbing her shoulder.

"I'm sorry to hear that, Mother Braxton," he said, trying to sound sympathetic.

"I closed my eyes and said Lord, let me make it to church this morning and here I am. Thank you, Jesus! God can do anything, but fail!" she said, waving her hands up in the air.

"Yes, ma'am," Terry responded, hoping she wasn't going to start preaching to him. Mother Braxton reached out and grabbed Terry's hand.

"Just look at you. You're the spitting image of your daddy, God bless his soul." "Where is your little brother, Warrick?"

"*Warren* didn't make it," he said, correcting her.

"Oh, that's right, it's Warren. I saw Pastor Freeman's wife a little earlier, but I haven't seen Reginald," she said, looking around the sanctuary.

"I don't think he's here, either, ma'am."

"What? That young man knows he should be here, especially with his father preaching on the church's fiftieth anniversary."

"I believe it's fifteen, Mother Braxton," he said, politely correcting her again.

"Fifteen? Isn't that what I said? Anyway, I just don't know about these young people today. When I was their age, my parents made sure I was in church every Sunday. You start moving away from the church, Satan will start moving into your heart."

"Yes, ma'am." Terry could tell Mother Braxton was getting ready to get on a roll, so he knew he needed to get away from her quickly, before it was too late. "I'm sorry to interrupt you, Mother Braxton, but I've got to catch up with my mother before she leaves."

"I saw your mother standing up in church this morning. She is such a wonderful, Christian woman. You be sure to tell her that Mother Braxton said hello."

"Yes ma'am, I'll tell her. It was really nice talking to you, Mother Braxton," he said, quickly walking away.

Before anyone else could approach him, Terry quickly walked over to his mother and uncle.

"Hey, momma. You look absolutely beautiful in that dress," he said, giving her a hug.

"And you are looking very handsome," she replied, straightening his tie. "You and the choir sounded wonderful."

"Yes, they did," Pastor Freeman said, giving Terry a hug. "Thank you again for coming today."

"No problem, Uncle Henry. I really enjoyed performing with the choir. Thanks for asking me to participate."

"It reminded me back in the day when you, Warren and Reggie were playing in the youth choir.

Even though we were a small church back then, we knew how to sing and praise the Lord," Pastor Freeman said, raising his bible up in the air. "I really appreciate you coming. It's nice to know I can depend on most of my family. Deacon Pedigrue did a great job filling in for Reggie on the drums."

"Maybe Reggie wasn't feeling well." Cora said, trying to be diplomatic.

"I guess it's hard to get up and come to church when you're out at the clubs all night and coming home at 4:30 am," he said, shaking his head.

"I've raised two sons, so I know what you're going through, Henry," Cora said, laughing.

"Hold on, momma. I didn't hang out at the clubs all night," Terry said, defending himself.

"No, you would just sneak into night clubs when you were under age," she said, looking at Terry with that motherly grin.

"I guess my son is going through that stage that most young people go through. I'm going to have to put in some extra prayers for him. Anyway, I need to head on down to the dining room so I can make sure I get a slice of your sweet potato pie, Cora."

"Don't worry. I baked a whole pie just for you," she replied.

"God bless you, Cora," Henry said, giving her a kiss on the cheek. "Terry, it was wonderful to see you in church today. I hope I'll see you here more often," he said, giving Terry a hug.

"Thank you, Uncle Henry." As Terry's uncle walked away, his mother reached out and gently grabbed her son's hand.

"He's right. It is wonderful to see you here at church again." As Terry gave his mother a hug and a kiss on the cheek, he wondered why everyone was making such a big deal about his coming to church today. Then it came to him. It had been almost two years since he had been inside his uncle's church.

Chapter 2

It was a slow Tuesday morning and I was dragging myself into my office at NexTech Solutions, a computer company located in Marietta. I worked in the sales department, so of course, I'm expected to sell a lot of computers, software and other related accessories. I already knew it was going to be hard to focus on my job during the upcoming week. In four days, our band was going to be in a talent competition at Club Elite, the most popular hip-hop club in the city. Each year, some of the most talented entertainers in the state would compete in Club Elite's Shining Star talent show. Talent scouts from the entertainment industry and record label executives from all over the country would come to this competition hoping to find that next superstar. I stopped by the break-room and made myself a cup of coffee, hoping it would help perk me up. As I slowly walked to my desk, I mumbled a few "good mornings" as I passed some of my co-workers. When I sat down at my desk, I noticed today's date was circled on my calendar. Suddenly, I remembered that today was my ten-year service anniversary with NexTech. As I took a sip of my coffee, I sat back, wondering how the hell I made it so long at this company. My original goal was to work here for a few years or until our band signed a lucrative record deal. I realized that after ten years with the company, I had gotten too comfortable with this job. Even though the job was stressful at times, it did pay all my bills. In addition to the money I made playing in the band, I had been able to live very comfortably. I reached over and turned on my computer, but the screen remained blank.

"Not again," I muttered to myself. My computer was down again. For the next twenty minutes, I was on the phone talking to the company's computer technician, who was trying to instruct me on how to fix my computer. Finally, I got my computer working and opened up my emails. Of course, my computer was operating very slowly. As I was going through my email, I noticed a message from Frank Gordon, my supervisor, dated yesterday at 3:55 p.m. I opened the email and it read: *Mr. Freeman, I need to meet with you in my office tomorrow morning at 9 am.* I glanced at the clock on my computer which read 9:06 a.m. Why did Gordon want to see me? I was coming to work on time. I was completing all of my office work. My sales quota was decent. I wasn't having any problems with any co-workers. Whatever the reason, I knew it couldn't be anything good. Frank Gordon was an arrogant white guy, divorced, in his mid-fifties, who thought he was smarter than most people because he graduated from an Ivy League school. When Gordon was transferred to my department three years ago, he made it very clear to me that he didn't like me and, after getting to know him, the feeling was mutual. I already knew Frank was going to say something stupid to piss me off, so I took a sip of my coffee, said a quick prayer, and headed straight to his office. As I reached his office, the door was closed.

"Here we go," I whispered to myself as I knocked on the door.

"Come in," I heard Gordon say, on the other side of the door. As I entered his office, Gordon was sitting at his desk, staring at his computer.

"You wanted to see me, Mr. Gordon?" I asked.

"Yes, close the door and have a seat." As I sat down in the chair across from his desk, I couldn't help but feel like an elementary student who had just been sent to the principal's office for misbehaving. "You're late, Mr. Freeman. My email said I wanted to meet at 9:00 a.m. It's now 9:08," he said, looking at his watch.

"Sorry about that. My computer was down for about thirty minutes this morning, so I just got your email message," I replied.

"I sent you that email yesterday at 3:55 p.m. and I believe the end of your work tour is 4:00. In every weekly meeting, I stress to everyone how important it is to check your email when you arrive in the morning and before you leave work. Had you checked your email before you left work, you would have known about this meeting, even if your computer was down this morning."

"Okay, Mr. Gordon, I'll keep that in mind. What did you want to see me about?" I asked calmly.

"I was looking at your numbers for the last month and your production has dropped down dangerously close to an unsatisfactory rating. If you don't increase your production numbers in the next few weeks, I'm going to have to put an unsatisfactory entry in your performance evaluation." Mr. Gordon opened up a file on his desk and began reading over it. "According to your personnel file, you have a satisfactory rating during your employment with the company. It would be very unfortunate if you were suspended or even terminated because you've let your production numbers go down. If you're having any personal problems or you need some additional training, just let me know and we can provide you with any assistance you need."

"Sure, I'll let you know. Is there anything else?" I asked, getting up from my chair.

"I wasn't finished, Mr. Freeman," he said, waiting for me to sit back down. "I also need to discuss your excessive telephone usage."

"What are you talking about?" I asked, starting to feel annoyed.

"Earlier, I noticed you were on the telephone around 8:25. I walked past your desk fifteen minutes later and you were still on the phone. Perhaps if you cut down on some of your personal phone calls, you might significantly improve your production."

I couldn't believe this pompous, jerk was talking to me like a child. It took my very best not to lose my temper and go off on this arrogant, egotistical, white man. If Gordon's goal was to piss me off, he was doing a great job. I took a deep breath and tried to talk calmly.

"I was actually on the phone for about twenty minutes, but I wasn't on a personal call. I was talking to the computer tech guy about my computer not working ... the same computer I told you wasn't working when we started this conversation."

Gordon glared at me with a look of annoyance all over his face.

"There's no need for any of your sarcasm, Mr. Freeman. It's my job as your supervisor to make sure you're using your time in a productive manner. I know you people have a problem with authority, but this is a place of business and company policy needs to be followed."

"*You people*? Careful, Mr. Gordon. It would be very unfortunate if I had to report you to Human Resources for racially-insensitive comments."

"Freeman, are you threatening me?" he asked, as his face began to turn red.

"No, just a friendly warning," I said, not backing down. I could tell by the look on his face that Gordon was livid and wanted to fire me on the spot, but he knew this was a battle he wouldn't win. "Is there anything else you need to talk to me about?" I asked politely.

"No, that will be all," he said, staring back at his computer. As I left his office, I closed the door behind me and started walking back to my desk.

"I've got to get the hell out of here," I said to myself. When I got back to my work area, Sandra Bryant, one of my co-workers, was putting a large stack of folders on my desk.

"Sandra, what's all this?" I asked, sitting down in my seat.

"Mr. Gordon just called me and told me to put all these accounts on your desk. He also told me to let you know that these accounts need to be completed by the end of the day."

I leaned back in my chair and shook my head as I looked at the mountain of folders piled on my desk.

"Terry, I'm sorry. I'm just following orders," Sandra said as she walked away.

Gordon certainly didn't waste any time retaliating, I thought to myself. I reached for my coffee and took a sip, which, of course, was cold. These were the times I wished I had listened to my best friend, Damon King, who would constantly tell me to stop wasting my time at my dead-end job and totally focus on turning Infinite Noise into a great and successful band.

Chapter 3

Terry and Damon met while competing against each other in their high school talent shows. Damon won the talent show in the tenth grade playing a bass guitar solo. Terry won the talent show in the eleventh grade playing the piano and singing. During their senior year, a three man rap group calling themselves, The Hard Ballers, entered the school's talent show. Damon and Terry knew it would be difficult to win the school's talent show against a new, rowdy rap group, so they decided to team up. They entered the talent show under the name of Two Smooth and ironically, their relationship changed from fierce competitors to talented musical partners. With Damon playing the bass guitar and Terry playing the lead guitar, the two were able to edge out the Hard Ballers and win the school's talent show. After high school, the two briefly went their separate ways. Terry attended Morehouse College and received a degree in music. During his sophomore year at Georgia State University, Damon's girlfriend became pregnant, so he dropped out of school and started working for a construction company to support his child. Damon and Terry kept in touch over the years and remained close friends. Terry was Damon's best man at his wedding and later became godfather to Damon's son, Darius. During the years the two friends were apart, Terry's brother, Warren and cousin, Reggie, worked hard to get into the music industry. Through hard work and hours of practice, Warren became an excellent keyboard player and his cousin, Reggie, became a very good drummer and rapper. A few years later, Terry and Damon decided to get back together and renew their musical careers. The two friends decided to form a new and exciting band, so they decided to add Warren and Reggie to their group. Months later, while playing the guitar in his uncle's church choir, Terry heard eighteen-year-old Layla Simmons, sing a solo gospel song. Terry was so impressed with her powerful voice and range of vocals, he asked her to join his band. With Terry playing lead guitar, Damon, the bass guitar, Warren, the keyboardist, Reggie, the drummer, and Layla, the lead vocalist, a new band was formed, calling themselves Infinite Noise.

Chapter 4

Peachtree Street was packed with cars and people eagerly trying to get inside Club Elite. Each year, Club Elite hosted the "Shining Star" talent competition for the top amateur bands and singers from all over the country. Admission was twenty dollars and you had to be twenty-one years of age or older to get into the club. The dress code was cosmopolitan and normally, it was strictly enforced. Tonight, however, the club was relaxing the dress code because of this annual talent competition. Infinite Noise was very familiar with this competition, having won the event two out of the last four years. Terry knew it would be great for his band to win this talent show again to re-establish themselves as one of the top bands in the city after a two-year hiatus. Their biggest rival would most likely be Marcus "Grill" Jones and his rap group, the Thug Lordz. Marcus was a self-proclaimed gangster, who formed a hardcore rap group, that pumped the crowd up with their loud, profanity-laden lyrics and crude on-stage behavior. Later that evening, Infinite Noise had just finished their performance and were waiting for the last group to perform. Performing on stage was an R&B group called Zenith Point. They were playing an old Kool and The Gang song called "Celebrate." As Terry listened to them perform, he could tell they were a very nervous and inexperienced band. Their drummer was a little offbeat and their bass player was playing too slowly. After Zenith Point finished their song, the crowd showed their appreciation by giving them a round of applause. The lights turned up and the DJ's voice boomed over the nightclub's sound system.

"That was our last band performing for the night. Ladies and Gentlemen, the judges have chosen our winners," the DJ said, reading from a piece of paper. "The third place winner of $1,000 dollars is "Sweet Heat!"

The all-female rock group walked onstage and accepted the check from the DJ and waved to the crowd. Terry took a deep breath and tried to look confident as the DJ made his next announcement.

"The second place winner of $2,500 is "Infinite Noise.""

The crowd cheered as the band walked onstage to accept their check. As the members of Infinite Noise walked off the stage, Marcus Jones looked at Terry with an arrogant look on his face.

"And now the first place winner of $5,000 and this year's Shining Star champion is . . . "The Thug Lordz!""

There was a loud smattering of cheers and boos as Marcus and his group ran up to the stage, flashing gang signs and grabbing their crotches.

"Yeah, that's right, that's right," Marcus screamed into the stage microphone. "We the Thug Lordz! We the baddest niggas in town and nobody can touch us."

Terry's cousin, Reggie, shook his head in disbelief as Marcus continued cursing and bragging about their first place win.

"What an asshole. I can't believe we lost to these guys," he said, glaring at Marcus.

Terry's younger brother, Warren, had not said a word since the band finished their performance. He was obviously pissed off about the band's second place finish and didn't want to talk to anyone.

"Come on, let's get out of here," Damon said to Reggie and the rest of the band.

As the band members walked over to the VIP room, reserved for all the performers, Terry immediately looked for Layla. Since she joined the band, Terry had taken it upon himself to watch and protect her. Men of all ages constantly approached her wherever they performed, which was understandable. She was a very attractive woman with a petite, curvy figure and exotic eyes. Even though Layla was small in stature, she had a very powerful singing voice that was a great addition to Infinite Noise. As the band walked to the VIP entrance, they were greeted by Big Brad Nelson, one of the club's bouncers. Standing at six-five and three hundred ten pounds, Big Brad was a very intimidating man. If anyone caused any problems in the club on his watch, you were either drunk, stupid, or both. He was a man of very few words but, when he did speak, everyone listened.

"Hey, what's up, Big Brad?" Terry said, extending his hand.

"I'm good, Terry. Y'all got robbed. You guys should have won first place," he said, patting Terry on the back with his huge hand.

"Hello, Brad," Layla said, walking up.

"Layla, you look absolutely stunning this evening." Brad said, looking down at Layla.

"Thank you," she said, giving him a warm hug.

"Hey, what about me, Brad? Don't I look stunning tonight?" Reggie asked, jokingly.

"Man, ain't nobody trying to look at your scrawny butt," Brad replied, getting a laugh from everyone.

A waitress walked up and brought everyone a glass of champagne.

"I'd like to make a toast to my favorite band, Infinite Noise," Damon said, lifting his glass in the air.

"And to good friends and family," Terry added, raising his glass.

As everyone started to mingle around the VIP room, Terry noticed all the various groups that had performed earlier. He noticed that some of the bands, like Sweet Heat, were talking with some talents scouts and record producers. Sweet Heat was an all-female rock band that didn't play or sing very well, but they sure looked sexy on stage. There were several attractive female groupies who had been invited into the VIP room who were talking and flirting with the various band members. As much as Terry was enjoying the atmosphere, he didn't want to stay too long. Marcus and his group would be arriving soon and he didn't feel like hearing his big mouth bragging about how they won this year's talent competition. Terry quickly finished his drink and began looking for the rest of his band members.

"Excuse me," a man's voice said from behind.

Terry turned around and noticed a distinguished looking black man, in his mid-forties approaching him. He looked familiar, but Terry couldn't seem to remember where he had seen him before.

"My name is Walter Caldwell. I'm a record producer with Galactic Records.

"I'm Terry Freeman," he said, shaking Caldwell's hand. "I saw you on the cover of Black Enterprise a few months ago. You were selected as one of the top music producers in the industry."

"I'm looking forward to the day when I will be selected as *the* top music producer in the industry," Caldwell said with confidence. "That's why I'm here tonight. I make a point of attending a lot of these competitions to see if there's some new talent out there. From what I saw and heard tonight, your band has a lot of potential. Our company is interested in producing a new, exciting band. Would you be interested in meeting with me and talking about a possible future with Galactic Records?"

"Yes, I would be very interested," Terry responded, trying to conceal his excitement.

"Call my secretary and she'll set up an appointment," Caldwell said, handing Terry his business card.

"Okay, thank you, Mr. Caldwell," he said, shaking his hand.

As Caldwell walked away, Terry closed his eyes and whispered, "Thank you, Lord." For the past few years, Terry's band had been waiting for a chance to land a recording contract with a major record label. After all their hard work and patience, he hoped that this would be the opportunity that Infinite Noise had been waiting for.

Chapter 5

It was 4:23 p.m. and I had just arrived at the annual Atlanta Business Symposium at the downtown convention center. The symposium was created twelve years ago for people in the business sector and the entertainment industry to convene here to discuss, share information, and network with others from all over the country. It had been two years since I attended one of these symposiums, but I knew I needed to re-establish my contacts with people in the music community if I was serious about making Infinite Noise a successful band. I also needed to look into finding a good attorney for our band. When Damon and I started our band, we always talked about hiring an attorney to handle our legal affairs, but we never found the right person for the job. Now that I was getting ready to meet with Galactic Records next week, I needed to start looking for a good attorney to represent our band. I walked around the large convention floor, amazed at the various and diverse businesses represented here such as AT&T, Time Warner, and Microsoft. As I looked around the room, I was temporarily stunned as my eyes locked onto a radiantly beautiful woman standing with a small group of well-dressed businessmen. I found myself mesmerized by this woman with her long, black hair that gently flowed over her shoulders and down her back. Her skin was a smooth, honey-brown, complexion. The short, blue dress she was wearing did an excellent job of showcasing her hour-glass figure and her toned, sexy legs. Suddenly, she began to walk away from the small group. The way she gracefully walked across the convention room floor in her high heels, gave me the impression she might be a professional model. As I slowly walked over in her direction, I couldn't help but notice that I wasn't the only man admiring this gorgeous woman. She was approached by several men, but it appeared she would politely speak to each man and then move on. I quickly decided that I had to meet this woman, but I needed to plan a good strategy. As I slowly, inconspicuously, made my way closer to her, she was approached by a distinguished-looking gentleman wearing a dark gray business suit. I eavesdropped on their conversation long enough to find out that the gentlemen was the owner of a restaurant located in Southeast Atlanta. The restaurant owner was trying his best to impress this lovely woman, but it didn't take long before she turned him into one of the many men who had tried and failed to win her interest. I didn't want to come off like I was trying to hit on her, even though I was, so I tried to think of something clever to say. No matter how hard I tried, I couldn't seem to come up with the right thing to say to her. There I was, standing a few feet away from this attractive woman, and I couldn't think of one intelligent thing to say to her. In all the years I had been meeting and talking to women, I was truly at a loss for words. I glanced over and saw this beautiful woman standing by herself. I finally decided to make my move before another guy approached her.

"Excuse me, Miss."

"Yes?" she replied, looking at me with her gorgeous, brown eyes.

"I'm with the convention center security staff and I've received a few complaints about someone fitting your description."

"Complaints? What are you talking about," she said, looking very confused.

"I've received some complaints that you've been crushing some male egos and throwing the remains all over this convention floor."

She looked at me curiously, not knowing whether to go off on me or whether to laugh. Fortunately, I discovered that she had a sense of humor.

"I haven't been crushing any male egos, thank you," she said with a smile.

"Are you sure? I followed a trail of crushed egos that led me right to you," I said, trying to sound like a detective during an investigation.

"If you're part of the convention security staff, why aren't you wearing gray pants and a blue jacket like the others?" she asked, obviously not believing my story.

"That's because I'm head of security, ma'am. I can wear whatever I want," I replied, trying to keep a straight face.

"Okay, Mr. Head of Security, I'll try my best not to crush any more male egos," she said as she turned and began to walk away.

"Ma'am, you're doing it again."

"Excuse me?" she said, looking somewhat annoyed.

"Here I am, trying to get to know you and you're just going to walk away without even telling me your name."

"Instead of trying to get to know me, shouldn't you be securing this place and making sure everyone is safe, Mr. Head of Security?"

"That's exactly what I'm doing, ma'am. I'm making sure that *you* are safe."

I could tell by the expression on her face that my head of security skit had gone from slightly funny to becoming annoying. I quickly went into my emergency backup plan.

"Okay, I have to be honest with you. I'm not head of security. "I just wanted the opportunity to meet you."

"Why didn't you just come over and introduce yourself?"

"I noticed a few guys tried that tactic and you quickly turned them away."

"Oh, really? You've been watching me all this time?"

"No, that would make me sound like I'm a stalker or something. I would prefer to say that I've been admiring you from afar. By the way, my name is Terence Freeman. My friend's call me, Terry." I said, extending my hand. "And you are?"

"Leaving. Good-bye, Mr. Freeman," she said as she turned and walked away, leaving me standing there with egg all over my face.

"Oh, no she didn't," I muttered to myself as I watched her walk away into the crowd.

As I stood there looking stunned and confused, I realized that I had become one of the several guys she had shot down. I'm glad she wasn't interested in me, I thought to myself, trying to soothe my bruised ego. I didn't have time to get involved with a woman, anyway. I was at the convention center for business reasons. If I was serious about signing with a major record label, I was going to need a good attorney to help negotiate a good contract for our band. Suddenly, I heard someone calling my name.

"Terry! Terry Freeman!" a man's voice yelled through the noise in the convention center.

I turned around and saw Carl Phillips, an old friend of my father, whom I had met several years ago when I was in college. Even though he had a lot more gray in his hair and had put on a little more weight, he still looked good for a man in his late fifties.

"Hello, Mr. Phillips," I said, extending my hand. Mr. Phillips grabbed my hand, pulled me toward him and gave me a firm hug.

"It's so good to see you. How have you been, young man?" he asked, finally releasing me from his bear hug.

"I'm doing good, sir."

"I think it's been about seven years since I've seen you."

"More like ten years, sir," I replied. "I was a junior in college when you became a city councilman."

"I owe a lot of that to your father. Your father was a very influential man in this town and his endorsement did a lot to get me elected."

"My father said that you'd be a good city councilman and he was right."

"Your father was a good man who loved this city. I'm proud to say he was one of my most trusted friends."

"Are you still in politics, Mr. Phillips?"

"No, I got out of that arena. I'm a legal consultant now. I work with several law firms all over the city. Here you go," he said, handing me his business card. "If you ever need any legal consultation, you be sure to call me. I'll hook you up with the best attorneys in this state," he said with confidence.

"Thank you, Mr. Phillips. As a matter of fact, that's one of the reasons I'm here. I've been looking for a good attorney. I'm looking to sign a deal with a recording label in the near future and I sure would like a good attorney to represent our band."

"I'm glad to hear that. You definitely have your father's musical talents. I was just talking to an old colleague of mine. He's an attorney with one of the largest law firms here in Atlanta. I think he's still here," Mr. Phillips said, looking around the crowded convention floor. "There he is. Come with me and I'll introduce you to him."

I followed Mr. Phillips into a crowd of people. We approached a short, chubby looking white man dressed in a dark grey, three piece suit, who was talking to a small group of people. I immediately noticed the attractive woman in the short, blue dress, that I had spoken to earlier. She had a very surprised look on her face as I walked up.

"Excuse me, Jack," Mr. Phillips said, getting his attention. "I'd like you to meet Terrence Freeman. Terrence, this is Jack Hamilton. He is one of the senior attorneys with Mason and Thompson Law Firm."

"Nice to meet you, Terrence," Mr. Hamilton said, shaking my hand. "And this is one of our interns, Miss Angela Greer. She's currently attending Emory Law School and hopefully will join our firm in the near future."

"It's nice to meet you, Mr. Freeman," she said, extending her hand.

"The pleasure is all mine, Miss Greer," I said, shaking her hand and trying my best to keep a straight face.

"Terrence is a very fine musician and he's looking to find a good attorney to represent his band," Mr. Phillips said, patting me on the back.

"Well, Terrence, our law firm is representing several local clients in the entertainment industry. We would love the opportunity to assist you and your band any way we can."

"I'm definitely interested in finding a good attorney to represent my band, Mr. Hamilton."

"Excuse me, Mr. Hamilton, don't forget you have a 3:00 meeting with the Orion Group," Angela said, politely interrupting.

"Thank you, Angela," he said, glancing at his watch. "Charles, I'm meeting with some city council officials. I would appreciate it if you would come with me. I could sure use some of your political expertise. After we're finished, I'll treat you to a steak at Giovanni's Grill."

"Jack, you're going to ruin my diet," Mr. Phillips said, laughing.

Mr. Hamilton turned to me and handed me his business card.

"Angela will get your information and set up an appointment for you. It was nice meeting you, Terrence," he said, shaking my hand.

"It was good seeing you again, Terrence," Mr. Phillips said, giving me a hug. As the two rushed off into the crowd, I turned and looked at Angela, who was looking slightly embarrassed.

"Okay, I guess I owe you an apology," she said, timidly.

"You guess?" I replied, looking very smug.

"Alright, I know I owe you an apology. Look, I've been here for almost two hours and I've been approached by at least fifteen guys with their creepy pick-up lines and indecent proposals. I assumed you were just another one of them." Not able to hold it in any longer, I started to laugh.

"The look on your face, when I walked up, was absolutely priceless."

"I'm sure you enjoyed every second of it," she said, smiling.

"Yes, I loved it."

"Anyway, can I get some information from you?" she asked, pulling out a pen and a small pad.

"Unfortunately, I'm on a very tight schedule and I don't have the time to do that right now," I said, glancing at my watch.

"Can you call our office next week and set up an appointment?" she asked.

"Yes, I could do that, but I have several questions about your law firm . . . and since you're representing your law firm, I would like to sit down with you and ask some questions. As a businessman, I have to make sure my band is going to be represented by the right law firm. Being a law student, I'm sure you can understand that," I said, sounding very business-like.

"Yes, I understand," she said, grudgingly.

"That being said, I'm very interested in talking to you about your law firm representing my band. Are you familiar with the Cheese Cake Factory downtown?"

"Yes, I've been there a few times."

"Let's do this," I said, taking the pen out of her hand and writing on her pad. "I have an extremely busy schedule coming up. Tomorrow will be my only free day. Here's my number. Call me tomorrow and we can meet for lunch or dinner. I'll leave that up to you. I look forward to seeing you tomorrow, Miss Greer," I said, handing her the pen, shaking her hand and quickly walking away.

As I merged into the large crowd, I felt a great sense of satisfaction knowing that it was my turn to leave Angela standing by herself, on the convention center floor, looking confused and speechless.

Chapter 6

Layla was in the bathroom, putting on the finishing touches of her makeup. As she looked at herself in the mirror, she frowned, thinking something didn't look quite right. She ran her fingers through her shoulder length, black hair, wondering if she should wear it up or down. She looked in the mirror wondering if the dark, green dress she was wearing complemented her small, curvy figure. She glanced at her watch and realized it was time to leave so she wouldn't be late for her performance tonight.

"Hey, mom, it's 6:04 p.m. I need to get there by 6:30," she yelled from the bathroom.

It had been almost two years since she and the band performed at the Peach State Tavern. Of all the places she had performed with Infinite Noise, this place was the most challenging for her. The Peach State Tavern was a very popular jazz club, located in mid-town Atlanta. The Tavern didn't have a stage and the patron's tables were so close to the performers, you could reach out and touch them. The first time she sang at the Tavern, she was extremely nervous being so close to the audience. She was so nervous, she forgot one of the lines to a song she was singing. Now, she was getting another chance to stand in front of a large audience and show them that she had become a confident singer and musician.

"Mom, are you ready?" she yelled, walking out of the bathroom.

"Yes, I'm in the kitchen waiting for you, dear," her mother responded. "What's the big rush? You said your show doesn't start until 7:00 p.m."

"Yes, but Terry always likes us to arrive early at all our shows," Layla replied. "How does this dress look on me, mom?" she said, slowly turning around like a professional model.

"Well, it looks like that dress is a little too short on you. And I don't think you need to wear all that makeup."

"Mom, I only have on a little eye liner and some lipstick. It would be nice if you could be a little more supportive."

"Supportive? Me and your father, God rest his soul, spent most of our life savings putting you through that performing arts college. I come to all your performances unless my arthritis flares up. I've been nothing but supportive of you."

"I'm sorry, mom. That was a poor choice of words. It just seems like you've never liked me performing with my band."

"I'll be honest with you. I've never wanted you to be in any kind of band. I've heard how these bands become popular and they turn into drug addicts and alcoholics."

"Mom, please don't start that up again."

"I'm not starting anything up, dear. I'm just saying that you are a wonderful singer and I think you're wasting your time singing in that band. When I think of all the money your father and I spent on violin lessons for you. Now, it seems like you spend more time playing on that big guitar than you do playing the violin."

"It's called a bass guitar and I enjoy playing it."

"Sweetheart, I just don't understand. You play the violin so beautifully. With your talent, you should be playing with the Atlanta Symphony Orchestra."

"Mom, that's why I enjoy playing with Infinite Noise. I get to sing, play the violin and I'm learning how to play other instruments, too."

"That's another thing, dear. I'm not too comfortable with some of the people in your band. There's talk in the church that Pastor Freeman's son has had some problems with the law. And then there's that young man, Warren."

"What about Warren?" Layla asked, looking confused.

"I can't put my finger on it, but there's something about him that rubs me the wrong way."

"Mom, how are you going to judge him like that?"

"I'm not saying he's a bad person. His mother, Cora, is a good Christian woman, so I know he has some good in him. I feel bad about what happened to his father, but there's something about him I just don't trust. I see the way he looks at you in church; the few times he does go to church."

"You've known Warren and the rest of the guys for years. You know they're good people."

"Sweetheart, how do you know they're not just using you?"

"Using me? What are you talking about, mom?"

"You are a very pretty girl. How do you know they're not just using your looks to attract a lot of filthy- minded men to come to your shows? I don't want people looking at you like you're some cheap floozy, shaking her butt onstage."

"Mom, I can't believe you said that! Is that the way you look at me?" she asked, feeling deeply hurt by her mother's comment. "You've seen me perform with the band many times. Have I ever dressed or done anything on stage that was crude or disrespectful?" Layla's mother didn't respond.

"Well, have I?"

"No, dear, you haven't."

Layla walked over and gently touched her mother's hand.

"Mom, I love you and I would never do anything to disrespect you or myself. You know why? Because my mother and father didn't raise me that way. I know you want what's best for me, but singing in this band is the second greatest thing that's ever happened to me."

"So, what's the greatest thing that's happened to you?" her mother asked, meekly.

"Having you and dad as my parents," she said proudly. Layla's mother put her head down as the tears flowed down her face. Moments later, her mother wiped the tears from her eyes and regained her composure.

"Layla, I guess we should leave now so you won't be late for your show."

"Okay, mom." As Layla walked to the front door, her mother stopped her.

"Layla?"

"Yes, mom?"

"I'm so blessed to have a wonderful daughter like you." Layla walked over to her mother and hugged her as they cried in each other's arms.

Chapter 7

Since she moved to Atlanta twenty one months ago, Angela had been approached by several men who wanted to date her. Some of the men were highly-educated, professional businessmen, while others were smooth-talking players, looking for their next conquest. Unfortunately, most of them reminded her of Kenya's father, Preston Seymour. Now, she had met a man who was different than the others. She wasn't quite sure how it happened, but she found herself becoming interested in Terry Freeman. Maybe it was because he didn't approach her like a suave, over-confident playboy. Or maybe it was because the first words out of his mouth weren't, *"Hey, what's up, shorty?"* Or the traditional, *"Damn, baby! You are sexy as hell!"* It was actually nice to have a man approach her without making her feel like a slab of rump roast at the local meat market. Even when she let him know that she wasn't interested, she admired the fact that he persisted in a non-aggressive way. With her classes at Emory Law School, her internship with the law firm and taking care of her eight-year-old daughter, she had abandoned any idea about dating or starting a relationship with any man. After her long, tumultuous relationship with Kenya's father, she definitely wasn't looking to get into any type of a serious relationship. When Angela called Terry to have lunch with him, she convinced herself it was for business reasons only. After all, part of the reason for being at the Atlanta Business Symposium was to make contacts with new clients for her law firm. But, after talking to him on the phone and making plans for lunch, she began to realize that she was actually looking forward to seeing him again. As she walked into the entrance of the Cheese Cake Factory, she looked around and noticed Terry standing at a table, motioning to her to join him. She was somewhat surprised to see him dressed in navy blue, pin-striped suit. Even though they were meeting for business reasons, she didn't think to come to the restaurant dressed in business attire. The moment she reached the table, Terry greeted her with a warm smile and a gentle handshake.

"It's good to see you again, Angela," he said, pulling out a chair for her.

"If I had known you were going to dress so formally, I would have dressed for the occasion," she said with a smile.

"I didn't want to be late for our lunch, so I came here straight from church."

"What church do you go to, Mr. Freeman?"

"It's called Keep the Faith Baptist church, located in Southwest Atlanta."

"I've been looking for a good church to attend since I moved here from Chicago."

"I think it's a wonderful church and I'm not just saying that because my uncle is the pastor."

"Maybe I'll make plans to attend your church one Sunday."

"Please do that. I'll be sure to save a seat for you. By the way, you look absolutely stunning," he said, gazing deeply into her eyes.

For a brief moment, Angela was speechless, totally caught off-guard by his charm and wit. She quickly tried to regain her composure.

"Anyway, I hope you don't mind if I record this short interview," she said, pulling out a miniature recorder from her purse.

"That won't be necessary," he said, handing her a sealed folder. "Here's everything you need to know about my band, Infinite Noise. There's a bio of each member, when our band started, the type of music we play, where we've performed, and our goals for the future."

"Well, you certainly came prepared. You know, Mr. Freeman, you could have just mailed all this information to me at the law firm."

"Yes, but then I wouldn't have had this opportunity to have lunch with you." Surprised by his comment, Angela felt herself blushing.

"Now that you've supplied me with all the information I need about you and your band, we're going to have a lot of free time on our hands."

"Not necessarily. I was hoping we could use this time to get to know each other better," he said, with a sly grin on his face.

"I guess you think you're pretty clever, don't you, Mr. Freeman."

"No, not at all . . . and please call me, Terry."

Angela looked at him, trying to see if there was something in his eyes or facial expressions, that could give her an indication if he was for real or just another smooth talker.

"Angela, I honestly would like to get to know you better."

She wasn't quite sure what it was, but something about him made her feel that she could trust him.

"Okay, Terry. What would you like to know?"

For the next hour, Angela and Terry talked, debated, laughed, and enjoyed their time together. She came to this lunch expecting to interview the typical pompous, egotistical musician with delusions of greatness. Instead, she met a man who was kind, intelligent, charming, and full of surprises. As much as she was enjoying his company, she glanced at her watch and realized it was time for her to leave.

"I hate to eat and run, but I have an important appointment I need to make," she said, standing up from the table. Thank you for lunch."

"No . . . thank you, Angela," he said, standing up, gently taking her hand and kissing it.

"I'll submit your information to one of our attorneys tomorrow and someone will be in touch with you."

"I hope that someone will be you," he said with a big smile.

"Good bye, Terry."

As she walked away from the table, she purposely put a little extra bounce in her step. She was very tempted to turn around to see if this charming man was checking out her booty as she walked away, but she decided to leave that as a mystery for now.

Chapter 8

I was nervous and extremely excited when I walked into the lobby of Galactic Records for my meeting with Walter Caldwell. I still couldn't believe my supervisor, Frank Gordon, gave me such a hard time about taking a half day off from work. If our band was offered a lucrative contract, I looked forward to quitting my job and telling Gordon to kiss my natural, black ass. I glanced at my watch, which read 10:54 a.m. I had planned to arrive at least twenty minutes earlier to have enough time to grab a cup of coffee and sit back and relax before meeting with Caldwell. Thanks to the traffic on Interstate 85 North, that wasn't going to happen. I remembered my father telling me about the importance of being on time. He felt that punctuality revealed a lot about a person's character. I walked up to the receptionist's desk where I was greeted by a very attractive, young woman.

"Hello, may I help you?" she asked, looking at me with a flirtatious smile.

"Yes, my name is Terry Freeman. I have an 11:00 a.m. appointment with Walter Caldwell."

The receptionist glanced at her appointment book, then picked up her phone.

"Mr. Caldwell, Terry Freeman is here to see you." She hung up the phone and looked up at me. "Mr. Caldwell is waiting for you in his office. Go down this hall and it's the second office on the left."

"Thank you," I said, giving her a friendly smile.

As I walked to Caldwell's office, I was very impressed at the lavish surroundings of expensive furniture and paintings on the walls. Just as I reached Caldwell's office, he greeted me at the door.

"Terry, how's my next superstar doing?"

"Hello, Mr. Caldwell," I said, shaking his hand.

"Please, call me, Walter. I would have met you in the lobby, but I was on a very important phone call with the CEO of the company.

Please come in and have a seat. I promise I won't take up too much of your time," he said as he walked to his desk and sat down.

As I sat down across from him, separated by a large, expensive office desk, I looked around his office and noticed several gold records and CDs that were encased in glass frames.

"Terry, I'll get right to the point. Last week, I was talking with the vice-president of Galactic Records. I told him that with a lot of hard work and the right guidance, I see a promising future for you and your band. I know you've established yourself locally as a very popular band, but I have a question for you."

Caldwell leaned back in his chair, which I assumed was my cue to respond to him.

"What question is that, Walter?" I asked, taking the bait.

"Do you think Infinite Noise is ready to take it to the next level? Are you ready for fame and fortune?"

"Yes, I definitely feel we're ready," I said, confidently.

"I feel you're ready, too. With my guidance, I know Infinite Noise can be very successful." Caldwell pulled out a folder, opened it and placed the paperwork on the desk. "After several talks with the vice-president and other executives, I've convinced them to offer your band the opportunity to sign a recording contract with us." I picked up the contract and started reading over it. "Terry, I'm offering you and your band the opportunity of a lifetime. I usually don't offer this amount of money to new artists, but I was able to convince the executives that your band has the potential for greatness."

As Caldwell continued to talk, I tried my best to listen to what he was saying while I stared at the $700,000 in the wording of the contract.

"Well, are you ready to take that next step?" Caldwell asked with a look of confidence on his face.

"Walter, I appreciate this opportunity, but I'll need to sit down with the rest of the group and go over this contract with them."

"Terry, I'm sure you wondered why I only invited you here instead of the entire band.

"Yes, I did wonder about that."

"I'm sure you've noticed the numerous awards on my wall," Caldwell said as he got up and began to walk around his office.

"I've managed and produced several successful groups and solo artists. In my fourteen years in the music industry, I've found that it's best to negotiate with one person, the leader of the group. You obviously are the leader of your group."

"Damon and I put this band together, but I usually handle the business side of things. However, we usually make decisions of this magnitude as a group," I said, trying to be diplomatic.

"Your sense of fairness is admirable, but in this business, it will bring you down. This isn't about fairness. This isn't about ego. This is about you making the best decisions for your band's success when the opportunity presents itself. There will be times when important decisions have to be made quickly and decisively. There will be times when there will be disagreements within your band. During those times, the leader has to be the voice of reason. Do you see all of the framed records and compact discs hanging on my wall? I was instrumental in turning these artists and their songs into gold. Like your band, they were raw, but had a lot of potential. These artists trusted me and allowed me to shape and mold them into the superstars they are today. That's what I need from you, Terry. I need you to trust me. Whatever decision I make for your band, you have to trust me. If you can do that, I'll turn Infinite Noise into one of the hottest bands in the country. Do you understand what I'm telling you, Terry?"

"Yes, I understand," I responded, still trying to read over the legal jargon in the contract.

"When I sign a new artist, I usually start them off at a base salary of $200,000 the first year; however, because I see the great potential in your band, I decided to offer you more. In addition to the two year $700,000 contract, I'm also including a $50,000 signing bonus. How does that sound?"

"So far, it sounds good."

"I'm meeting with some of the company executives next Tuesday. I would like to have that signed contract in my hand when I meet with them, so I need to have your decision by Friday."

"This Friday?" I asked, looking at the numerous pages in the contract.

"Is that a problem?" he asked, looking confused.

"I'm going to need a little more time. I need to sit down and go over this contract and, of course, consult with my attorney," I said, knowing I don't even have an attorney to consult.

Walter leaned back in his chair, looking somewhat annoyed.

"Do you realize what I'm offering you? There are several other artists our company is evaluating, so we can't waste too much time on this."

"Walter, I appreciate this opportunity, but this is a major step for me and the band. As I said earlier, I've always been responsible for the business decisions for our band, so I have to make sure this contract is right for us. As a business man, I'm sure you can understand that."

"Okay, Terry. Take the contract home with you, go over it with your people, and get back with me no later than Monday morning. We need to get this done as soon as possible," he said as he stood up and extended his hand.

"I'll be here Monday morning at 9:00 a.m." I replied, shaking his hand.

I picked up the contract and left his office feeling elated, but at the same time I felt a little uneasy. As I walked out of the building and to my car, my head was spinning as I tried to process everything that Caldwell and I talked about. This was a great opportunity for our band. This is what I've always wanted, a contract offer with a major record label. So, why was I feeling so apprehensive? Why did I have these feelings of doubt? Maybe I was just overreacting. Maybe I was just nervous and excited over the contract offer. Then it became clear to me. I knew exactly why I felt so uncomfortable. For years, I had been responsible for making most of the financial decisions for Infinite Noise. This seemed like a great opportunity for our band and I didn't want to blow it by making the wrong decision. As I stood outside my car, I reflected back on something my father always told me. "Anything that seems too good to be true, usually isn't." It became clear to me what I needed to do. I pulled out my cell phone to make an important call.

"Hi, Angela. This is Terry. I just received a contract offer from Galactic Records. I really need some legal counseling. Can you schedule an appointment for me sometime this week with one of your attorneys so we can go over this contract? Great, I'll see you on Friday. Bye."

I was so excited, I threw my cell phone up in the air and nearly dropped it on the ground on its way back down. It was turning out to be a wonderful day. Not only did our band get a contract offer from a major record label, but I would get a chance to spend some time with Angela on Friday. All of a sudden, I was feeling a whole lot better about the contract offer. There was no reason for me to get stressed out. I was going to have a legal expert go over the contract and help me make the right decision for our band. Everything was going to work out just fine. Maybe this was the break I had been waiting for all these years and the start of something great for Infinite Noise.

Chapter 9

It was 5:23 p.m. on a Thursday evening when Terry arrived at his mother's house in SWAtlanta, anxious to share the news about the contract offer from Galactic Records. Knowing his mother, she was probably in the kitchen preparing dinner. As he walked to her front door, he noticed that the grass in the front lawn had gotten very high. A sense of guilt came over him when he realized that he hadn't visited his mother in over two weeks. As Terry rang the doorbell, he could already smell warm cornbread baking in the oven. The door opened and Terry was greeted by his mother's warm smile.

"Well, hello, stranger. I was beginning to think you had forgotten where your mother lived."

"Hey, Momma," he said, giving her a big hug.

"Come on in and have a seat. Dinner is almost ready," she said, heading to the kitchen.

"No, that's okay, Mom. I can't stay too long. I have to take care of a few errands."

"It's a shame you can't stay for dinner. I've made smothered pork chops, mashed potatoes, string beans, macaroni and cheese, cornbread, and some ice cold, sweet tea," she said with a grin on her face.

"Well, I guess I can stay for a little while."

Forty minutes later, Terry was leaning back in a recliner chair, wondering why he had eaten so much food. He looked over at the dining table and noticed his mother smiling at him.

"Are you sure you had enough to eat?" she asked as she began taking plates and glasses into the kitchen.

"I'm sure. I can't eat another bite. Hey, let me help you clear the table."

"No, I've got it. You sit back and relax."

"Momma, why do you always cook so much food?" he asked, rubbing his stomach.

"I guess I've just gotten used to cooking for you and Warren, even though I hardly see my sons anymore."

"Yeah, I'm sorry about that, momma."

"Is everything okay with your brother?"

"Yeah, he's fine. He's probably too busy running after females," Terry said, jokingly.

"Does he still have a crush on little Layla Simmons?"

"Momma, she's not little anymore. She just turned twenty-one a few weeks ago."

"What? It seems like just yesterday she was turning eighteen and singing her first solo in the adult church choir. Oh, Lord, your Momma is definitely getting old."

"You are aging like a fine wine," he said, walking over and giving her a hug.

As Terry looked at his mother, he realized she had gotten a little older. He noticed a few more wrinkles and little more gray hair, but she still had that warm, beautiful smile that could light up an entire room.

"Layla is a special young lady," Cora said proudly. "I was so happy when she joined your band. She has a wonderful personality and a beautiful voice."

"Don't tell Warren I said this, but she definitely puts a big smile on his face whenever they're together."

"I'm so glad to hear that. Your brother has been through a lot since we lost your father and he needs a special woman like Layla in his life."

Cora had become very quiet for a few moments as if deep in thought. Then she looked at her son with a sly grin on her face.

"What about you? I'm sure there's a special woman out there for a wonderful man like you."

"Are you sure you don't need any help clearing the table?" he asked, trying to change the subject.

"Am I going to have to drag it out of you? You know I will."

"Okay, I see you're not going to let this go," he said, giving up. "I have met someone."

"That's wonderful!" she said, excitedly. "Tell me a little bit about her."

"Her name is Angela Greer, she's thirty-years-old, never been married, but she does have an eight-year-old daughter named Kenya. I really admire her. She takes care of her daughter, goes to Emory Law School, and works part-time at a law firm."

"She sounds like a hard-working, independent woman. Where is the father of this little girl?"

"I think he's living somewhere in Chicago. From what Angela tells me, he hasn't been much of a father to their daughter. He's been in and out of their lives over the years."

"That is so sad," Cora said, shaking her head.

"Anyway, we've been seeing each other for a few months and so far everything is going great. I have to admit it's very different dating someone with a child." Terry noticed a certain look on his mother's face. It was the same look she would give him whenever something was troubling her. "Okay, I know that look. What's on your mind?"

"I'm not trying to meddle in your relationship, but I think you should take your time and get to know this young lady. Getting involved with someone with a child can be very difficult at times."

"Don't worry, Momma. I'm not rushing into this blindly."

"Well, I hope I'll get a chance to meet both of them in the near future. Maybe you can invite your lady friend and her daughter over here for dinner."

"Sure, that would be great. I really want you to meet her so you can see what a wonderful person she is." Terry didn't want to get into a deep conversation about his love life, so he tried to change the subject again. "Momma, I have some good news to share with you. Our band got a contract offer from Galactic Records. They're a major record company located in Duluth."

"Congratulations, son!" she said, giving him a big hug. "Your band has worked so hard for this. I'm so happy for all of you."

"I just got the contract offer a few days ago and I haven't talked to any of the band members, yet. I need to sit down with an attorney and read over all the legal jargon in the contract and make sure we're getting a good deal. I'm meeting with Angela and one of the attorneys from her law firm tomorrow evening."

"This is wonderful news. God is so good."

"He sure is, Momma."

After giving her son another big hug, Cora pulled away from him.

"By the way, I didn't see you in church this past Sunday. I guess you must have been sitting in the back row where I couldn't see you," she said, trying to look serious.

"Sorry, I didn't make it to church. There's just so much going on right now. Things are getting hectic at my job and of course the band keeps me pretty busy. I just don't seem to have enough time for anything else," he said, defensively.

His mother reached out and gently touched her son's face.

"Terry, no matter how busy you get, you should always have time for the Lord."

"You're right, Momma, but sometimes . . . it's just so hard," he said, softly.

Cora looked at her son and she could see the hurt and pain in his eyes. She rarely talked about her husband's death to her son, but this was one of those times she felt it was necessary.

"I understand, son. It was a terrible thing that happened to your father. Sometimes, terrible things happen in our lives that can bring us down. During those times when you're down, you've got to call on God and He will pull you right back up. Keep your head up, son. I want you to stay strong and keep the faith. It's what your father would have wanted you to do."

"Yes, I know, Momma. Hey, I've got to get going," he said, glancing at his watch."

As he walked to the front door, he stopped and turned around to face his mother.

"I'll be back this weekend to cut the grass."

"Okay, son. I love you," she said with a warm smile.

"I love you, too, Momma."

Chapter 10

I should have known the traffic on Interstate 285 East would be congested around this time period. It took me an hour and a half to drive from my job in Marietta to Angela's apartment complex in Alpharetta. I glanced at the digital clock on my car's dashboard and noticed that it was 5:52 p.m. I still remember when this apartment complex was being built about four years ago. I actually thought about moving into this complex until I found out the rent for a one-bedroom apartment was $1,800 per month and that didn't even include the utilities. I reached into my pocket to find Angela's address I had written down on a piece of paper.

"There it is. Building sixteen, apartment c," I read aloud.

I got out of my car, reached over and grabbed a folder containing paper work and a dozen roses I bought from the florist right down the street. As I walked toward her building, I couldn't help but notice the very expensive cars in the parking lot. I stopped to admire a brand new harvest gold, Porsche 928S, parked next to a silver-colored, Mercedes Benz CLS550. It was very obvious Angela lived in a very upper-class neighborhood. Even though we had been dating a few months, this was the first time she had invited me over to her apartment. As I walked to Angela's door, I started feeling a little nauseous. At first, I tried to blame my queasy stomach on the two chili dogs and onion rings I had for lunch at the Varsity restaurant, but then I realized I was nervous about seeing Angela. I rang her doorbell, then put the roses behind my back to conceal them. It was strange, but I almost felt like a teenager going out on his first date. I hadn't felt so nervous dating a woman since I was a freshman in high school.

"Stop being nervous. Be a man," I whispered to myself.

As Angela opened the door, I felt my heart skip a beat.

"A man who is right on time. I like that," she said, looking at me with those pretty brown eyes.

"Are you impressed?" I asked, trying to regain my composure.

"One of the things you should know about me is that I'm not a very easy person to impress."

"Okay, I'll be sure to remember that."

"Be sure that you do, Mr. Freeman"

"Mr. Freeman? I didn't know we were being so formal."

"This is a business meeting. Come on in," she said, gently grabbing my arm to lead me inside.

"Okay, but first, these are for you," I said, pulling the roses from behind my back.

"Terry, these are beautiful. Thank you very much." she said, taking the roses from me.

"Okay, I'm not overly impressed, but you're definitely getting there."

"So, where is Kenya?" I asked, looking around the apartment.

"She's over at a friend's house."

"I was hoping I'd finally get a chance to meet her."

"When you do meet Kenya, keep in mind that she can be a little distant until she gets to know you. So, don't take it personally."

"That's okay, her mother was the same way, but I found a way to get past her defenses," I said, arrogantly.

"Yes, you certainly did." As I leaned over to kiss Angela, she slowly pulled away.

"Mr. Freeman, I think we need to get down to business."

I was curious as to why Angela was being a little distant, but suddenly, I understood. I heard the sound of a toilet flushing and shortly afterward, a slim-looking guy, wearing a dark blue suit, walked into the room to join us.

"Terry Freeman, this is Paul Jefferson. He's one the attorneys at Mason and Thompson Law Firm. Paul was kind enough to meet us here so he can help us go over your contract."

"Hello, Paul," I said, shaking his hand.

"Nice to meet you, Terry."

"Okay, now that we've got the introductions out of the way, we'll start going over that contract for you," Angela said, sounding very professional. "Did you bring that business plan we talked about?"

"Yes, I've got everything right here," I said, handing her my folder.

As she reached for the paperwork, I gripped it tightly so she couldn't pull it from my hand.

"In case you didn't know, you *are* on the clock," she said, looking at her watch.

"You sure know how to take the fun out of a meeting."

Angela put on her reading glasses and began reading over my business plan.

"Paul, you can sit at the dining room table. That should give you plenty of space to go over the contract." Paul walked into the dining room area, spread the paperwork on the table and began to read over my contract.

"That was very nice of Paul to take time out of his busy schedule to come here to your apartment," I said to Angela, sarcastically.

"Before you get the wrong idea, Paul is doing this as a favor to me," she whispered, not wanting Paul to hear her. "Had we met at the law office, your bill would not have been pretty."

"Thank you for setting this meeting up for me. By the way, you are looking so sexy in those glasses," I whispered to her.

Angela didn't respond, but I noticed a small smile on her face. "I think I should go in there with Paul so we can go over your contract."

"Why don't you go in there and tell Paul to go out for some dinner and come back a little later?" I said, putting my arm around her waist.

"I have a better suggestion," she said, gently pushing me away. "Why don't you go into the den and entertain yourself? I'm sure there's some kind of sporting event on TV that you can be watching while we go over your contract."

"Now that you mention it, I think the Atlanta Braves are playing right now," I said, walking toward her den.

"Don't get too comfortable in there. I have to pick up Kenya from her friend's house in a couple of hours."

"A couple of hours? I have a much better suggestion for us," I said, with a mischievous smile.

"Please go watch your baseball game," she said, pointing to the den.

"Okay, I can take a hint."

As I walked into her den, I couldn't help but notice the expensive tables, chairs, and paintings on the walls. I sat down on a plush, suede sofa and gazed at what appeared to be a fifty-two inch, high-definition, big screen TV. Angela must be making some serious money to afford a nice apartment like this, I thought to myself. After flipping through the channels, I finally found the Atlanta Braves game. It was the top of the third inning and the Braves were leading the Los Angeles Dodgers 3-2. I laid back on her sofa, relaxed and watched the game. About forty minutes later, Angela walked into the den.

"Sorry to interrupt your game, but we've finished looking over everything."

"It's okay, I'm anxious to hear what Paul has to say about that contract."

I got up and followed Angela into the dining room, where Paul was sitting at the table, reading over the contract.

"So, what do you think, Paul?" I asked.

"After going over your contract, I've found a few issues," he replied.

"What kind of issues?" I asked, looking bewildered.

"Well, first of all, I noticed in your contract that you're only getting five percent for royalties on the sale of albums or CDs. Most new artists should try to get at least a ten to twelve percent royalty. How many people are in your band?"

"We have five members," I replied, wondering where Paul was going with this.

"It's very important that you understand that the five-percent royalty is for the entire band. "If you're in a five-member band, each member would receive a one percent royalty."

"What?" That can't be right," I responded, reaching for the contract.

"It's all in the fine print. This is why it's so important to have an attorney look over all of your contracts before you sign them. There is another important detail you need to know about this contract," Paul said, pulling out a small calculator. "Galactic Records is offering you a two-year $700,000 or $350,000 per year contract plus a $50,000 signing bonus," Paul said, tapping on the calculator.

"That would leave you with roughly $142,000 a year after taxes." Paul pulled out a piece of paper and handed it to me to look over. "Then you have to look at all your other expenses. For example, you need to factor in the cost of recording in a studio. Recording costs for new artists can range from $40,000 to $150,000 per year. "Next, if you're seriously thinking about being successful in the music industry, you need to put together a good business team to help you. I noticed in your business plan, you don't have a business team."

"What type of business team are you talking about?" I asked, starting to feel a little confused.

"You're going to need a good business manager to help you make important business decisions and to help handle your financial affairs. Trust me, you don't want the IRS looking into your band's finances. A business manager will charge you around fifteen to twenty-percent of your earnings. You're also going to need an agent to help you with booking concerts, radio, and television appearances. You definitely need to hire an attorney to look over all of your contracts and other legal matters. Most attorneys will charge you around $150 per hour. If you're interested, I would be willing to represent your band for around $75 per hour. If you choose to hire some or all of these people on your business team, it's going to cost you roughly $20,000 to $40,000 per year. Other things I need to point out are the expenses for compact disc artwork and marketing which can range between $10,000 to $100,000 depending on how elaborate you want the project to be. The most important thing you need to know is that your band will be totally responsible for paying for all of these expenses."

"Are you serious? I thought Galactic Records would be responsible for paying most of these expenses," I said, scanning over the numerous contract pages.

"On page sixteen, paragraph four, it states that *"the record company will not be responsible for expenses incurred by the artist."* As I listened to Paul explain the details of high costs and expenses, I began to realize how little I knew about the legalities of my contract.

"Let me get this straight, Paul. You're basically telling me that by the time our band gets through paying for all these expenses, it's very possible we could go over the $350,000 in the first year."

"Yes, that's right and keep in mind, that $350,000 is before Uncle Sam gets his cut. Remember, this is a business and everyone wants their piece of the pie. Of course, you can cut a few corners here and there to save some money, but the bottom line is, you won't be making a profit in the first year or two. Does your band have a website?"

"No. Do we really need one?"

"I would highly recommend creating a website to help promote your band and to keep your fans currently updated about your music and concert appearances. A website is an expense that will definitely pay for itself in the long run."

"Okay, that makes sense," I said, trying to soak in all of the information.

So far, I was very impressed with Paul. He appeared to be around my age, but he seemed to possess a great deal of knowledge and experience in the music industry. I thought Paul was going to be one of those uppity, arrogant, black guys when he walked into the room with his high-yellow complexion and his nerdy looking, wire framed glasses. I obviously misjudged this guy. As I continued to listen to Paul, I realized that this guy definitely understood the business side of the music industry and I had a lot to learn.

"Terry, there's something else I need to bring to your attention. This may not be important to you, but on page fourteen, paragraph three, it states that the record company will have creative control over all of your band's music."

"Oh, hell, no! That clause in the contract will definitely have to be changed," I replied.

"Good luck with that," Paul said, with a smirk on his face. "I've heard that Caldwell doesn't like to negotiate, especially with new artists. He makes you an offer and you either take it or leave it."

"I'm not going to let him take advantage of us, so he's going to have to work with me on revising this contract," I said, firmly.

"I guess it wouldn't hurt to give it a try. Well, I guess we're all done here," Paul said, standing up from the table. "By the way, I did a little research on your band and I was very impressed with what I found. Two years ago, you were voted best new artists by Hotlanta Magazine. You were also voted as the number one band in the Southeast by Top Charts Magazine. Then for two years, I didn't see any information about Infinite Noise. What happened?"

"We . . . decided to take a little break . . . from performing," I said, hesitantly.

"Your band took a two-year break? That's a very long break for a band that was highly successful."

Paul continued to press the issue and it began to annoy me.

"Look, after the concerts and traveling all over the South, we were burned out. We needed a break. Why are you making such a big deal about that?" I said, sounding a little defensive.

"I apologize if I was being too personal. I just want to prepare you for what any record company might ask you during contract negotiations."

All of a sudden, I felt embarrassed for getting an attitude with him. Paul was obviously trying to help me and I was acting like a paranoid jerk.

"No, I should be apologizing to you. You're right, I need to be prepared for any questions that might be asked about our band. Paul, I really appreciate your taking time out of your schedule to go over my contract."

"If you decide you need an agent or business manager to represent your band, please feel free to call me," he said, handing me his business card.

"Thank you," I said, shaking his hand.

"Thanks again for coming over, Paul," Angela said, walking Paul to the front door.

As the two walked out of the room, I stood there feeling a little angry and very disappointed. When Angela came back into the room, I tried to put on a positive attitude.

"I'm glad I found out this was a bad contract before I signed it," I said, forcing a smile.

"I'm sorry, Terry. I know you must be disappointed."

"No, it's cool. Who knows? Maybe I can get Caldwell to re-negotiate this contract." I replied.

Even though my contract offer turned out to be bad news, I thought I could salvage the evening by asking Angela out on another date.

"Angela, if you're not busy Sunday, I was hoping we could get together."

"Terry, you know I enjoy spending time with you, but I don't have a lot of free time right now."

"Come on, Angela. We haven't gone out together in over a week. I know with your classes, working at the law firm and taking care of Kenya, you have a very busy schedule. At some point, you owe it to yourself to have some fun. And if you go out with me, you know you're going to have fun." Angela looked at me and smiled, knowing she couldn't disagree with me.

"There's this place downtown I know you would really enjoy."

"I doubt I can find a babysitter for Kenya on such short notice."

"You don't need a babysitter," I said, being persistent. "Kenya can come with us."

"Well, I'm not sure," she said, hesitantly.

"The place is called the Action Zone. It has a lot of indoor games and activities for kids young and old. Trust me, you won't be disappointed."

"It sounds very nice, but . . ."

"Oh, come on," I said, cutting her off. "Do it for Kenya. She will absolutely love this place and it will give us a chance to get to know each other," I said, pleading my case.

Angela pondered for a moment, then looked at me with a big smile.

"Okay, we'll join you."

"Great, I'll call you tomorrow and work out all the details. By the way, how much do I owe you and Paul for all of this expert legal advice?"

"There's no charge," she said with a mischievous smile.

"What? I thought you said I was on the clock."

"Yes, I did say that, but I wanted to see how serious you were about getting some legal representation. If you were willing to pay us for legal advice, that tells me you're serious about your band. Paul came over here to look over your contract as a favor to me.

However, if you decide to hire a business manager for your band, I'm sure he would appreciate your considering him for the job."

"I have to admit, Paul sounds like he really knows his stuff."

"Don't get a big head, but he thinks your band has what it takes to be very successful. I happen to agree with him. I also did some research. You guys were a very popular group a few years ago."

"Does that mean you're impressed?" I asked, gently grabbing her hand.

"Like I said before, it takes a lot to impress me."

"Thanks again for all your help and advice," I said, giving her a hug.

As I started to pull away, Angela wrapped her arms around my neck and gave me a passionate kiss.

"Goodnight, Mr. Freeman."

"Goodnight, Miss Greer."

As I walked to my car, I couldn't help but feel excited about seeing Angela on Sunday and meeting her daughter, Kenya, for the first time.

Chapter 11

Infinite Noise had just finished a long, but productive practice at Gerald's Warehouse. The owner of Gerald's Warehouse, an old friend of Terry's father, had been kind enough to allow the band to practice in his warehouse for the last two years. The large, spacious warehouse helped to simulate the acoustics of a huge arena and it was located away from any nearby businesses to give the band total privacy. Terry and Damon had written a new song for the band that allowed each member to play a small solo and showcase their talents. Since the band started performing again after a two-year hiatus, the practices had been long and tedious. Tonight was different. It was one of those practices where the music flowed smoothly and everyone played with energy and confidence. In three days, Infinite Noise was going to perform at the Waverly Ballroom, a very exclusive hotel located in the affluent Buckhead District and Terry wanted to make sure the band would be ready.

"Hey, everybody, let's have a short practice on Friday around six o'clock to go over a few things!" Terry yelled.

Damon noticed Reggie rushing to the exit door to leave. "Reggie, did you hear that?"

"Yeah, I heard, Friday, at six. Later, guys." Reggie said, quickly dashing out of the door.

"Reggie must have a hot date tonight," Terry said, unplugging his guitar from his amplifier.

"What's wrong with these young guys today? I've never run after a female," Damon said, confidently.

"Oh, really? What about Rosa Hernandez?" Terry asked with a big grin on his face.

"Who is Rosa Hernandez?" Layla asked as she walked by.

"Rosa was this very cute Hispanic girl that Damon had a crush on in the tenth grade."

"She almost broke my heart," Damon said, trying to look sad.

"Almost? She broke, crushed and ripped out your heart," Terry said, laughing.

"Man, you are dead wrong for bringing her up. Hey, what time do you have?"

"It's 6:23," Terry replied, checking his watch.

"Damn, I need to be running out of here myself," Damon said, grabbing his bass guitar and case. "I promised Gail I would be home by seven to take her and Darius out to a movie tonight."

"I suggest you start running. You do not want to make Gail angry."

"Yeah, you got that right. See you Friday," Damon said, sprinting toward the exit door.

Warren was unplugging his keyboard and putting it inside the protective case when he noticed Layla getting ready to leave.

"Hey, Layla, can I walk you to your car?"

"Yes, that would be nice," Layla said, giving him a warm smile. "By the way, thanks again for the Atlanta Braves t-shirt. It's a perfect fit," she said, spinning around to model the shirt.

"No problem. It's one of the rare benefits of working at Super Star Sporting Goods."

Warren opened the door for Layla and they walked outside to the parking lot.

"Are you excited about performing at the Waverly this weekend?" she asked.

"It's more exciting when we perform at larger venues like the Atlanta Civic Center or the Peachtree Playhouse."

"Oh, that's right. You enjoy performing in front of thousands of people instead of a few hundred."

"Layla, when you have all this talent, you should share it with as many people as possible," he said, sounding very cocky.

"You are so conceited," she said, punching him lightly in the arm.

As they got closer to Layla's car, Warren tried getting up the courage to ask her out on a date. It had been almost two months since the last time they went out together and it didn't go very well. When Layla joined the band a few years ago, she saw for herself how women practically threw themselves at Warren before, during and after the shows. Layla made it very clear to him that he was a nice guy, but she didn't want to be part of his harem of women. Yes, he admitted that he got caught up living the life of a "player," but he insisted, those days were far behind him. He was determined to prove to Layla that he was a changed man and that he wanted her to be the only woman in his life. As they reached Layla's car, Warren stepped in front of her, blocking her way.

"Layla, do you have any plans for tonight?"

"I sure do. I'm going home and taking a long, hot bath. After working all day at Macy's, then coming here to practice for almost two hours, I just want to go home, relax, and finish a book I've been reading."

"Wow, it doesn't get any more exciting than that," he said, sarcastically.

"I know my evenings are nothing compared to your wild, all-night partying, but I enjoy it."

"First of all, I don't go out partying all night anymore. Second, I enjoy spending a nice, quiet evening at home reading a book, too."

"Warren, when was the last time you read a book or magazine other than Playboy or Hot Hooters?" she said, laughing.

"For your information, I just finished reading a book called, *Give it a Chance.*"

"Oh, really? Tell me a little bit about this book," she said, putting him on the spot.

"It's about a guy who meets this shy, beautiful woman and falls in love with her. No matter how hard he tries, she doesn't give him a chance to prove his love for her."

"Hmmm, this story sounds very familiar. Are you sure you're not talking about a real life story?"

"I guess it's possible that the author of this book was writing from personal experiences. As I was saying, the poor guy gives her beautiful flowers, writes her romantic poems, and even composes a love song for her. After several months, the woman finally gives the guy a chance and she agrees to go out with him. I really admire a strong woman, with a kind heart, who can give a good man a chance to prove his love."

"It's easy for a strong woman with a kind heart to give a man a chance, when the man isn't a full-time player," she responded.

"Full-time player? Is that what you think of me?"

"I didn't mention any names, but a hit dog will holler," she replied, putting her hands on her hips.

Warren leaned forward and gently grabbed her hand. For several moments, he looked deep into her warm, caring eyes.

"Listen, I know I've messed around with a lot of females in the past, but I'm not like that anymore."

"The few times we've gone out on a date, I really had a great time, but you and I both know that you're not ready to commit to one woman."

"That's not true. Since I've gone out with you, I haven't been interested in any other woman."

"Oh really? What about a few months ago at the Buckhead Diner?"

"I already told you, she was just a friend. I went out with her a few times and that was it."

"Warren, this woman walked up to our table, threw your drink in your face and threatened to kick my ass. That woman was crazy."

"Exactly! That's why I stopped dating her!"

"Maybe you should be more careful about the women you sleep around with."

"Layla, I never had sex with that woman," he said, defensively.

"Okay, now you sound like Bill Clinton."

Warren could feel himself becoming frustrated, so he turned and slowly walked away from her. Even though Layla didn't want to get into a relationship with Warren, she still cared about him and didn't want him to be upset. She walked up to Warren and gave him a hug.

"Don't be mad. I believe you, okay? I'm just trying to prevent myself from getting hurt. I hope you can understand that."

"Layla, I would never hurt you," he said, sincerely.

As Warren put his arms around her, she shuddered as she felt his slim, but muscular frame pressing against her body. As he pulled her closer, she wondered if he could feel her heart beating like a drum. She tried to tell him to let go, but as she opened her mouth to speak, nothing came out. This was not what she wanted. She couldn't deny the desire she felt for this man. Standing at five foot ten, Warren appeared to tower over her. As he leaned down to kiss her, she closed her eyes, anticipating his warm lips pressing against hers. Suddenly, the front door to Gerald's Warehouse opened, startling both of them, as Terry came walking out carrying his guitar and amplifier.

"Layla, don't you know better than to be hanging out in dark parking lots with strange men?" Terry said, jokingly. Layla regained her composure and pretended to throw punches at Warren.

"Don't worry, I have a black belt in karate. I know how to handle guys like this."

"Warren, make sure Layla gets home safely," Terry said, putting his musical equipment into his car.

"Go on home, old man. She's in good hands," Warren said, putting his arm around Layla.

As Terry drove away into the night, there was an awkward silence between Warren and Layla. Finally, Layla broke the silence.

"Well?" she asked.

"Well, what?"

"The book you were reading, how did it end?"

"The woman fell madly in love with the guy, they got married, had four kids and lived happily ever after."

"You are such a liar," Layla said, laughing.

"What are you talking about?" he said, with a serious look on his face.

"You didn't read any book called, *Give it a Chance*. You made all of that up."

Warren tried his best to keep a straight face, but he couldn't hold back any longer and began to laugh.

"Okay, maybe I made up the story about the book, but you have to admit it sounded very romantic," he said, gazing into her eyes.

"Yes, I admit it sounded very romantic," she replied, trying to conceal her nervousness.

"I'm hoping one day you'll give me a chance to show you how happy I can make you."

As Layla looked into his eyes, she could feel herself becoming drawn to his confidence and charm. As much as she was attracted to him, she didn't want to develop any romantic feelings for him. She knew that Warren enjoyed living the life of a single man and she didn't want to be one of his several girlfriends. She looked at her watch and convinced herself it was time to leave before her emotions began to take over.

"Hey, it's getting late. I really need to be getting home. Thank you again for walking me to my car."

"The pleasure was all mine," he said, kissing her hand.

For several moments, no one said a word. There was so much they wanted to say to each other, but they realized that it wasn't the right time. Layla smiled at him and quickly got into her car. She started her car and rolled down her window to talk to him.

"Okay, I guess I'll see you Friday."

"Drive safely," he said, with a warm smile.

"Bye, Warren."

As Layla slowly drove away, she looked into her rear view mirror. She noticed Warren standing in the dimly-lit parking lot, watching her drive away. Her heart was tempting her to stop the car, turn around and throw herself into his arms, but her head was telling her to keep looking forward and drive home. On this particular night, her head won out over her heart.

Chapter 12

It had been almost three months since Angela started seeing Terry and things were going surprisingly well. She initially had reservations about dating him, but after getting to know him, she realized that she misjudged him. Maybe there are some good guys left in this world after all. After a lot of soul searching, she had finally decided that is was time for Kenya and Terry to meet each other. When Terry suggested getting together so he could meet Kenya, she agreed it was finally the right time. It was 4:25 p.m. on a humid Sunday evening. After driving around for several minutes, Angela finally found an available space in the parking lot of the Action Zone. Terry chose to meet at this venue because it was a family-oriented amusement center, known for its fun video games and good food. He felt it would be better to meet Kenya at a place like this, so she wouldn't feel like he was invading her space at home. Angela truly wanted Terry to meet her daughter, but she was feeling extremely nervous. Even though she had dated a few men since she left Kenya's father almost two years ago, Terry was the first man she had felt comfortable with meeting her daughter. As she and Kenya walked around the indoor amusement center, she tried to start up a conversation with her daughter.

"My friend thinks you will really enjoy this place. What do you think about it so far?"

"I guess it's okay," Kenya replied, sounding very disinterested.

"My friend says there are over a hundred video games to play here."

"There sure are a lot of people in this place," Kenya said, looking around the large room.

Suddenly, Angela's cell phone began to chime, indicating that she had received a text message. She took the cell phone out of her purse and noticed she had received a text message from Terry.

"Is that your . . . friend?" Kenya asked, sarcastically.

"Yes, it's my friend, little smarty mouth. He's letting us know he has a table reserved for us."

As they walked over to the restaurant area, Angela couldn't resist smiling at her daughter's little remark. She just hoped Kenya wouldn't do or say anything to embarrass her in front of Terry. From across the room, she spotted Terry standing next to a table waving at her.

"There he is," she said to Kenya. As Angela walked toward Terry, she found herself comparing him to Kenya's father, Preston. At five foot nine, Terry wasn't as tall as Preston, but he had a physique any man would be proud to have. Terry was one of those guys that could make casual looking blue jeans look extremely sexy. The blue, silk shirt he was wearing did a great job accentuating his muscular chest and arms. She was usually attracted to men who were clean-shaven, but Terry looked very handsome with his trimmed mustache and goatee.

"Hi, I'm glad you could make it," he said, giving Angela a gentle hug. "And who is this pretty, young lady with you?"

"This is my daughter, Kenya. Kenya, this is my friend, Terry Freeman."

"Hello, Kenya. It's nice to meet you," he said, extending his hand.

"Hi," she said, softly.

"Okay, this is our table," he said, pulling out a seat for Kenya.

"Thanks," she said very quietly.

Angela glared over at Kenya and gave her the "you better act nice" look. Suddenly, a waitress walked up to their table.

"Hello, welcome to the Action Zone. My name is Ashley. Is everyone ready to order?"

As much as Angela wanted to order the burger and wing combo, she thought about how snug her jeans were feeling on her hips and decided to order something more calorie friendly.

"I'll have the garden salad and a glass of water," she said, reluctantly.

"Kenya, what would you like to eat?" Terry asked, looking over the menu.

"I'm not really hungry," Kenya said, meekly.

"Sweetheart, I'm sure there's something on the menu you like." Angela said, giving her daughter a piercing stare.

Terry looked at Angela with a sly grin on his face, letting her know that he was up to something.

"Ashley, I would like to order a pizza, but I'm not sure what I want on it." he said, mulling over the menu and trying to look confused. He put the menu down and looked at Kenya.

"Kenya, what toppings do you like when you order a pizza?"

"Well, I like sausage, pepperoni and extra cheese on mine."

"That sounds good to me. Okay, I'll have a large pizza with sausage, pepperoni, and extra cheese."

"What would you like to drink, sir?" the waitress asked politely.

"I'll have some sweet tea and a large strawberry milkshake for this pretty, young lady."

"Okay, your food will be ready shortly," the waitress said, picking up their menus and walking back to the kitchen.

"How did you know I like strawberry milkshakes?" Kenya asked, with a confused look on her face.

"Sometimes, if I concentrate really hard, I can read people's minds," Terry replied, trying to look serious.

"Mr. Freeman, you can't read people's minds," she said, rolling her eyes.

"Okay, your mother might have mentioned to me that you like strawberry milkshakes. By the way, please call me Terry. Calling me, Mr. Freeman, makes me feel like an old man."

"Well, you are kind of up there in age, sir," she replied with a little smile.

"I might be a little old, but I bet I can beat you in any video game in this place."

"I bet you can't," she fired back.

"Okay, after we eat, I'll let you choose any game you want to play and I'll destroy you."

"Yeah, whatever."

"Whatever? Little girl, I will bring tears to your eyes."

"Oh, no you won't."

"Okay, you guys." Angela said, interrupting their verbal sparring. "You two can settle this after we eat."

When the waitress arrived with their food, Terry continued to make conversation with Kenya by asking her questions about school and other areas of interest. As Angela listened to Terry and Kenya's conversation, she couldn't help but feel a sense of admiration for him. Even though Kenya had been giving him a hard time, he found a way to get her to interact with him. After finishing their meal, the three walked around the large room filled with various video games and other fun activities.

"Okay, let's see what you've got, little girl. You pick any game you want to play and I'll crush you." Terry said, sounding like one of those professional wrestlers promoting a pay-per-view event.

"Let's play that one over there," Kenya said, pointing at a game.

Angela couldn't help but smile when she noticed the game Kenya had chosen. Of all the games in this building, her daughter decided to challenge Terry in *Guitar Hero*, a video game simulating the playing of an electric guitar. Angela walked over to Kenya and put her arm around her little shoulder.

"Sweetheart, maybe you should pick another game."

"Mom, I have this game at home. I'll slaughter him," she said with confidence.

Angela looked at Terry who had a big smile on his face.

"Ladies first," Terry said as he followed Kenya to the video game.

Angela walked up to Terry and gently grabbed his arm.

"You'd better go easy on her," she whispered in his ear.

"This is going to be fun," he said with an evil laugh.

For the next hour, Terry and Kenya competed against each other in various video games. It warmed Angela's heart to see Kenya having such a good time with Terry. Since they moved from Chicago two years ago, Kenya hadn't fully adjusted to life in Atlanta. Angela knew it was difficult for Kenya leaving her school and all of her friends behind, but she had to do what was best for herself and her daughter. Angela knew she couldn't go through another year of pain and anger with Preston. She got tired of finding women's numbers in his car or women texting him whom he claimed were business clients. She put up with his lying and cheating for years because she didn't want to deprive Kenya of having her father in her life. Angela knew how hard it was for her growing up without a father and she didn't want her daughter to go through the same pain and emptiness she went through. It took years, but she finally found the strength to leave Preston. It was difficult for Angela that first year she moved to Atlanta, but once she started receiving Preston's child support checks, it made her situation so much better. Angela knew it didn't make things any easier on Kenya when she started working part-time at the law firm. She tried to keep Kenya busy by getting her involved in gymnastics and taking piano lessons, but she still felt guilty because she didn't have a lot of quality time to spend with her daughter anymore. It warmed Angela's heart as she watched her daughter laughing and having so much fun.

"Angela, get over here!" Terry yelled, breaking Angela out of her daydreaming. "Kenya wants to challenge us in a race car game."

"Racing cars? I don't think so. I have problems driving my own car around in this city," she replied.

"Come on, Mom," Kenya said, grabbing her mother's arm. "Even if you crash, nobody gets hurt."

Seeing the big smile on her daughter's face was all the convincing she needed.

"Okay, let's do this," Angela said, sitting down in a car seat attached to the video game screen. She glanced over at Kenya, who was staring at the screen of the video game, waiting for the race to begin. "Are you having fun, sweetheart?" Angela asked over the roar of the race car engines.

"Yes!" she replied, not taking her eyes off the video screen. After several minutes of racing and several crashes, Angela stood up from the video game seat, feeling very humbled.

"Mom, what are you doing? The next race is getting ready to start!" Kenya said, excitedly.

"No, that's it for me. I'm tired of finishing in last place. Anyway, it's getting late and you know you have school tomorrow."

"Please, Mom, just one more race," she pleaded.

"No. I know you, Kenya. One race will turn into two races and then you'll be trying to talk me into staying here for another hour."

"Yeah, let's get out of here, Kenya. I've beaten you enough today." Terry said, sounding very cocky.

"You got lucky," Kenya replied, trying to conceal her smile.

"I'll admit, you're pretty good for a little girl. We can always come back another day and I'll give you a rematch."

"Sure, I guess we could do that," Kenya said, trying not to sound too excited.

As they walked out of the amusement center, Terry escorted both of them to Angela's car.

"Thank you for the meal and showing us a great time," Angela said, giving Terry a kiss on the cheek. She glanced over at Kenya, who was trying her best to act disinterested. "Kenya, did you have a good time?" she asked, giving her daughter the, "act like you have some manners," stare.

"Yes, I had a good time. Thank you, Mr. Freeman," she said in a monotone voice.

"You're welcome, Kenya. It was nice meeting you, and remember, it's okay to call me Terry.

"I'll try to remember that, Mr. Freeman." she replied.

Angela could feel herself getting very annoyed with Kenya's behavior. After all the fun she had this evening, she couldn't believe her daughter was still giving Terry such a hard time.

"Alright, let's go, young lady," she said, giving Kenya a firm nudge in the back.

"Hey, Kenya," Terry whispered to her before she got into the car. "I sure hope your mother drives this car better than she drives on those video racing games."

She tried her best not to laugh, but Kenya began to giggle at Terry's comment.

"Kenya, you'd better make sure you put your seat belt on," he said, causing her to burst out laughing.

"Oh, that's funny?" Angela said, gently pushing Kenya into the car and closing the door. "Thank you for showing her a great time," she said, getting in the car. "I'll call you later. Bye."

As Terry watched her drive away, he felt very pleased knowing his first meeting with Kenya turned out quite well. He realized that his relationship with Kenya would most likely determine how close he and Angela would become in theirs. Even though it had only been a few months since they started dating, Terry had developed strong feelings for Angela. It had been several years since he felt that way about a woman and he was willing do whatever it would take to make their relationship work.

Chapter 13

It was Wednesday morning and Reggie was sound asleep in his bed. Suddenly, the blaring sound of his alarm clock resounded loudly in his ears. Reggie rolled over and put the pillow over his head to drown out the noise. His father, Henry Freeman, was knocking on his son's door for the second time.

"Reginald, do you know what time it is? You need to wake up!" Reggie sat up in his bed feeling tired and annoyed.

"I'm up, dad. You can stop banging on my door."

"Open the door, Reggie," his father yelled on the other side of the door. Reggie finally dragged himself out of the bed, unlocked the door, and opened it.

"I said I was up. Why do you keep banging on my door?"

"I've been knocking on your door for the last twenty minutes, trying to wake you up. Can you please turn that alarm off while I'm talking to you?" Reggie walked over to his night stand and hit the snooze button, then flopped back down on his bed.

"Reginald, what are you doing? You need to get up and get ready for work."

"I'm not going to work today. I don't feel so good. I think I'm coming down with something," he said, pulling the covers over his head.

"The only thing you're coming down with is a hangover. I heard you coming into the house around 4:30 a.m. Just look at you. You're still wearing the same clothes you had on when you went out last night. I know you've been drinking because I could smell the alcohol the minute you opened your door."

"Come on, Dad, don't start that up again," he said, rolling over and putting a pillow over his head.

"Reginald, sit up and look at me when I'm talking to you!"

"Alright, alright, I hear you," Reggie replied, sitting up in the bed.

"You need to get up, shower and go to work," Henry said, trying to remain calm.

"I told you, I'm not going to work today."

"Son, you just started working at this job last month. You don't need to start taking days off from your job just because you were out partying all night."

"Dad, don't get upset, but I'm not working at the store anymore."

"Why not?" Henry asked, with a stunned look on his face.

"The supervisor at the store said I was being insubordinate and told me not to come back to work."

"Are you telling me you got fired from another job?"

"Hey, it wasn't my fault. My supervisor kept ordering me around like I was his slave. He was disrespecting me and I wasn't going to put up with that. No matter where you go, the white man is always trying to keep the black man down."

"What are you talking about? I met your supervisor and he's a black man."

"Yeah, he's black, but he thinks like a white man."

Henry's patience with his son was wearing very thin. It was times like this that Henry was glad to be a religious man because he was very tempted to pick up the baseball bat lying next to the bed and knock some sense into his son's head.

"Reginald, I am so tired of you pulling out the race card and blaming the white man whenever you get fired from a job. You need to grow up and be responsible for your own actions."

"I am responsible. I'm not going to be sitting around the house broke. I'll still have money coming in. I've got a gig coming up next week with the band. Don't worry. I'll have enough money to help pay the bills around here," he said, sprawling back down on his bed.

Henry was feeling very frustrated, but said a little prayer to himself to regain his composure.

"Son, this isn't about you having money to help pay the bills. I'm concerned about how you're living your life. You go out almost every night with your friends, partying at the clubs, drinking, and coming home whenever you want to. Trust me, you don't want to get in trouble with the law by hanging around the wrong people. I'm sure you know how difficult it is being a young, black man with a police record."

"You act like I hang out with a bunch of criminals. Those people happen to be my friends."

"Do you mean the same friends you were hanging out with when you got arrested a few months ago?"

"Oh, my God! How many times are you going to bring that up? I told you, it wasn't my weed!"

"It doesn't matter, Reggie! You were in a car with illegal drugs when the police officer pulled you over!" Henry didn't want to get into a shouting match with his son, so he took a deep breath and tried to talk calmly. "You were very lucky you didn't get charged with illegal drug possession. Next time, you might not be so lucky."

"Let's face it, Dad. You never like anything I do. When I grew my dreadlocks, you didn't like it. When I got my tattoos, you didn't like it. When I got this diamond put in my ear, you didn't like it. I'm always going to be wrong in your eyes."

"Son, growing dreadlocks, getting tattoos and putting a diamond in your ear doesn't make you a man. All I'm asking is for you to show me and your mother a little respect."

Reggie walked over to his dresser and turned on his CD player. Music started to play, followed by rap lyrics. "*All these bitches in the club, I can have my pick. These niggas want to be like me, y'all can suck my dick.*"

"Reggie, turn that garbage off," Henry said sternly.

"It's not garbage," Reggie said, turning off the CD player. "It's a rap song I wrote and recorded on a CD," he said proudly. "I don't understand why you have a problem with that."

"The problem is, I don't want to hear rap songs that are insulting and degrading to black people."

"It's what people want to hear. If black people felt like rap music was degrading, they wouldn't go out and buy the music."

"Let me explain something to you, Reggie. Traditionally, black people are a very strong and proud race. We've encountered many obstacles over the last 400 years such as slavery, the Jim Crow Laws, the Ku Klux Klan and segregation. There is one obstacle standing before black people that is more powerful than anything we've ever encountered," Henry said, looking deeply into his son's eyes. "Our own black people," Henry stated, passionately.

"Come on, Dad. Stop being so dramatic about this."

"I'm not being dramatic. We have black gangs killing other black gangs. We have black drug dealers selling illegal drugs to other black people. We have black people robbing and killing other black people. And then we have black music artists disrespecting, insulting, and degrading other black men and women."

"You can't honestly say that rap music is responsible for all of that."

"No, I'm not saying that. What I am saying is that music is a very powerful medium that reaches out and influences millions of people. Rap music can be a wonderful form of entertainment and enlightenment if used in a positive way. Unfortunately, a lot of these hip-hop artists use rap in a negative way because record labels are paying them millions of dollars to do so."

"Okay, we're not in church. You don't need to preach to me. I already know I'm a big disappointment to you. I'm never going to live up to your "holier than thou" standards."

"That's not true, Reggie. All I've ever asked is that you respect our home. I don't think that's asking too much."

"When are you going to stop treating me like a child? I'm twenty-five years old. I'm a grown man, I can stay out late and do whatever I want to do!" he said, defiantly.

"Not while you're living under my roof!" Henry fired back.

"That's cool. Maybe it's time for me to move out and get under my own roof!"

"If you can't follow the rules of this house, maybe that's what you need to do!"

"No problem," Reggie said, getting out of the bed and walking over to his closet. "I'll be out of your house by tonight," he said, throwing his clothes from the closet to the floor.

"Reggie, are you sure this is what you want to do?"

"Yeah, it's time for me to get my own place."

Henry stood quietly as his son continued to empty clothes and other items from his dresser drawers. He's tempted to talk his son out of leaving, but deep down he realized that it was time to show his son some "tough love." Maybe it was best for his son to get out on his own, he thought. Maybe his son needed to find out for himself how hard life can be without Mom and Dad to depend on all of the time.

"There's a large travel bag in the basement if you need it," Henry said, already feeling the sadness building inside him.

"Okay, thanks," Reggie responded without looking up.

For a brief moment, Henry considered talking to his son again, but, instead, he decided to walk out of his son's room, closing the door behind him.

Chapter 14

Angela was quickly walking into the lobby of the Westin Peachtree Hotel, located in the heart of downtown Atlanta. "Late again," she said to herself, as she looked at the time on her cell phone, which read 6:26 p.m. When Terry offered to take her out to dinner for her birthday, she didn't anticipate her baby sitter cancelling out on her. It had been a long time since she had gone out and celebrated her birthday and she wanted to make it very special. Ever since she moved to Atlanta, she had wanted to have dinner at the famous Sun Dial Restaurant. This upscale restaurant, located seventy three floors above the city, rotates 360 degrees every hour, giving diners a magnificent view of the beautiful Atlanta skyline. As she walked into the entrance of the hotel, she noticed Terry standing in the lobby, looking very suave, wearing a dark brown Armani suit. As she approached him, he greeted her with a warm smile and a kiss.

"Terry, please don't give me a hard time about being late."

"Hey, I was going to give you a compliment. You're only twenty seven minutes late this time," he said, glancing at his watch. "You're getting better," he said, jokingly.

"It's not my fault. My baby sitter calls me at the last minute and tells me she can't watch Kenya, but, I do have some good news to make up for being late. Kenya is going to spend the night with one of her friends, so I don't have a curfew tonight," she said, giving Terry a flirtatious smile.

"Now that's what I call good news."

"I hope that makes up for my being late."

"Don't worry about that. I got a little hungry waiting for you, so I just walked down the street to Burger King and ate a burger and some fries."

"Terry, why would you do that!?"

"Hey, I was starving," he replied, rubbing his stomach. Before Angela could say another word, Terry put his arms around her and gave her a hug. "Calm down, pretty lady. I was just kidding."

"That wasn't funny," she said, giving him a light punch to his chest.

"I made reservations for six o'clock, so we better get going."

As they walked to the elevators, Terry couldn't help but admire how stunning Angela looked this evening. She was wearing a short blue Versace dress which hugged her rounded hips and showcased her silky, smooth legs. He was totally captivated as he watched her gracefully walk across the lobby floor in her matching blue pumps. As they entered the elevator, Angela looked at herself in the reflection of the glass elevator doors.

"There's no need to make any adjustments. You look absolutely beautiful."

"Thank you. I have to say, you're looking very handsome in that suit, Mr. Freeman."

"Well, thank you, Miss Greer."

As the elevator continued to rise up to the top floor, Angela began to smile, knowing this was going to be a memorable birthday dinner. She put her arms around Terry's waist and gave him a firm hug.

"Thank you again for bringing me here for my birthday."

"You know, it would have been nice if you could have brought Kenya with you to celebrate your birthday. Then I could have picked you both up instead of meeting you here like we're on our first blind date. After all, we've been seeing each other for about three months now."

"It's been two months and twenty-three days to be precise."

"I'm surprised you don't know the hours, minutes, and seconds," he said, sarcastically.

"I really want you and Kenya to get to know each other. I just want to take it slowly so she can gradually adjust to the new man in my life."

"The new man in your life? I like the way that sounds. Anyway, I just thought you might have wanted to spend some time with her on your birthday."

"No, I need a little time away from being a mommy. It's been a few years since I've celebrated my birthday. I'm going to eat a nice dinner, have some adult drinks, and who knows what can happen later tonight?" she said with a sensuous smile.

"Oh, believe me. This could be a birthday night you'll never forget."

"Okay, don't you start getting a big head. This elevator isn't large enough to handle that. I probably shouldn't ask, but how high does this elevator go up?" she asked, looking outside of the glass elevator.

"It goes about seventy-three stories high."

"Oh, God. Are you serious?" she said, holding tightly onto Terry's arm.

"That's right, just hold on to big daddy's arm. I'll protect you."

As Angela tightened her grip on Terry's arm, she was relieved to hear the soft chimes in the elevator indicating that they had reached the top floor. The elevator doors opened and they walked to the entrance of the restaurant.

"This place is so elegant," she said, excitedly. "Have you ever been here before?"

"Yes, a few years ago," he replied.

As they reached the entrance of the restaurant, they were greeted by a distinguished-looking gentlemen dressed in a black tuxedo.

"Good evening. Welcome to the Sun Dial Restaurant. May I help you?" the greeter asked politely.

"Yes, I have a table reserved under the name of Terrence Freeman."

"Yes, I see you had a reservation but unfortunately, that table is no longer available. Your reservation was for 6:00 p.m. and it is now 6:34," he said, looking at his watch. "We can only hold reservations for thirty minutes."

"How long will it take for another table to become available?"

"One moment, I'll check on that for you, sir," the greeter responded, looking over his notepad.

"It looks like the next available table will be approximately forty minutes."

"Is there any way you can squeeze us in? It's my friend's birthday."

"Happy birthday, ma'am," the greeter said, glancing over at Angela. "No, I won't be able to squeeze you in, sir."

"Excuse us for a second," Angela said, gently grabbing Terry's arm and pulling him away from the greeter. "This is my fault for being late," she whispered. "Let's just go somewhere else."

"No, it's your birthday and this is the place you chose to celebrate it. Wait here, I'll be right back." Terry walked over to the greeter. "Excuse me, Mr. . .," Terry paused, waiting for a response.

"Jennings. Raymond Jennings," he replied.

"Mr. Jennings, I understand we're a little late, but can you help me out here? It is her birthday."

"I'm sorry, sir, but that's the restaurant policy."

Terry began to become a little frustrated. He really wanted Angela to have a memorable birthday, so he reluctantly tried a different approach.

"Mr. Jennings, is Charles Duncan here tonight?"

"Sir, Mr. Duncan is not available for this type of situation. If you would like to speak to a supervisor, I can . . ."

"No, thank you," Terry said, cutting him off. "Please tell Mr. Duncan that Terrence Freeman would like to speak to him." Mr. Jennings pulled out a cell phone from his jacket and made a call.

"Mr. Duncan, there is a gentlemen here at my station that is requesting to see you. His name is Terrence Freeman. Very good, sir. I'll let him know." Mr. Jennings slid the cell phone back into his jacket and walked over to Terry and Angela. "Mr. Duncan will see you shortly," he said dryly, walking back to his station.

"Let's just go," Angela said in a soft voice."

"Relax, I've got this," Terry said with confidence.

A few moments later, a middle-aged, chubby, white gentleman, in a black three-piece suit, approached the entrance of the restaurant.

"I'm sorry to have disturbed you, Mr. Duncan, but this gentleman . . ."

"Terry Freeman!" Mr. Duncan said, cutting off Mr. Jennings. "It's so good to see you."

"Hello, Mr. Duncan. It's been a while," Terry replied, shaking Mr. Duncan's hand.

"How's your mother doing?"

"She's doing fine."

"I heard that your band is back together."

"Yes, we've been doing some performances for a few months now."

"I'm so glad to hear that. We need to make plans to get you back in here." Mr. Duncan noticed Angela standing behind Terry. "And who is this lovely, young lady?"

"This is my friend, Angela Greer. Angela, this is Charles Duncan, the owner of the Sun Dial Restaurant."

"Nice to meet you, Mr. Duncan."

"No, the pleasure is all mine," he said, gently taking her hand and kissing it.

"Today is Angela's birthday and I wanted to take her to the best restaurant in town.

Unfortunately, we got here a little late and lost our reserved table," Terry explained.

"I'm sure we can take care of that," Mr. Duncan said with a wide grin. "In case you didn't know, the Georgia Grits Gang is performing tonight. I'll be sure to get you a table near the stage." he said, motioning to Mr. Jennings. "Raymond, could you please escort my guests to table three?"

"Yes, Mr. Duncan," Raymond responded.

"I really appreciate this, Mr. Duncan," Terry said, shaking Mr. Duncan's hand.

"No, problem. You two enjoy your evening. Happy birthday, Ms. Greer," Mr. Duncan said as he walked back to his office.

Angela and Terry followed Mr. Jennings to a small table for two, near a stage where four middle aged gentlemen were performing. The dimly lit chandeliers, the floral arrangements, and the sound of live jazz music cascading throughout the room, created a very romantic atmosphere.

"This is so nice," Angela said, smiling, as Terry pulled out a chair for her to sit. As Terry walked over to his chair and sat down, he noticed Angela looking at him with a curious look on her face.

"What?" he asked, looking bewildered.

"You're just full of surprises, aren't you?"

"What do you mean?"

"When I asked you earlier if you've ever been here before, you didn't mention that you knew the owner of one of the most exclusive restaurants in Atlanta."

"I met Charles Duncan about four years ago. When he became the owner of this restaurant, he started booking live bands to entertain the dinner guests. I guess he really liked our music because he would book our band to perform here once or twice a week."

A waitress walked up to their table to take their order. While waiting for their dinner, Angela peered out of the nearby glass window to admire the view of the city.

"This is so beautiful. I can't believe we have a table so close to a window. Thank you, Terry," she said, leaning over and giving him a kiss.

"I want this to be a birthday you'll always remember."

After twenty minutes of playing, the jazz band took a short break. One of the band members, a bald, chubby gentleman, in his late fifties, walked up to Terry and Angela's table.

"Terrence Freeman. I thought I recognized you sitting over here. How have you been, young man?"

"I'm doing well, Leo," Terry said, getting up from his seat and giving him a hug. "You guys sound great tonight. Your rendition of "Aisha" was very smooth."

"I appreciate that, but no one can play it quite like John Coltrane. You know Aisha was one of your father's favorite songs."

"Yes, I remember." Leo noticed Angela sitting in her seat listening to their conversation.

"I see you have company. I didn't mean to interrupt your dinner," he said, looking at Angela with a smile.

"Please excuse my bad manners. This is my friend, Angela Greer. Angela, this is Mr. Leonard Fontaine, trumpet player for the Georgia Grits Gang."

"Nice to meet you, Leonard." she said, shaking his hand.

"Please, call me Leo. All my friends do. I hope you're enjoying the show."

"Yes, I grew up listening to jazz. My mother was a big fan of Thelonius Monk and Miles Davis."

"Did Terry tell you his father use to play with Thelonius Monk's band back in the day?"

"No, he never mentioned that," she replied, looking at Terry with a surprised look on her face.

"I had the honor of performing with Terry's father many years ago. Bobby Freeman was a very talented and gifted musician." Leo noticed that Terry had gotten very quiet and hoped talking about his father hadn't brought back any bad memories. "Okay, I'm going to let you young people get back to your dinner. It was a pleasure meeting you, Angela."

"Thank you, Leo" she said with a warm smile.

Leo walked over and gave Terry a hug. "I really like her. She's a keeper," he whispered in his ear.

As Leo walked backstage to join his band, Angela leaned over and lightly hit Terry on his hand.

"You never told me your father played with Thelonius Monk."

"It was a long time ago. I was just a young kid around ten-years old," he replied.

"What instrument did your father play?"

"He played the saxophone, guitar, and piano."

"I think that is so awesome. Did your father . . ."

"Hey, this is your special night," he said, cutting her off. "Let's focus this night on you."

"Okay," she responded, feeling a little confused.

Moments later, the sound of applause filled the room as Leo and the Georgia Grits Gang walked back to the stage area.

"Thank you, ladies and gentlemen. We hope everyone is having a wonderful time this evening," Leo said into the stage microphone. "To start our next set, we would like to play a song by a jazz legend. Since we're high up in the sky, overlooking this beautiful city, I can't think of a more appropriate song to play than "Groovin' High" by Dizzy Gillespie." Leo picked up his trumpet and began to play as his band joined in. As Terry listened to the music, he couldn't help but reflect back on the fond memories of his father performing with his band, the Jazzy Gents. He still remembered, many years ago, sneaking into a nightclub to watch his father play. At the age of fourteen, he wasn't old enough to get into the club, but he was determined to watch his father perform. The smoke-filled club was crowded and extremely loud that night, but it seemed like his father was oblivious to all the noise and chaos going on around him. He was totally focused on his upcoming performance. Terry was amazed as he watched his father mesmerize everyone in that packed night-club playing his saxophone. The crowd howled and cheered their approval as chants of "Bobby, Bobby" reverberated throughout his father's performance. Terry felt a great sense of pride knowing his father was blessed with so much musical talent. Suddenly, Terry's flashback is interrupted by the sound of applause. The Georgia Grits Gang had just finished playing their song and Leo was bowing to the crowd.

"Thank you, everyone. You're too kind. The next song we'd like to play was composed by the great jazz legend, Thelonius Monk. At this time, I would like to make a special request. In the audience is a very talented musician I've known since he was a young boy," he said, looking at Terry. "I used to play with his father in a band called the Jazzy Gents many years ago. I would be honored if this young man would come up here and play one of his father's favorite songs, "Round Midnight." There was a small spattering of applause as Terry sat stunned in his chair. Ladies and gentlemen, may I present Mr. Terry Freeman."

Terry looked over at Angela who was clapping and urging him to join Leo on stage. Terry reluctantly stood up and walked toward the stage, still shocked that Leo would put him on the spot like that. While the crowd continued to applaud, Terry could feel the nervous butterflies in the pit of his stomach. As he walked onto the stage, he was greeted by the band members. Even though it had been several years since he had seen them, Terry remembered them all. Playing on drums was Thomas Boyd, Eddie "Big Feet" Stevens on the upright bass and Donald "Duck" Johnson on the piano, and of course, Leonard "Leo" Fontaine on the trumpet. Terry had met most of these talented musicians as a young boy when they performed with his father over fifteen years ago. Terry quickly walked around the stage to shake hands with all the band members. He turned around to see Leo walking from the back of the stage carrying a gold colored guitar, very similar to the one his father would sometimes play with the Jazzy Gents. "Here you go. It's already tuned and ready to play," Leo said, handing Terry the guitar. Terry put the guitar strap around his neck and let the guitar rest comfortably on his body. He gently stroked the strings on the guitar, making sure they were all tuned. To help calm his nerves, he closed his eyes and tried to focus. He could hear the soft clanking of metal utensils against dinner plates and the gentle rumble of numerous voices talking in the spacious dining room. When he opened his eyes, everyone in the room appeared to be focused on the stage, waiting in anticipation of a special musical performance. As Terry looked around the room, he noticed Angela sitting at their table watching him intently. This was the first time she would watch him perform without the other members of Infinite Noise and Terry didn't want to disappoint her. Suddenly, the lights in the room dimmed, leaving Terry and the rest of the band standing in the glow of the stage lights. The entire room became quiet as everyone turned their focus on the musicians on the stage. As Terry adjusted the microphone stand to accommodate his height, it suddenly occurred to him that he hadn't played "Round Midnight" since his father's death. "Round Midnight" was one of Terry's favorite songs. The song was a slow, beautiful ballad that featured very moving harmonic sequences with smooth chord progressions. For the past two years, Terry avoided playing this song because he felt it would bring back too many painful memories. After all, it was the first jazz song his father taught him to play when he was ten-years old. He wasn't sure why, but tonight he felt compelled to play this song. Maybe it was because he was playing with some of his father's old friends or maybe it was because he needed to prove to himself that he could move on with his life and leave all the hurt and pain behind him. Terry quietly cleared his throat and leaned toward the microphone.

"Good evening, everyone. I would like to dedicate this song to my father, Bobby Freeman," he said softly.

Terry glanced over at the drummer and nodded his head, letting him know he was ready to begin. The drummer tapped his sticks together to start the song and Terry began to play. The moment Terry strummed the first chord of the song, he felt an electric tingle surge throughout his entire body. At first, he assumed it was his nervousness of playing in front of a packed dinner crowd, but he realized the feeling was more of an ethereal presence. As Terry looked out into the audience, he noticed a gentleman sitting by himself at a table near the back of the dining room. In the dimmed lighting of the room, the gentleman almost looked like his father. Of course he knew it wasn't him, but he closed his eyes and imagined that the man at the dimly-lit table was his father, watching his son perform. As Terry continued to play, he released all of his emotions, putting his heart and soul into the song that would always remind him of his father. He could feel the tears begin to well up in his eyes, but he held them back, determined not to cry in front of a room full of strangers. The audience was totally captivated by the pure energy and emotion Terry was releasing through the playing of his guitar. Each note and every chord he played emitted a sound that gracefully flowed throughout the room. Several people sitting at their tables began to bob their heads and tap their feet to the beat of the music. Terry was so immersed into his playing that he didn't notice that the drummer and the bass player were the only band members playing along with him. The other band members had stopped playing and were listening to Terry play his rendition of this popular jazz song. At the end of the song, the audience erupted in applause, many giving him a standing ovation. Terry looked over at the table where the lone gentleman had been sitting, but no one was there.

"Thank you," Terry said meekly into the microphone. Leo walked over to the center of the stage, looking at Terry like a proud parent.

"Great job, son," he said, giving Terry a hug. "Your father would be so proud of you."

"Thanks, Leo."

Terry placed the guitar in a stand and quickly left the stage before Leo tried to get him to play an encore. When he reached his table, Angela greeted him with a big hug. As they both sat down, Angela continued to look at Terry in amazement.

"That was beautiful. I didn't know you could play like that."

"I started off a little slow," he said, modestly. "I didn't expect Leo to put me on the spot like that, but I'm glad you enjoyed it."

Angela reached over and gently touched his hand as the band began playing another song.

"I thought it was so sweet of you to dedicate that song to your father. You played it with so much emotion. It was absolutely wonderful. I wish your father could have been here to listen to you play."

"For a brief moment, I think he was," he said, smiling, as the mellow sounds of smooth jazz played in the background.

Chapter 15

Reggie was dining inside Frank Ski's Restaurant & Lounge, taking the last bite of his rib-eye steak. He realized it wasn't a very smart decision to spend $36.95 for his dinner and drinks, but it was a little too late now. It had been five days since he moved out of his parent's house and he was learning the hard way how difficult life could be out on his own. After paying his dinner bill, he looked inside his wallet and realized he had gotten himself into a bad situation. The $300.00 he took out of the bank on Tuesday for his motel rent, partying, dining out, and gas for his car was supposed to hold him over until next week. Unfortunately, he decided to spend $165.00 last night at the Magic City strip club. At the time, it felt good impressing his friends, buying them drinks and treating them to table dances. Now, after paying his dinner bill, he had $5.16 left to last him through the rest of the weekend. As he left the restaurant and walked to his car, he tried to assess his current situation. The rent at the motel where he had been staying was sixteen dollars a night. It was Saturday night, all the banks were closed until Monday and he didn't have a bank card to withdraw any money from an ATM. He pulled out his cell phone and noticed he had one bar left on the battery charge. He opened his car door and frantically began looking inside to find his cell phone charger, but it was nowhere to be found. He called his cousin, Warren, but after several rings, no one answered. "Damn, he doesn't even have voice mail for me to leave a message," he muttered to himself. He considered driving over to Warren's apartment, but as he looked at the gas indicator on empty, he knew he didn't have enough money for gas to get him there. He quickly began searching the contact list on his cell phone for friends to call. He found the name of a close friend he had known since high school.

"I sure hope he's home," he said as he dialed the telephone number. "Hello, Joey?"

"Yeah, who is this?"

"It's me, Reggie."

"What's up, my nigga?"

"Nothing much, just trying to survive."

"I feel ya. Hey, me and some of the boys are getting ready to drive downtown and check out some strip clubs. You wanna hang with us?"

"No, not tonight."

"Come on, Reggie, it's Saturday night!"

"Sorry, my cash flow is a little low right now. I was hoping you could loan me a little money until Monday."

"If you need some money, I've got some merchandise you can sell for me."

"No, I'm going to have to pass up on that."

"What's up with you, man? We use to get out there and hustle and make money back in the day."

"Joey, we did that shit back in high school. I don't do that stuff anymore."

"Oh, you think you're too good to hang out and hustle with me. I guess you think you're special because you play in that little band of yours, or maybe you've finally turned into daddy's little preacher boy."

"You need to chill with that kind of talk. I never said I was too good to hang out with you. I'm just trying to stay out of trouble."

"Don't give me that bullshit. All these years, guys have been sayin' you were a soft-ass punk, but I always had your back. I guess the homies were right about you all along."

"You can call me whatever you want. I'm not going to get busted selling drugs," Reggie replied.

"Awww, man, are you still trippin' about us gettin' busted with that weed? Nobody got in trouble except for Darnell and that was his dumb-ass fault for trying to hide it under the car seat."

"It was your weed, Joey!"

"Man, stop bitchin' about that! You need to grow some balls and stop actin' like a pussy."

Reggie was very tempted to tell Joey to kiss his ass, but he realized that he wasn't in a position to anger someone who might be able to help him.

"Look, Joey, I'm in a tight situation. Can you loan me the money or not?"

"Loan you some money? Nigga, I ain't no bank."

"No, you're not a bank, you're an asshole!" Reggie said, disconnecting the call.

Reggie leaned back in his car seat and tried to calm down. After regaining his composure, he continued to go through his contact list on his cell phone and attempted to call another friend.

"Hey, Nick. This is Reggie."

"Hey, bro. What's good?"

"I need a place to chill for a couple of days. Can you help me out?" Reggie asked, almost pleading.

"Sorry, I don't have room for anybody to stay here. I guess you gonna have to call somebody else."

"Come on, Nick. My cell phone is getting ready to die on me. I just need a place to stay until Monday."

"Sorry, I can't help you."

"Can I at least get the thirty dollars you owe me?"

"Sorry, I don't have it right now."

"You're sorry? No, I'm sorry I wasted my time calling your broke ass!" Reggie said, yelling into the phone. "I can't believe I thought these trifling, no expectation having, deadbeats were my friends," he said, talking to himself. "They're always asking me for money or favors. The one time I need help from them, they can't help me."

Reggie continued frantically looking through his cell phone's contact list, hoping to find someone who could help him. Suddenly, he came across a name in his cell phone that put a smile on his face.

"Here we go. I can call sweet little Kim Matthews. She won't let me down," he said as he dialed her phone number.

"Hey, Kim. How are you doing, baby?"

"Who is this?" Kim asked, not recognizing his voice.

"It's me, Reggie."

"You mean the same Reggie that I haven't heard from in two months?"

"Baby, I'm really sorry about that. I've been so busy performing with my band and then I misplaced your number."

"Well, do me a favor and misplace my number again."

"Come on, baby, don't be like that. Just give me a chance to . . . hello? Kim, are you there?"

Reggie looked at his phone and realized his cell phone battery had gone dead.

"Damn, I don't believe this!" he yelled to himself.

Reggie sat back in his car seat and closed his eyes, trying to figure out his next move. It was beginning to get dark and he knew he didn't want to sleep in his car in this part of town, especially with his drum set packed inside his trunk and back seat. He contemplated calling his father and asking if he could come back home, but his pride wouldn't allow him to make the phone call. He drove to a nearby gas station and put his last five dollars in the gas tank and prayed that he could make it to someone's place. After a twenty-five minute drive, Reggie drove into his cousin's apartment complex. He looked at the clock on his car's dashboard, which read 10:14 p.m. He felt a sense of relief as he noticed Terry's black Chevrolet Camaro parked in front of the apartment building. As he walked up to the apartment door, he contemplated what he could say to convince his cousin to let him stay for a few days. He softly knocked on the door hoping Terry didn't have any female company. After knocking on the door several times, Warren began to worry when no one came to the door.

"What the hell am I going to do if he's not home?" he thought to himself.

Suddenly, the door opened and Terry was standing in the doorway with stereo headphones draped around his neck.

"Hey, Reggie," Terry said, looking a little surprised.

"Hey, T. I'm sorry to drop by on you like this."

"No, it's cool. Come on in."

Reggie walked inside and immediately noticed Terry's guitar hooked up to some computer equipment.

"Sorry about the mess," Terry said as he cleared some sheet music paper off of a chair for him to sit. "I was going over a few songs for our show next week. So, what's going on?"

"Me and Daddy Jesus got into an argument last week and he kicked me out."

"That must have been a serious argument for him to kick you out."

"Man, he was trippin' about me coming home late a few times. I'm sick and tired of him treating me like a kid." Reggie felt himself getting upset so he walked over to a chair and sat down. "Anyway, I know you don't want to hear about my problems. I need a small favor. I'm a little low on cash right now. If it's cool with you, I was hoping I could stay here until Monday. Then, I can go to the bank, get some money, and find another place to stay. Before you ask, I've already tried calling some friends, but they all said no."

"Reggie, you're family. You know you can stay here."

"Thanks, I knew I could count on you," he said, feeling relieved. "By the way, is it okay to leave my drums in my car?"

"Just to be safe, let's bring your drums inside and put them in the guest room."

Terry followed Reggie outside to his car and helped him carry his drum equipment and two luggage bags into the guest room. Finally, relieved that he had a place to stay for the weekend, Reggie laid down on the bed and closed his eyes. Looking at Reggie sprawled on the bed, Terry could tell that his cousin was exhausted.

"If you're hungry, there's some pizza in the fridge," Terry said.

"No, I'm good. All I want to do is take a nice, hot shower and get some sleep.

"The bathroom is down the hall, first door on the right. There are clean towels in the closet."

"Thanks, Terry. I really appreciate this."

"No problem. Anyway, we'll be performing at the Rialto Lounge next Thursday night, so I need to make sure my drummer gets plenty of rest so he won't be falling asleep during our show," Terry said, jokingly.

"Don't worry, I'll be ready," Reggie said, getting up and heading to the bathroom.

Terry waited until he heard the shower running, then he picked up his cell phone to make a call.

"Hi, Aunt Lori. No need to worry anymore. He got here about twenty minutes ago. Yes, he's fine. Right now, he's taking a shower. He's going to stay here for a few days. I'll keep in touch with you and Uncle Henry and let you know what's going on. Okay, bye."

Terry walked back over to his sofa, picked up his guitar, and continued to practice.

Chapter 16

Angela was scampering around her apartment trying to get herself ready for her law class. When she found out her second quarter law classes were only going to be offered on Tuesday and Thursday evenings, she was in a dilemma because she didn't know who could watch Kenya for those days. She was pleasantly surprised when Terry offered to watch Kenya after he got off work. They both decided it was a good idea since not only would it help Angela attend her classes, but it would also give Terry a chance to form a closer bond with Kenya.

"It's already 5:27 p.m. Where are my car keys?" Angela asked frantically, looking through her purse.

"Calm down, Angela. Your keys are right here on the kitchen counter," Terry said, handing her the keys.

"Okay, I'm calm," she said with a nervous smile. "Here's the number to the school and you have my cell phone number. Terry, are you sure you can handle this?"

"Yes, I've got this. I promise I'll call you if anything comes up."

Okay," she said, apprehensively.

"You might want to take an umbrella," Terry suggested. "I think it's supposed to rain tonight."

He could tell she was feeling very stressful, so he walked over and gave her a reassuring hug.

"Hey, don't worry, everything's going to be fine."

"Thank you for watching Kenya for me."

"I told you, it's not a problem."

Angela walked over to Kenya and gave her a hug and a kiss.

"Sweetheart, be a good girl while I'm gone, okay?"

"Okay, mom," Kenya replied.

"Don't worry, Kenya and I are going to have a great time while you're in class. Right, Kenya?"

"If you say so, sir," she said, walking back to her bedroom.

"Okay, I need to go. I should be back around 8:45 p.m." Angela said, giving him a quick kiss as she rushed out of the door.

As Terry locked the door behind her, he walked toward Kenya's room. He peeked into her bedroom and noticed Kenya sitting on her bed, reading a book.

"Are you hungry or want something to drink?" he asked.

"No sir," she said, not looking up from her book.

"Kenya, you don't have to call me, sir. All of my friends call me Terry."

"Okay," she replied.

"Hey, I brought some movies that I thought we could watch. "I've got some action movies, comedies, science fiction, and a few Disney movies." Kenya doesn't look up, still reading her book. "I also brought some microwave popcorn and some candy," he said, hoping that might get her somewhat excited.

"I've already eaten dinner and my mom doesn't like me eating junk food after dinner," she said in a nonchalant tone.

Terry tried not to get frustrated, knowing that little girl was trying her best to ignore him.

"What type of movies do you like?" he asked.

"I'm not allowed to watch TV or movies until I finish my homework and I'm trying to finish it now," she replied, sarcastically.

"Sorry, I didn't know you were doing homework. Alright, I guess I'll leave you alone and let you finish. I'll be in the den if you need anything, okay?"

"Okay," she said, not looking up from her book.

Terry walked into the den, turned on the TV remote and began searching through the channels for something good to watch. A few moments later, he found "Crimson Tide," one of his favorite Denzel Washington movies. He had probably seen this movie over fifty times, but he never got tired of watching it. Thirty minutes into the movie, he heard a distant rumble that sounded like thunder. He had hoped it wouldn't storm so Angela wouldn't have to drive home in the pouring rain. A flash of lightning crackled outside and the lights in the room dimmed momentarily. He reached over, grabbed the remote control, and turned off the TV. He went into the kitchen and began looking for a flashlight or candles just in case the storm knocked the power out. After rambling through a few drawers, he found a small, yellow flashlight. He turned it on and a dim light emanated from the bulb. The batteries were obviously weak and he had no idea if Angela had any new batteries or where to look for them. Suddenly, there was a loud thunder strike and the lights went completely out in the apartment. With only the small beam of light shining from the tiny flashlight, he slowly walked toward Kenya's room. Kenya's door was closed, so he softly knocked.

"Kenya, can I come in?" he asked.

She didn't answer, so he slowly opened the door and entered her room. The dim glow of the flashlight barely allowed him to see anything in her room. He slowly shined the flashlight around her room and stopped when he saw an empty bed with no pillow.

"Kenya, are you in here?"

When she didn't respond, Terry began to wonder if this little girl was playing games with him. Suddenly, he heard a faint noise in the corner of the room and aimed the small flashlight in that direction. Sitting on the floor, clutching a small pillow, was Kenya. Even in the dim glow from the flashlight, Terry could see the look of fear on her face.

"Are you okay?" he asked as he slowly walked over to her. "Is it okay if I sit next to you?"

"Yeah, it's okay," she whispered.

As he sat down and gently slid next to her, he could feel her little body trembling with fear. He placed the small flashlight upright on the floor to help illuminate the room.

"That sure is a loud storm out there," he said in a soft voice. "It looks like the storm knocked out everyone's power in the apartment complex." Suddenly, they heard a loud thunder strike, followed by a big flash of lightning. "Wow, that was a big one!" he said, excitedly.

"I hate storms," she said, meekly.

Terry realized the best thing to do was to get her mind off the storm.

"Did you know that I play in a musical band?"

"Yeah, my mother told me you're in a band called Infant Noise."

"That's close, but the name of the band is Infinite Noise. Believe it or not, the name of our band was created during a storm."

"How did you come up with a name like that?" she asked.

"Many years ago, my best friend and I were at my house trying to come up with a great name for a band we were forming. We were in my room writing a new song. I was playing the keyboard and my friend was playing his bass guitar when suddenly, all the lights went out. For several seconds, my friend and I were sitting in total darkness. My dad came walking into the room with a flashlight and said everything was okay. He said there was a big storm and the lightning knocked out all the power on our street. I think my dad knew we were a little scared, so he stayed in the room with us. My keyboard was battery-operated so it could still be played without any electricity in the house. For thirty minutes, my dad talked and played on my keyboard to keep us from being afraid of the dark. We told my father we were trying to write a new song, but we had run out of ideas to finish it. He explained to us that music is like numbers; it's infinite, continuous, and never-ending. He said if composed correctly, even the noise from the storm could be turned into good music. My friend and I looked at each other and thought that would be such a cool name for our band. So, we used the two words, infinite and noise, to come up with the name of our band."

"Yeah, Infinite Noise does sound pretty cool," she said softly.

Terry felt relieved knowing that talking to Kenya was helping to keep her mind off the storm outside, so he continued to talk to her.

"When I was your age, I was afraid of bad storms, too. I would jump whenever I heard the loud thunder or the bright flash of the lightning. My mom would tell me that thunder and lightning means that God and the devil are having an argument."

Suddenly, there was a loud boom of thunder. Kenya jumped and grabbed Terry's arm tightly.

"God and the devil must really be mad at each other tonight," she said, slightly trembling.

"Hey, it's okay to be a little scared. The important thing to remember is that God is not mad at you."

"But what if the devil is mad at me?" she asked softly.

"Always remember, too, that God will never let the devil harm you. As long as I'm around, I will never let the devil or anyone harm you, either."

"You promise?" she asked, looking up at him with her adorable, brown eyes.

"Yes, I promise."

Kenya leaned over and put her head on Terry's shoulder. He put his arm around her and gave her a gentle hug. It had taken a little more than three months, but Terry felt like he was finally creating a bond with Kenya and that put a big smile on his face.

Chapter 17

Preston Seymour was sitting at his desk at work, staring at his computer screen. "Damn," he muttered to himself, trying to remember the password to pull up his online banking account. After several attempts, he finally saw his banking account information appear on the screen. As Preston scrolled down the computer screen, he looked somewhat disappointed with the $87,203.43 in his savings account. When he scrolled down to his checking account balance, he shook his head in disbelief at the $18,105.16 balance in his checking account. He realized he had a bad habit of spending too much money on designer clothes and leasing expensive cars, but he felt he should have more money in his account for someone making a little over $135,000 a year. It didn't help that he was dating several women and spending hundreds of dollars a week to impress them. With his charm, good looks, and a six-figure income, he felt he could have any woman he desired. At six-two, two hundred fifteen pounds, Preston was an impressive looking man. He was blessed with dark, wavy hair, handsome features, and a physique most women would pay good money to see if he decided to become an exotic dancer. From the time he was a teenager in high school, Preston knew that he was a lady's man and he did his part to play that role. It definitely helped that he was raised in an upper middle-class family. His mother was a successful real estate agent and his father, a manager for a large accounting firm. He attended private schools during his high school years and then attended Northwestern University, where he received his business degree. After college, Preston began working at his father's accounting company. Sure, he heard the whispers from other employees that he was only hired because of his father, but he didn't care. It didn't matter what any of them said or thought about him. He was one of the top-paid accountants in the company and that's all that mattered to him. He continued to read over his current monthly expenses, which started with $4,200 for rent and utilities for his condominium. His other expenses included $786.00 for suits and shoes, $450.00 for a personal trainer, $65.00 for a haircut, $110.00 for a pedicure and $567.00 for dinner dates. After looking at all of his monthly expenses, the one that stood out the most was the child support payment. Suddenly, the door to Preston's office opened and one of his co-workers, Greg Day, walked in.

"Preston, you want to go out and grab some lunch with me?"

"You need to knock before you come barging into my office," Preston responded, with a foul attitude.

"Hey, I'm sorry. Don't bite my head off."

Preston realized that he was over-reacting because of his financial situation and tried to regain his composure.

"Come on in, Greg. I didn't mean to snap at you like that."

Greg closed the door and sat in a chair in front of Preston's desk.

"So, what's going on? Let me guess. You got busted by that female you've been dating," Greg said, jokingly.

"Man, I cut her loose about two weeks ago."

"Are you serious? You let that fine ass Tracy get away? Damn, I see why you're in such a shitty mood."

"Her name was Stacy, not Tracy," Preston responded.

"Stacy, Tracy or Macy, it doesn't really matter," Greg said, laughing. "You know you didn't care about her. You go through females like I go through my money. That's why I stay broke most of the time."

"I just got through looking at my bank account statements and I'm getting ready to join you."

"Preston, stop lying. I've seen your paycheck, so I know you're making some serious money. Your finances should be the least of your worries."

"I know I blow a lot of money on unnecessary shit, but child support is an expense I don't need in my life."

"It sounds like your baby's momma is hitting your wallet pretty hard," Greg said, trying to sound sympathetic.

"Don't call her my baby's momma. That sounds so ghetto. Her name is Angela," Preston said, looking annoyed.

"I'm not trying to get into your business, but how much money are you paying Angela for child support?"

"I send her a check for $5,000 each month."

"Five thousand freaking dollars! Even with bonuses and overtime, I don't make that much money in a month. When you went to child support court, did they think you were Tiger Woods? Or maybe they thought you were Tyler Perry," he said, jokingly.

"Do you think you're a damn comedian?"

"Relax, Preston. You know I'm just messing with you."

"For your information, most of that money I'm paying is from two years of back child support. I agreed to that amount because I thought she and I would be getting back together, but it doesn't look like that's going to happen."

"Damn, for $5,000, you need to make it happen."

Greg noticed a framed picture on Preston's desk. He reached over and picked it up.

"Is this Angela and your daughter?"

"Yeah, Angela sent me that picture from Atlanta last year."

"Whoa! Angela is fine as hell!" Greg said, excitedly.

"I know you're not in my office lusting over my woman's picture."

"Calm down. I was just complimenting you on your good taste in women. By the way, your daughter is a real cutie. How old is she?"

"I think Kenya is seven, no wait, she's eight-years old. She's got a birthday coming up next month."

"Jesus Christ! Do you realize you'll be paying child support for the next ten years?"

"Hey, I already know all that. I don't need you to remind me. Angela moved to Atlanta about a year and a half ago, so it's been hard for me to work things out with her. I know I made some mistakes in the past, but that was a long time ago. I want us to be a family, but she just won't give me a chance."

"Preston, I've known you for a little over a year and I know you enjoy living the life of a single man. Hell, if I was collecting a paycheck like yours, I'd be trying to sex every hot female in town. Are you sure you're ready to give all that up?"

"Maybe I'm getting old, but I'm tired of waking up next to some fake-ass female I don't even know or care about. I'm ready to settle down and be a real father to my daughter. I know you don't believe me, but I've changed."

"Maybe you have changed. In the time that I've known you, I've never seen you put a picture of any of your females on your desk," Greg said, putting the framed picture back on the desk.

"My daughter has a birthday coming up next month, so I've made plans to fly out to Atlanta in three weeks to see her. While I'm there, I'm going to convince Angela to move back here to Chicago, so we can be a real family."

"Preston, have you even considered that Angela might be involved with someone."

"I don't care if she's involved with someone or not. Angela is my woman and Kenya is my daughter. I'm going to Atlanta to take back what's mine!" he said with confidence.

"You are the man!" Greg said, giving Preston a high five.

"You're damn right, I am! Now, let's get out of here and grab some lunch."

Chapter 18

Damon was standing in front of his apartment door, fumbling with his keys. He was holding his bass guitar case in one hand while trying to unlock the door with the other. As he opened the door, he saw his seven-year-old son, Darius, sitting in front of the television.

"Hey, daddy!" his son yelled, running to his father. Damon set his guitar case down, picked up his son and gave him a big hug.

"Hey, little man, how was school today?"

"It was okay. We went over a bunch of words."

"Daddy is starving. What did mommy make for dinner?"

"I don't know. She made me a bowl of veggie soup," he replied, going back to watching his television show.

Damon picked up his guitar case and walked into the bedroom just as his wife, Gail, was coming out of the bathroom.

"It's almost 6:30. You're just now getting home?" she asked, sounding irritated.

Damon could tell from the tone in her voice that she wasn't in a good mood.

"After I left work, we had a short band practice," he replied, leaning his guitar case against the wall.

He walked over to give Gail a kiss, but she pulled away.

"Another band practice? Didn't you just have a band practice earlier this week?"

Yeah, we're going to perform this week at the Peachtree Gardens Center. Why are you giving me attitude?"

"If I have an attitude it's because you work all day at the post office, then you go straight to your band practices. You hardly have time for me and your son. While you're out with your friends, your son and I are stuck in this small apartment."

"You're not stuck in this apartment. You have a car. You can go anywhere you want to go."

"Go where, Damon? I'm not working. I barely have money to put gas in my car or to buy me and Darius something to eat if we go out."

It was obvious to Damon that his wife was in one of her foul moods. Instead of getting into an argument with her, he tried to change the subject.

"So, what's for dinner? I'm starving," he said, walking toward the kitchen.

"Do you want me to make you a bologna sandwich?" she asked.

"A bologna sandwich? Gail, is it asking too much to have a nice, hot dinner ready when I get home from work?"

"I could make you a hot dinner if I had enough money to buy the food," she fired back.

"I just gave you a hundred dollars last week for groceries."

"Even using coupons, that hundred dollars didn't buy that much food. As much as you and your son eat, I'm surprised we have any food in that kitchen at all."

"Okay, I get paid this Friday, so I'll have some money for you to buy more groceries."

As Damon searched the refrigerator for something to eat, he noticed the frustrated look on his wife's face.

"What's wrong now?"

"The car dealership called again. They want to know when you're going to make this month's payment."

"I'll give them a call tomorrow morning and work something out."

"You make sure you call them. I don't want to look out of this apartment window and see the repo man towing my car away."

"Okay, okay, I said I would handle it!" he replied, starting to get aggravated.

"You're making me feel very uncomfortable with our living conditions. Your job at the post office is barely paying all the bills. I know you like playing in your band, but maybe you need to give that up and find a second job to bring in some extra money."

"Come on, Gail, don't start that up again," he said, walking out of the kitchen.

Damon could feel himself becoming angry with his wife's constant whining and complaining. He walked into the bathroom to give himself some space away from her.

"Damon, I know you're not walking away from me while I'm talking to you."

"Damn, woman! Can I take a piss, please? Go ahead and talk, I can hear you."

The sound of liquid splashing into the toilet only seemed to agitate Gail further.

"You can try to ignore me, but you know I'm right, Damon. You have to face the facts. You've been trying to make it big with your band for almost four years. You are thirty-two years old, not twenty-two. You have a responsibility to take care of your family."

Damon walked out of the bathroom looking very annoyed.

"What the hell are you talking about, woman? I take good care of this family."

"You're constantly struggling to pay the rent each month. Bill collectors are always calling because you haven't paid them. I'm constantly worried about our money situation and its really stressing me out."

"Okay, I might be a little late paying some bills, but they get paid! I didn't hear you complaining about money when I bought you that brand new Lexus parked outside!"

"Stop yelling at me! I'm just making a suggestion to help out our financial situation."

Damon could feel himself ready to explode and lose his temper. He walked over and closed the bedroom door so his son wouldn't hear them arguing.

"Gail, let me explain something to you. Playing in this band isn't some meaningless hobby. There are times I make more money playing in the band than I do at my full-time job. Since you're so stressed out about our money situation, I have a suggestion for you, sweetheart. Why don't you get off your lazy ass, get a job and help pay some of the bills around here?"

"If I get a job, who is going to take care of Darius?" she asked, putting her hands on her hips. "If I put him in daycare, that's going to be more money you'll have to pay for someone to watch him."

"Then find a night job, then I can watch Darius when I get home from work."

"Are you serious? There is no way I'm going to work at night. It's too dangerous for a woman to be working at night."

"It will be even more dangerous if we can't pay the rent and have to live out on the streets," he replied.

"Okay, Damon, I see I'm wasting my time talking to you about this. Just remember that you have a wife and a son to support and we should come first before anything," she said, walking out of the bedroom.

It had been a long day and the last thing Damon wanted was to come home and hear his wife complaining to him about finances. All he wanted to do was take a long, hot shower and get a good night's sleep. As he tossed his car keys on the night stand, he noticed an opened envelope that appeared to be the electric bill. He pulled the bill out of the envelope and began to read it. At the top of the bill, he stared at the words in bold letters: "Payment Overdue."

Chapter 19

Terry was at home, relaxing on his sofa, trying to find something entertaining to watch on TV. Suddenly, the telephone rang. He glanced at the caller ID to see if he recognized the name or number. To his surprise, he saw the letters WRPP FM appear on the caller ID screen. WRPP 101 was the number one hip hop radio station in Atlanta. Terry assumed the station was calling for some type of radio promotion. Out of curiosity, he answered the phone.

"Hello?"

"May I speak to Terry Freeman?" a female voice asked.

"This is Terry."

"Hi, Terry, my name is Brenda Thornton. I'm the producer of the Thurman Payne Morning Show on WRPP. I hope I'm not disturbing you?"

"No, you're good. What can I do for you, Brenda?"

"The reason I'm calling is that our radio station is putting together a show about the controversy of hardcore rap music and its possible negative effects on its listeners. We're putting together a panel for our show and I would love to have you on that panel."

"Why do you want me on your panel?" he asked.

"I'm very familiar with you and your band, Infinite Noise. Your band is well known for its wide range of music genres. We already have a rap artist on our panel and it would be great to have someone like you on our show, who has a different perspective."

"Let me get this straight, Brenda. You want me to be on a panel speaking about the negative side of hardcore rap music on a radio station that plays nothing but hardcore rap music."

"Well, our station does play two hours of gospel music on Sunday mornings."

"Oh, great, that changes everything," Terry said, laughing.

"Terry, I could have asked several artists from numerous bands around this city, but I specifically chose you. I've been a fan of Infinite Noise ever since I saw your band perform at the Fox Theater two years ago. I was absolutely blown away by your music and your performance on stage. Your band is unique and refreshing and I can tell that you take pride in the type of music you play for your fans. I respect and admire what you and your band represents. I would really appreciate it if you would be on our panel to share your thoughts and feelings about today's music."

Even though his instincts were telling him to say no, he felt himself drawn to accept her invitation.

"When are you planning to do this show?" he asked.

"We're planning to do the show on September 12, which is four weeks from this Friday."

For a brief moment, Terry pondered her request. Even though he was feeling very reluctant about being on her radio talk show, he realized that appearing on one of the city's largest radio stations could be a big boost in helping Infinite Noise regain its popularity.

"Okay, Brenda. I'll be on your panel."

"Great! Thank you so much, Terry. I'll be calling you sometime next week to fill you in on all the details. Good-bye."

As Terry hung up the phone, he suddenly began to question his decision. He had listened to the Thurman Payne Morning Show on many occasions and he knew how vicious and rowdy the listeners to his show could be when riled up. Terry laid back on his sofa, hoping he hadn't gotten himself into something he couldn't handle.

Chapter 20

It was Tuesday morning and Terry was at work, looking at the numerous accounts piled on his desk. As he looked at the time on his computer screen, which read 11:46 am, his eyes began to blur.

"It's time for a break," he said to himself.

He knew what would help perk up his day, so he picked up the phone and called Angela. After several rings, she answered the phone.

"Hey, Angela, guess who?"

"Is this Bill? Or is this Tony?" Angela asked, trying to sound confused.

"Check you out, trying to be funny and I do emphasize *trying*."

"Okay, I guess that was kind of lame," she said, laughing. "Anyway, how are things going at work, Mr. Freeman?"

"I was sitting here working on an eighteen-million dollar account, but I put it aside to give you a call."

"You put aside an eighteen-million dollar contract to call me? That was so sweet of you, even if I don't believe you."

"Okay, it's only an eighteen-thousand dollar account, but I still put it aside to call you. How is your day going?" he asked.

"It's a little stressful right now. I was just going over the invitation list for Kenya's birthday party this Saturday. I didn't realize she had invited so many friends."

"How many friends did she invite?"

"There are twenty-three kids on this list and that's not counting the parents that will probably stay for the party. It looks like I'm going to have to order more food and more ice cream and cake. Then, I just got a call from Zarnack the Magician. His grandmother died, so he has to go to Tennessee to attend her funeral this weekend. Of course, that means he won't be able to perform at Kenya's birthday party. Anyway, I've got three days to try to find some kind of entertainment to replace him. Of course, nobody is available at this short notice."

"Sorry to hear that," he said, being sympathetic.

"I just can't believe Zarnack cancelled out on me at the last minute."

"Zarnack's grandmother should be ashamed of herself for dying on you like that," he said, sarcastically.

"I'm sorry. I guess that did sound very insensitive."

"It's okay, I understand. Where is Kenya's birthday party?"

"I made reservations at the Funtastic Village. I've never been there, but I've heard it's like an indoor play center. She had such a great time with you at the Action Zone, I thought she might like this place, too.

"I'm glad Kenya had a good time. I really hope she and I can become friends."

"I know she gave you a hard time, but she thinks you're pretty cool."

"If she thinks I'm so cool, why didn't she send me a birthday invitation to her party?"

"Terry, you know you don't want to go to a birthday party with a bunch of loud, screaming kids."

"Are you kidding? I love kids' birthday parties. You get to play games, eat ice cream and cake and run around screaming and yelling. What time does her party start?"

"The party is from 2:00 p.m. to 4:00 p.m."

"I have a suggestion. Would you like Infinite Noise to perform at Kenya's party?"

"That's very nice of you but, honestly, I don't think I can afford to pay your band. I've already gone way over my budget for her party."

"You wouldn't have to pay us. It will be our birthday present to Kenya."

"Terry, are you sure? That's a lot to ask of your band members to play for free."

"We don't have any shows lined up until next week and we could use the practice. I'll call the band and we'll have everything set up for her party this Saturday."

"That would be so wonderful. Kenya will love it. Thank you for doing this on such short notice. By the way, Kenya is spending the night with a friend Thursday night and I don't have any classes, so it looks like I'll have some free time."

"That sounds great. What do you feel like doing?"

"I haven't been out dancing in a while."

"I think I can find a good dancing spot for us," he said confidently. "I'll see you Thursday night. Bye."

As Terry leaned back in his chair, he smiled, feeling that his relationship with Angela was growing into something very special.

Chapter 21

Angela was in her bathroom, staring in the mirror, wondering if she should put on the red lipstick or just a little lip gloss. It had been a long time since she had taken the time to get her nails done and going to the hair salon. As she slowly spun around, modeling herself in the mirror, she smiled, knowing she looked good in her red halter dress that showed off her curvy figure. Since she left Kenya's father two years ago, Angela's main focus had been on her daughter and her career. Now that Terry was in her life, she had finally met a man that inspired and motivated her to look and dress like a beautiful woman again. Kenya was spending the night with one of her classmates so she and Terry decided to take advantage of this opportunity to go out dancing. As she was putting on the finishing touches of her makeup, she heard a knock at the door. She glanced at her watch and noticed that Terry had arrived to pick her up much earlier than expected. She smiled thinking, it was better to date a man who was a little early than a man who is always late with a poor excuse. As she rushed to the door, she wondered if he was going to surprise her with another bouquet of roses. She opened the door and her smile quickly disappeared when she saw Kenya's father, Preston Seymour, standing in front of her.

"Preston, what are you doing here?" she asked, feeling temporarily stunned.

"By the expression on your face, you must have been expecting someone else . . . but, to answer your question, I came here to see you and my daughter."

"A phone call would have been nice," she said, coldly.

"I was going to call you from the airport, but my cell phone died on me. I must say, you look very stunning in that dress. I assume you're going out on a date."

"You assume correctly," she replied.

"That's strange. Whenever I call you, I'm always hearing about how busy you are with law school, your job and taking care of Kenya"

"That's all true, but when I do have some free time, I try to take advantage of it."

"Well, I can't say I'm surprised. You are an attractive woman so I'm sure you're approached by a lot of men." Angela's only response is an annoyed look on her face. "Since you're all dressed up and going out on a Thursday night, is someone coming over to watch our daughter?"

"Kenya is fine. She's staying over at a friend's house."

"That's very convenient for you," he said, grinning. "Anyway, I have a birthday present for Kenya and I was hoping to give it to her in person," he said, holding up a small, wrapped gift in his hand.

"You can leave it with me and I'll make sure she gets it," she said, taking the gift from him.

"Angela, can I please come inside and talk to you? I just need three minutes of your time."

"Okay, you've got exactly three minutes." Angela opened the door, stepped back and allowed him to walk inside.

"I just love what you've done with your place," he said, looking around the room.

"I'm sure you don't want to spend your three minutes admiring my apartment."

It became obvious to Preston that Angela wasn't going to fall for any of his old bullshit lines, so he tried to get right to the point.

"Angela, I know I've made some mistakes in the past, but nobody's perfect."

"I never asked you to be perfect. The only thing I've asked from you is to be a good father to our daughter."

"How can I be a good father to Kenya if you won't let me be in her life? You were the one who moved down here to Atlanta."

"I had to leave. I got tired of being your main ho' while you tried to screw every female in Chicago. I needed to get my life back on track and I couldn't do that with you slithering in and out of my life."

"There you go again, bringing up old shit from the past. Why can't you just let all of that go?"

"After five years of your lying and cheating, I finally let *you* go," she replied. "I had to think about what was best for me and my daughter."

"Don't you mean *our* daughter? I'm sure I don't need to remind you that I send you a very nice check each month to provide for our daughter."

"It takes more than sending a check every month to be a good father. You've been in and out of her life since she was born. You just started paying child support two years ago and that's only because it was court-ordered."

Preston was getting frustrated and felt himself ready to lose his temper, but he knew that wouldn't help his case. If he wanted to win back Angela's heart, he was going to have to use a different tactic. He lowered his head and tried his best to look despondent.

"You're absolutely right. I know I messed up. You were the best thing that ever happened to me. It's so true what they say; you don't realize you have a good thing until it's gone. I know I've hurt you and you never deserved that. I just hope you can find it in your heart to forgive me. I've done a lot of things in the past that I regret, but the thing I regret the most, is not being a part of my daughter's life." Preston paused to look at Angela and noticed that her expression had mellowed. He sensed that he may have found a way to soften her heart - through their daughter, Kenya. "I've missed so many important events in Kenya's life, like the first time she walked and the first words she spoke. It hurts so much . . .," he paused, pretending to be choked up with emotion. "It hurts so much knowing those are special moments I'll never be able to experience with her." Angela had become very quiet as she listened to him open up and pour his heart out to her. "I would really appreciate it if you would let me spend a little time with my daughter on her birthday."

"I've already made plans for her birthday," Angela responded. "She's having a party this Saturday with some of her friends."

"Well, maybe I can just drop by and give her my birthday present."

"No! I mean . . . I don't think that's a good idea. Kenya is still . . . adjusting to things and it's been a while since she's seen you," she stuttered, nervously.

Just the thought of Preston coming to Kenya's party and confronting Terry sent a feeling of dread throughout her whole body.

"Angela, I understand that you're angry with me and you don't want to give me another chance. I only ask that you'll let me to be a part of my daughter's life. I don't think that's asking too much."

"I just need some time to think things out," she said meekly.

"Okay, I understand. I'm staying at the Atlanta Prestige Hotel. Here's my room number or you can call me on my cell phone if you need to contact me," he says, handing her his information on a small sheet of paper. "I'll be flying back to Chicago Sunday morning." Angela takes the paper from him without looking at it. "Will you at least think about letting me see my daughter on her birthday?" he asked, trying to look sincere.

"I'll call you after her party and see what we can work out," she said, walking Preston to the front door.

"Thank you, Angela," he said giving her a hug.

Preston noticed that she barely hugged him back. He pulled away and looked into Angela's eyes. "Before I leave, I just want you to know that I love you and Kenya and I want us to be a family," he said, trying to look sincere. "Please think about everything I've said."

Even though she was acting very cold and distant, he could tell her heart was beginning to soften. Preston turned and walked out of the apartment, feeling confident that he was breaking down her resistance and getting closer to winning back Angela's love.

Chapter 22

Terry and his band were in the final stages of setting up their musical instruments and equipment for Kenya's party. Layla was softly singing into a microphone to make sure the volume was correct. She looked up and noticed Terry walking toward her with a concerned look on his face.

"Layla, I have a phone call for you," Terry said.

"Who is it?" she whispered.

"It's Damon. He needs to talk to you," he said, handing her his cell phone.

"Hi, Damon. Where are you?"

"Hey, Layla," Damon said, on the other end of the phone. "My car broke down on Interstate 20 East. I'm on the side of the road waiting for a tow truck."

"How long will it take you to get here?"

"I won't be able to make it there for another forty-five minutes," Damon replied.

"Forty-five minutes? Damon, we're getting ready to start our show in fifteen minutes!"

"I know. That's why I'm calling you. You're going to have to fill in for me on the bass until I get there."

"What? Are you serious?"

"Yes, I'm very serious. Terry has the bass guitar you've been practicing on. Remember to make sure it's tuned before you start the show. Look, I've got to go, my cell phone is dying on me. Bye."

"Damon, hold on! Wait!" Layla looked at the cell phone and saw that the call had been disconnected.

"Did Damon explain everything to you?" Terry asked.

"Yes, he explained everything," she said, handing him the cell phone.

"I'm looking forward to hearing you play the bass on "Evening Bliss."

"I don't know if I'm ready to do a bass solo," she said nervously.

"Layla, you've been working with Damon on this song for three months. I've heard you play the bass to that song so many times, I hear it in my dreams. No more stalling. It's time for you to play."

"Maybe we should wait until Damon gets here," she replied. "I'm sure everyone will understand if we start a little late."

Terry walked up to Layla and put his hands on her shoulders.

"Layla, listen to me. If Damon says you're ready to play, you are ready. You need to trust him. You need to trust me. What's even more important is that you need to trust yourself."

"Okay, I'll give it a try," she said, forcing a smile. Layla walked up to the bass guitar resting on a stand, picked it up and began to tune the strings. She felt a queasy feeling in the pit of her stomach as she practiced a few notes. "Why is Terry doing this to me?" she whispered to herself. Then she remembered that Terry was only doing what she asked of him seven months ago. She didn't want to be just a pretty face and sexy body in the band, so she asked Terry if she could do more than just sing. He volunteered to teach her how to play the keyboard, but she let him know that she always wanted to learn how to play the guitar. She thought it might be cool to learn the bass guitar, so Terry set up practice sessions with Damon. After six years of violin lessons, she assumed it wouldn't be difficult to learn how to play a guitar with only four strings. For the first month, Terry taught her the basics of playing the bass guitar. Then, the next three months, Damon taught her the more advanced stages of playing the bass. Now, after seven months of training and several hours of practice, Terry felt that she was ready to perform in front of a live audience. As she began to warm up, Warren walked up to the area where the band was to perform. He noticed Layla nervously playing her bass guitar, so he decided to give her some much need encouragement.

"I hear the beautiful Layla Simmons is going to be playing the bass today," Warren said.

"I'm going to try," Layla said meekly. "I just wish I had known sooner. Maybe I could have prepared myself better."

"Listen, I know you're nervous, but keep in mind you're just playing in front of some little kids and their parents. Even if you mess up, they won't even notice," he said with a grin.

"Thanks for the vote of confidence."

"Relax. I'm just joking with you." Warren reached out and gently grabs her hand. "Just believe in yourself and you'll do just fine. "Remember, we've got your back."

"Thank you, Warren," she said, forcing a smile.

Terry walked up behind Layla and Warren and put his arms around them.

"Okay, everybody, it's almost showtime. Are you ready, Layla?" he asked.

"No, not really. Maybe we should give Damon about ten minutes."

"The show starts at 1:00 p.m. It's now 12:57," Terry said, looking at his watch. "You know we always try to start on time. I understand you're nervous, but I know you can do this. We're all counting on you. You're not going to let us down, are you?"

"Of course not," she said, trying to force a smile.

"Layla, you can do this. Remember, just relax and let the music flow from your body."

Even though Layla was feeling very nervous, she felt excited at the same time. This was her first opportunity to play the bass guitar during a live performance and she didn't want to let her friends down.

"Let's do this," she said, feeling a burst of confidence.

From out of the crowd, Angela walked up to the stage area and began speaking into one of the microphones.

"Good afternoon." I'd like to thank everyone for coming here to celebrate Kenya's ninth birthday. We have a special treat for everyone. Performing for us is a very popular band who I know is going to put on a great show for us. Everyone put your hands together for Infinite Noise!"

As the audience from the birthday party yelled and applauded loudly, the band started the show by playing "Let's Go Crazy," an upbeat, funky song by Prince, to get everyone pumped up. Moments later, young kids and parents were on the dance floor bumping and gyrating to the music. The band then transitioned into a song called "Evening Bliss. It was a funky, hip-hop song that Damon and Terry wrote specifically for Layla's first bass solo performance. At the start of the song, the birthday crowd was bobbing their heads and clapping their hands to the beat. Just before the song reached the point where Layla played her bass solo, Terry glanced at her, winked his eye and smiled. That look from Terry gave Layla a boost of confidence. As she began to play her solo on the bass guitar, the children and parents in the audience started cheering and applauding loudly. Hearing the approval of the crowd gave Layla a burst of energy that flowed into each note she played on her bass guitar. She looked up and noticed Terry and Warren had both stopped playing and were focused on her. The only music being played was the smooth, deep sound of her bass guitar and the rhythmic beats of Reggie's drums. Chants of "go Layla, go Layla" reverberated throughout the room. When Layla's solo part was over, Terry and Warren joined in and began playing again. At the end of the song, the audience erupted into loud cheers and applause. Terry walked up to Layla and gave her a big hug.

"You were great!" he said, excitedly. Terry turned and walked up to a microphone stand to address the crowd. "Thank you, everyone. Before we take a short break, I'd like to introduce you to the members of our band. On drums, Reggie Freeman. On keyboards, Warren Freeman. I'm Terry Freeman on lead guitar. And on bass guitar, the lovely and talented, Layla Simmons."

The audience cheered loudly and began to chant Layla's name. Terry motioned to Layla to step forward and take a bow. As she peered out into the cheering crowd, she noticed a familiar face.

Damon was standing in the front of the cheering audience, smiling at Layla like a proud parent. She slowly walked up to him and gave him a hug.

"I can't believe you set me up like this," she said, giving him a soft punch in his arm.

"Hey, it wasn't just me. We were all in on this," he said, laughing. "We decided this was the only way we could get you in front of an audience and play that bass guitar. You were fantastic. I am so proud of you."

"Damon, thank you for believing in me," she said, giving him another hug.

"It was my pleasure," he said proudly.

As Terry watched Layla and Damon hug each other, he was filled with great pride knowing that these two people were more than his close friends. They were more like family. From out of the crowd, Angela walked up to Terry.

"Everyone is enjoying the show, especially Kenya. Thank you again for doing this for her," she said, giving Terry a kiss on the cheek.

The band took a break and began to mingle with the birthday crowd. It gave Terry great satisfaction talking to the audience and hearing them express how much they enjoyed the band's music. After their break, the band began to perform again. Kenya was all smiles as the band got everyone to join in and sing happy birthday to her. As a special treat, the band asked Kenya to join them on the stage. They played Kenya's favorite song, "Angel" by Anita Baker as she sang for all of her birthday guests. When Kenya finished singing the song, everyone cheered and gave her a standing ovation. To the delight of the crowd, Kenya took a bow and waved at everyone like a true professional singer. Kenya was so happy and thrilled about her first solo singing performance that she walked over to Terry and gave him a big hug.

"Thank you, Terry," she said, holding him tightly.

"Happy Birthday, Kenya," he said over the noise of the crowd that was still cheering and applauding.

Terry could tell by the big smile on Kenya's face, that this would be a birthday she would never forget.

Chapter 23

One of the interesting things I had learned about Angela is that she was very big on special occasions. It was my birthday and she had invited me over to her apartment for dinner to celebrate my special day. As I sat back and relaxed, watching TV in Angela's den, I heard the faint sounds of a piano playing in another room. Kenya had been practicing on the piano for about twenty minutes while I was watching re-runs of the "Cosby Show." Listening to her practice reminded me of when I was taking piano lessons from my father. I was only six-years old at the time, but my father insisted that I learn to play a musical instrument. He said it would open up my musical horizons. I didn't quite comprehend what he meant back then, but now I truly understood because music was so important in my life. My thoughts were temporarily interrupted by the tantalizing aroma coming from the kitchen. I got up, walked to the kitchen, and stuck my head into the doorway.

"Whatever it is, it sure smells good," I said.

"It's spaghetti and meatballs," Angela said, slowly stirring the sauce with a large spoon. "I hope I didn't put too much garlic in the sauce."

"Maybe you should let me sample that for you," I said, walking over to the stove with a small spoon.

"No, thank you. Now, could you please get out of my kitchen?"

"Hey, it's my birthday. Don't I get a little special treatment?"

"Not when it comes to cooking my first dinner for you. Why don't you go back into the den and watch TV or something?"

"Fine, I know when I'm not wanted," I said, walking out of the kitchen.

As I walked back to the den, I again heard the faint sounds of a piano coming from down the hall. Whatever Kenya was playing, I could tell it was a rather complicated song. Out of curiosity, I walked down the hallway to a room adjacent to the den. The door to the room was closed, but I decided to at least go inside to say hello to her. I slowly opened the door and saw Kenya, with her back to me, playing on a small piano. As I quietly stood in the doorway, not wanting to disturb her, I was very surprised to hear how well Kenya played at such a young age. As she got to a difficult part of the song, her playing became uneven and erratic. She became very frustrated and stopped playing.

"Hey, that was pretty good," I said, slightly startling her.

"No, it wasn't," Kenya said, staring at the music sheet.

"It sounded like a very complicated piece. Is that Beethoven or Bach?"

"It's Wolfgang Amadeus Mozart," she responded, correcting me.

"I used to play a little Mozart when I was taking piano lessons."

"You play the piano?" she asked, sounding surprised.

"Yeah, I play a little. When I was your age, I was playing Sunday school songs like "Amazing Grace.""

"I've never heard of it. Is that one of those old school songs?" she asked, sarcastically.

"It's a simple little song. It's very easy to play and . . . uh, never mind," I said, sensing that Kenya was not interested.

"How long have you been playing?" I asked.

"Around three years," she replied, going back to her piano practicing.

"You play very well, Kenya."

"That's not what Mr. Volkoff tells me," she said, quietly.

"Who is Mr. Volkoff?"

"He's my piano teacher. He wants me to play in his piano recital next month, but I don't think I'll be ready by then."

Kenya began to play the song again and I listened very carefully. As I watched her play from the music sheet, I was impressed with how well she read music and how rarely she looked at the piano keys while playing.

"Okay, let's try this. Play it again, but this time, play it *espressivo*," I said with a Spanish accent.

"What's that?"

"Espressivo means playing with expression and feeling." Kenya looked at me with a confused look on her face. "May I sit next to you?" I asked politely.

"Sure, go ahead," she said, sliding over on the piano stool. I sat down next to her and started playing some old songs I learned when I was taking piano lessons.

"Pretend you're telling a story through the music. If it's a happy song, play it with joy and happiness," I said as I played a happy song. "If it's a sad song, play it dark and gloomy," I said, playing a sad song. "That is espressivo. Okay, now you try it with the song you've been practicing." As Kenya began to play, she made a few mistakes and stopped playing. "It's okay, just take your time. It will come to you." Kenya began playing again and after about fifteen minutes of practice, she was able to play through the entire song. "That was very good, Kenya. Mr. Volkoff would be very proud of you."

"Yeah, I guess it did sound pretty good," she said with a look of accomplishment on her face.

"If you practice like this every day, I know you'll be ready for that piano recital next month."

"Okay, I'll do that," she said, smiling. "What was that song you were playing earlier?"

"Do you mean this song?" I asked, as I began playing a song.

"Yes, I really like it. Did you write that song?"

"My brother wrote most of it and I've been trying to add a little bit to it."

"Is it hard to play?"

"No, it's a pretty basic chord progression. You play this chord, followed by these eighth notes," I said as I demonstrated on the piano. After a few minutes we began playing the song together.

Suddenly, I heard this melody in my head.

"Why did you stop playing?" she asked.

"I just got an idea. Kenya, will you play this part for me?" I asked as I demonstrated to her what I wanted her to play.

Kenya began playing the bass chords I showed her and then I added a few lead chords to play along with her. After we began to play, I started playing a new melody to the song.

"Wow, did you just come up with that?" she asked, in amazement.

"Yes, I did. Thank you, Kenya," I said, giving her a big hug.

"What was that for?" she asked with a surprised look on her face.

"For several months, I've been trying to find the right melody for this song and you just helped me figure it out. I'm going to make a recording of this song and make a copy for you, okay?"

"That would be so cool," she said, excitedly.

"Hey, dinner is ready!" Angela yelled from the kitchen.

"Are you staying for dinner?" Kenya asked.

"Is that an invitation?"

"I guess you might as well stay since you're already here."

"Thank you. I feel honored."

"Whatever," she said, nonchalantly.

"Just remember to keep practicing and you'll become a great piano player,"

"Hey, Terry?"

"Yes, Kenya?" I asked, somewhat surprised that she called me by my first name.

"Thank you," she said softly.

"No problem. We musicians need to stick together. Come on, let's eat."

As we walked out of Kenya's room, I was feeling very upbeat. It appeared that Kenya was finally beginning to open up to me. Maybe there was hope that she and I could actually develop a friendship.

Chapter 24

Warren wiped the sweat from his forehead as he turned the air conditioner switch on "high" in his car. He realized it was a waste of time since all he could feel was hot air blowing out of the vents. Warren was not looking forward to getting out in the hot sun and cutting his mother's big, front lawn. As he pulled into his mother's driveway, he smiled as he noticed the front lawn had been freshly cut. Even though he had planned to cut his mother's lawn today, he was happy to see that someone else, most likely his brother, had already taken care of it. A feeling of depression slowly crept inside of him as he saw his father's 2004 black Cadillac Seville parked in the driveway. He noticed the broken side mirror on the driver's side, which was a constant reminder of that tragic night. Warren thought back on the numerous times he and Terry would help their father wash and detail his car. He remembered the many vacation trips his family enjoyed riding in that car. Seeing his father's car now only gave him a feeling of loss and sorrow. He glanced at his watch which read 5:17 p.m. If his timing was correct, his mother would have already finished cooking her Sunday after-church dinner. He rang the doorbell, already envisioning the wonderful dinner waiting for him inside. Warren laughed to himself as he heard his mother unlocking the numerous locks on the front door. When the door finally opened, he was greeted by his mother's warm smile.

"Hey, Momma."

"Well, look who's here?" his mother said, giving him a big hug. "Come on in and get out of that heat," she said, gently grabbing his arm and leading him inside. "I'm just getting home from a late church meeting, so I haven't had a chance to cook, yet. I think I have some leftover meatloaf in the refrigerator. I can warm that up for you if you're hungry."

"No, that's okay, Momma. I'm not that hungry," he said, trying to hide his disappointment.

"Your brother tells me you've been dating that pretty girl, Layla. She seems like a fine, young lady."

"Yeah, she's nice, but we're just friends. It's nothing serious." Warren could tell his mother was getting ready to pry into his love life, so he quickly tried to change the subject. "By the way, one of the reasons I came by was to cut your lawn, but I see someone beat me to it."

"Your brother was nice enough to stop by the other day and cut it for me. He mentioned to me how well you and the others are doing with your band."

"Yeah, we've been doing okay. I just wish Terry would loosen up a bit and let us do some new stuff."

"Maybe in time, he'll do that. I still remember when Terry and Damon started writing music together and then a few years later, you and Reggie joined the band. I thought it was so wonderful when Layla joined your group. She has such a beautiful voice."

"Terry has done a good job with our band, but we're never going to make it to the top if he keeps holding us back."

"How is he holding you back?"

"Momma, the music business can be very complicated. It's a little hard to explain."

"Excuse me? Have you forgotten that I was married to a man who played in a professional jazz band? I probably understand the music business better than you."

"Okay, Momma," he said, laughing at her comment. I'll try to explain it to you. Today, most successful groups are into hip-hop or rap music. Our band plays basically jazz and R&B music." Reggie and I have written some very good rap lyrics, but Terry never lets us use any of our stuff during our performances."

"Do you mean rap lyrics like that foul mouth rapper, King Krunk, I've heard on the radio?"

"Yeah, his lyrics are a little strong, but he's getting paid big time. I want Infinite Noise to make it big like that."

"You make it sound like your band hasn't been successful," she said. "Do you know how many great articles I've read over the years about Infinite Noise?"

"Most of that stuff you read about our band was about two years ago. Back then, Infinite Noise was doing well and we were very popular, but things are different now."

"Well, I think Infinite Noise is still a great band," she said proudly.

"Come on, Momma. Our band hasn't been the same since . . ." Warren abruptly stopped talking.

"Since we lost your father," she said, finishing his sentence.

"Momma, you know things have changed. Our band didn't perform together for almost two years after what happened to Dad. Those years away from performing really hurt us. We fell out of the spotlight. Now, it's like we're starting all over again. I'm tired of living from paycheck to paycheck at that sports shop. I want to experience the finer things in life. There are so many things I want to do, so many places I want to see. I want to be able to take care of you and buy you anything your heart desires."

"Warren, please listen carefully to what I'm about to say. Everyone deals with tragedy in their own way. After we lost your father, Terry needed some time away from the band to get his head together and to heal. I hope you understand that and don't hold that against him."

"No, Momma, I would never do that. After what happened to dad, we all needed to take some time off from the band, but we were out of the music scene for a long time. Now, we need to focus on getting back to where we were. Don't get me wrong, Terry has done a good job making Infinite Noise a very good band, but times have changed. If our band doesn't change with the times, we're going to become like the prehistoric dinosaurs and become extinct. Hip-hop music is our key to fame and fortune. Look at rappers like Jay-Z, Eminem, and Lil' Wayne. Those guys are multi-millionaires because of hip-hop music. I honestly feel we need to change the direction of our music if we're going to be successful."

"Son, success isn't always about how much money you make." Cora walked over to a table in the den and picked up a framed picture of her late husband. "When your father was part of the Jazzy Gents, he would always tell me that if you play good music, people will listen and enjoy it, no matter what type of music you play. Your father loved playing in that band. It didn't matter if he was performing in a small nightclub or in front of thousands in a packed auditorium, he was never ashamed of the music he played. Lord knows, he didn't make millions of dollars playing with the Jazzy Gents, but that didn't matter to him. To him, it wasn't about the money. What was most important to him was seeing how his music made so many people happy. Your father felt blessed playing in his band and he always tried to pass his blessings on to others around him. That is what true success is all about."

"Okay, Momma, I hear what you're saying, but things have changed since Dad was performing. Sometimes, you have to make sacrifices with your music to make it to the top. If Dad and the Jazzy Gents were performing in today's world, they wouldn't be getting any record deals."

"You don't know that, Warren. Believe it or not, there are a lot of people who love jazz music. Just like there are people who love rock and roll, country, or classical music. There are a lot of people, like me, who love a variety of music. I can listen to a gospel singer like Yolanda Adams and five minutes later, I can be listening to Trey Songz."

"Momma, what do you know about Trey Songz?" he said, laughing.

"Your Momma might be getting old, but she's not dead." Cora walked over to her son and sat next to him on the sofa. "I just want you to know that I'm very proud of you and your band. When I come to your shows, I look around and see mothers and fathers singing with their children. When my friends and church members tell me how much they enjoy watching Infinite Noise perform, I'm filled with great pride and happiness. If your father was here today, he would be so proud, watching all of you making so many people happy with your music. And believe me, your father loved every member of Infinite Noise."

Warren could feel himself becoming emotional, but he was determined not to show his feelings in front of his mother. He remembered why he didn't feel comfortable coming over to his mother's house anymore. It brought back too many painful memories. He didn't want his mother to see this side of him, so he began to act tough and hard.

"Momma, I hear what you're saying, but I'm going to be a star with or without Infinite Noise. I'm going to be one of the greatest hip-hop artists of all time," he said, standing up and strutting around the room. "I'm going to be a superstar and when I become rich and famous, I'm going to buy you the biggest house in Atlanta," he said, picking his mother up and spinning her around.

"I believe you, now put me down!" she said, laughing.

As Warren gently put his mother down, she grabbed his arm firmly.

"Listen to me, Warren. You don't have to yell and curse into a microphone to be successful. You are a talented musician and I'm proud of you."

"Okay, Momma," he said, giving her a hug.

Just holding his mother began to bring back fond memories of his mom and dad when he was younger. Unfortunately, the memories also brought back feelings of hurt and sadness. The sadness started to engulf him like a raging river. He didn't want to feel the pain anymore so he knew it was time to leave his mother's house.

"I wish I could stay longer, but I have some things to do before it gets too late," he said, looking down at the floor, hoping his mother wouldn't see through his lie.

"I'm glad you were able to stop by and spend some time with your mother," she said, giving her son a kiss on the cheek. "Take care, son. I love you."

"I love you too, Momma."

Warren quickly walked out of the house, still trying to shake the feeling of sadness inside of him as the tears welled up in his eyes.

Chapter 25

As Terry drove down the narrow street leading to Keep the Faith Baptist Church, he noticed his uncle's dark blue Buick Regal, parked in a designated spot marked *Reserved For Pastor*. He was surprised to see so many cars in the parking lot two hours after church service had ended. He assumed there must be a bible study class or church meeting going on. He glanced at his watch and noticed the time was 3:36 p.m. As he walked into the church, he was greeted by a few church members, who were mingling in the lobby area.

"Terrence, it's so good to see you," said Mrs. Black, a long-time member of the church.

"Hello, Mrs. Black," he said, giving her a hug.

"I wish you were still in the church choir. It's just not the same without you."

"Thank you, ma'am," he said as he opened the exit door for her.

As Terry walked into the sanctuary, he suddenly realized it had been several months since he had performed at the church's anniversary program. He reached down and picked up a rolled-up church program lying on one of the benches. He opened the program and discovered that his uncle's Sunday sermon was "God Can Heal Your Pain." He smiled, wondering if his uncle's sermon was a message to him. He looked up and noticed a drum set, a bass guitar, a piano, and that old pipe organ on the church stage. He still remembered how many years it took before his uncle finally let him play his guitar in the church choir. Once Terry started playing in the choir, people would come to the church from all over the city just to hear him play. His uncle may never admit it, but the addition of a lead guitar, bass guitar and drums, greatly improved the choir, which in turn, increased the church's membership. As Terry walked onto the stage, he began thinking about how much fun he had performing in the church choir. He sat down at the piano and started playing one of his favorite old gospel songs, "*I Need Thee Every Hour.*" It was a simple little song, but back in the day, he thought it was one of the greatest gospel songs of all time.

"I remember the first time you played that song in the youth choir," a familiar voice said from behind. Terry turned around and standing there was his uncle, Pastor Henry Freeman.

"Hey, Uncle Henry. Or should I call you Pastor Freeman since we're in a church?"

"Uncle Henry is fine with me," he said, giving Terry a hug.

"I hope my playing didn't disturb you."

"No, not at all. It's good to hear you playing some of the old gospel songs."

"Yeah, it's been a long time," Terry said, going back to playing the piano.

"Is everything alright?"

"Yes, I'm fine. I just thought I'd come by, say hello to my uncle, and play a little gospel music."

Terry's uncle had always been a very observant man, so he knew that something was troubling his nephew.

"Talk to me. What's wrong?" Henry asked, sounding concerned.

Terry stopped playing the piano, turned, and faced his uncle.

"I'm okay, Uncle Henry. I guess I'm just confused about the direction of our band," he said, sounding depressed.

"Terry, don't get frustrated. You and your band are very talented. It's just a matter of time before the right person or record company sees the talent that you young people have."

"As a matter of fact, I met with a record producer last week. Our band was offered a recording contract."

"That's wonderful news!" Henry said, excitedly.

"I'm not sure. I know I should be happy, but it just doesn't feel right. I've been reading over the contract and it appears this record producer, Walter Caldwell, wants to change our image and have control over the music that we play. I'm meeting with Caldwell tomorrow morning to give him my decision."

"How do the other band members feel about the contract offer?"

"Well, I haven't really told them about the contract yet," Terry replied, feeling somewhat guilty.

"That's a pretty big decision to make by yourself, don't you think?"

"I just don't want the others to get caught up in the dollar signs and we end up being slaves to the record company. I don't know. Maybe I'm wrong. Maybe I am living in the past thinking our band can control our own style of music. I was hoping our band could put something positive out there for people to listen to. Maybe our band does need to make a change."

"Do you honestly want to put out music that refers to black men as niggers and our black women as bitches and whores? Is that the type of message you want to send to our young, black people?"

"No, of course not, but that seems to be the music people want to hear these days. Our band performed at a high-school graduation a few months ago and we almost got booed off the stage because we didn't play any hardcore rap songs. I'm starting to feel like I'm wasting my time trying to make this band work. Nobody really wants to hear our type of music anymore," Terry said, feeling dejected.

His uncle walked over, pulled up a chair and sat next to his nephew.

"You are the leader of your band. As a leader, you owe it to yourself and to your band to do what you feel is right. You do whatever you have to do to make this right. More important, you are a fine young man and nobody, not even me, should tell you to be something that you're not. Your mother and father raised you to be your own man."

"It's bad enough I have to deal with problems outside of our band, but it seems like I'm constantly bumping heads with Warren and Reggie about what type of music we should play."

"Lord knows that I've bumped heads with my son on many occasions. I've talked to Reggie a few times since he moved out, but there's still a lot of tension between us."

As Terry looked at his uncle, he could see the hurt and concern in his eyes.

"I really feel bad about what happened with you and Reggie," he said, sympathetically.

"Don't feel bad, Terry. I know it's been hard on Reggie growing up with a father who is the pastor of a church. For years, his mother and I tried our best to talk to him, but he didn't want to listen. Finally, I gave him the option of getting his life together or moving out. He didn't want to respect the rules of the house and decided to move out. I'm just glad he decided to move in with you. His mother and I feel better knowing he's staying with a responsible family member."

"So far, it's worked out pretty good. I think this has given me and Reggie a chance to rekindle the bond we had when we were younger. By the way, he told me last night that he's moving into his own apartment next week."

"I really appreciate you giving Reggie a place to stay. Here, I wanted to give you this," Henry said, pulling out his wallet. He opened the wallet and gave Terry a check made out to him for one hundred dollars.

"Uncle Henry, I can't accept this. We're family," Terry said, trying to give the check back to him.

"No, please take it. Reggie's been staying with you a few weeks and I know how much food my son can eat," Henry said, jokingly. "I am so proud of you, Terry. I thank God Reggie and Warren got involved in your band. There are so many negative influences out there for young, black men. I think you've been a positive influence on both of them."

"Me? A positive influence? I'm not so sure about that. If anything, I've been a big disappointment," Terry replied, putting his head down.

"Why would you say that?" Henry asked, looking bewildered.

"Because it's true."

Pastor Freeman could tell that his nephew was going through some personal issues. He reached over and put his hand on Terry's shoulder.

"Are you ready to tell me what's troubling you?"

Terry was tempted to tell him that everything was fine, but he knew his uncle would see right through his lie. He was tired of holding in all of his frustrations, so he decided to open up and talk to his uncle.

"When Damon and I started Infinite Noise several years ago, we had this dream of becoming a great, successful band. We were going to be this unique band that played jazz, rock and roll, hip-hop, R&B and gospel music. Then after what happened to Dad, I lost my focus. I stopped writing songs and I stopped trying to push this band to be the best it could be. For almost two years, our band went into limbo because I went into my own little shell. Now, Reggie and Warren think our music is old and outdated. Maybe they're right. Maybe I just need to leave the band and let the others take over. Since we lost Dad, I feel like I've lost my drive and passion to push our band to the top. Maybe I'm holding our band back from becoming successful."

"Terry, don't be so hard on yourself. Sometimes, it takes a long time to heal from losing someone you love. When we lost your father, it felt like a part of me died with him. To this day, I pray for the Lord to give me strength. I look at you sometimes and it warms my heart because I see so much of your father in you. He was a very strong and confident man who made his own decisions. I see a lot of those qualities in you. Don't worry about what other people say or think about your music. You do what makes you happy."

"I don't know how you do it, Uncle Henry. There are so many times I have to argue about decisions being made in our little five-member band. You've been the pastor of this church all these years and you never have major problems with any of your church members."

"That's not always true, Terry. I've learned that part of being a good leader is listening to the people you're trying to lead. As a leader, it's important to let everyone know that their voice will be heard when it comes to making important decisions. That's one of the first things I had to learn when I became pastor of this church. When I have meetings with my church members, we don't always agree on the direction of our church. The important thing is that I give everyone a chance to voice their opinions. I don't always agree with everyone's opinion, but I listen."

"I know I definitely need to do a better job of listening. It seems like Warren and Reggie have changed so much over the last few years. I owe you an apology, Uncle Henry. All those years, you were trying to explain to me how our band has a responsibility to promote good positive music. I didn't want to listen to you because I didn't understand what you were saying. Now, I understand. I see how a lot of young kids are listening to some of today's music. They watch some of these hardcore music videos and they really do have an effect on a lot of our young people. I was at the park the other day and these little boys, around eight-years old, were cursing and yelling at each other like grown men."

"You should hear some of these kids in our bible school classes," Henry said, chuckling. "Most of them can't tell me one verse out of the bible, but they know every curse word in some of these rap songs. We adults need to stop complaining about the disrespectful music and do something to save our young people."

"You're right, Uncle Henry. I guess that's why I agreed to be on a radio talk show."

"You're going to be on the radio?" his uncle asked, sounding very surprised.

"I'm going to be on station WRPP next month," Terry replied.

"Isn't that the radio station that plays nothing but rap music?"

"That's the one. I was asked to be part of this panel to talk about hardcore rap music and its possible negative influence on young listeners. At first I thought it might be a good idea, but now, I think I'm making a big mistake."

"Terry, I think this is a great opportunity for you to express your views," Henry said, excitedly.

"I've talked to friends and co-workers about some of this music that promotes drugs and violence and they say I'm a sellout or an Uncle Tom for not supporting our black rap artists. They tell me I should support these rappers because black people need to stick together."

"Yes, black people do need to stick together, but not if it means supporting a cause that you know in your heart isn't right. Do you remember any of the scriptures from the bible I asked you to read at your father's funeral? Do you remember 1 Peter 3:13-14? *"Who is going to harm you if you are eager to do good? But even if you should suffer. . ."*

"But even if you should suffer for what is right, you are blessed." Terry said, finishing the scripture.

His uncle looked at Terry with a proud look on his face.

"Very good, Terry. That was one of your father's favorite scriptures. Always remember that scripture and it will help to guide and strengthen you whenever your faith begins to waver. What is it you young people say? You have to keep it real. Many great men have expressed their views on different issues and everybody didn't always agree with them. I remember back in the sixties during the early period of the civil rights movement, black leaders like Martin Luther King and Malcolm X were very outspoken in their views. When it came to civil rights in this country, Malcolm X believed in making changes by any means necessary. Dr. King, on the other hand, believed in non-violent change. There were many blacks who disagreed and even hated these men. During the civil rights movement, Dr. King's life was constantly threatened. He was ridiculed, stabbed, imprisoned, and eventually killed for standing up for what he believed in. A lot of white people felt Dr. King was a trouble-maker while some black people felt he was an Uncle Tom because he believed in non-violent change. No matter what obstacles came before him, Dr. King never wavered and never gave up. What I'm trying to say is that everyone is not going to agree with your religious beliefs, your political views, or your philosophy on life. Be strong in your faith. You have to believe in what you feel is right and make a stand."

"Maybe that's the problem. It seems like I've lost a lot of my faith over the years."

His uncle leaned over and put his hand on Terry's shoulder.

"I know how hard it's been for you since we lost your father."

"I just don't understand why it happened to him."

"Sometimes tragic things happen in our lives that we don't understand. Your father was a good man. He treated everyone with kindness and respect. His faith was strong. He was a great brother and a wonderful father. Believe me, losing my brother was like losing a part of me. I understand what you're going through. When we lost your father, my faith began to waver. I began to question God's love and wisdom."

Terry was so shocked to hear this from his uncle that he's left speechless. All he could do was look at his uncle with a stunned look on his face.

"Yes, it's true. My faith was shaken. I felt lost and confused . . . the same way you're feeling now," he said, looking at Terry as if he were looking into his very soul.

"You're right, Uncle Henry. I am lost. I'm angry, hurt, confused, and I don't know what to do," he said, pouring out feelings he had been holding inside these past few years.

"It wasn't easy for me, Terry. I prayed day and night for strength and understanding. Then, one day, my eyes were opened. Then, I realized, who was I to question God? Who was I to question the Father who sacrificed His beloved Son, so all our sins would be forgiven. This is when you truly have to draw on your faith. I have to believe that God had a reason for calling my brother home. It's not my place or yours to question God's will. We must have faith and believe in Him. I don't understand all of God's reasons or His master plan, but I do know that we were blessed to have your father in our lives. Hold my hands, close your eyes and ask Him," he said, extending his arms and hands to Terry.

"Ask Him for what?"

"Ask Him for whatever you feel you need."

"I don't need anything."

"Yes, you do. Please, take my hands," he said, holding his open palms out to his nephew.

"It's getting late," Terry said, looking at his watch and standing up. "I need to be going."

"It's okay, Terry. When you're ready, He will be there for you."

His uncle picked up a church program and handed it to Terry.

"Here, take this with you. Remember to keep the faith. It isn't just the name of our church . . . it's the way we should live our lives."

"Okay, Uncle Henry, I'll remember that."

"One last thing. Don't worry about being on that radio station. You're going to do just fine. I'll be praying for you," he said, giving Terry a hug. "Just say what you feel in your heart. It's what your father would have wanted you to do."

Chapter 26

This was not the way I wanted to start off my Monday morning. It would normally take me about forty minutes to drive from my apartment in Riverdale to the city of Duluth, but after running into the morning rush hour traffic on Spaghetti Junction, it had taken me over an hour. As I pulled into the parking lot of Galactic Records, I grabbed my briefcase containing the contract from the car seat and quickly jogged to the building. There was no way I was going to be late for this very important meeting with Walter Caldwell. As I walked up to the receptionist's desk, I noticed the clock on the wall read 8:54 a.m. I had made it to my meeting with six minutes to spare.

"Good morning, Mr. Freeman," the receptionist said as I walked up to her desk.

"Good morning to you," I replied.

"You can go down to Mr. Caldwell's office. He's expecting you."

"Thank you," I responded, trying to conceal my nervousness.

When I reached Caldwell's office, the door was closed.

"Come on in," Caldwell responded as I knocked on his door.

As I entered his office, Caldwell was sitting at his desk, talking on the telephone.

"Listen, Martell, I'm not wasting any more time with you," Caldwell said, angrily. "You've become a liability to the company and I'm letting you go. I don't have the time or the patience to keep bailing you out of jail every time you fuck up. Don't call me, anymore!" he said, hanging up the phone.

"That didn't sound good," I said, trying to lighten up the mood.

"That was a prime example of someone who didn't want to follow my guidance and now his music career is over. Anyway, have a seat. Let's move on to more pleasant matters. I assume you had time to look over the contract."

"Yes, I did look over the contract, Mr. Caldwell," I replied, sitting down in a plush leather chair.

"So, is your band ready to take that next step toward success with Galactic Records?"

"Yes, I feel we're ready, but I had some concerns about portions of the contract."

"Terry, we don't have time for delays. We need to get this ball rolling. As I mentioned to you last week, I'm meeting with some executives tomorrow to talk about the future of your band. I need to have that contract signed and in my hand when I meet with them. Did you sign the contract?"

"No, I didn't. There were a few things in the contract I was hoping we could discuss," I said, pulling out the contract from my briefcase.

"What did you want to discuss?" he asked, looking somewhat puzzled.

"On page fourteen, paragraph three, I'm not comfortable with that part about the record company having control of our image and our music."

"That is a standard clause that most major record companies require when signing new artists. Our company is investing a lot of time, resources, and money into your band. We need to be able to guide you in the right direction to insure your success . . . and ours. I've been doing this for awhile. I know what I'm talking about."

"With all due respect, I understand what you're saying, but our music and our image is very important to us."

Caldwell leaned back in his chair, looking very frustrated.

"Your image? If you're serious about becoming successful in the music industry, your band's image is the first thing you need to change."

"What's wrong with our image?" I asked.

"I'll tell you what's wrong. I was at your show at Club Elite a few weeks ago. Your performance was fine, but the guys in your band looked like tired, old men, and the young lady looked like an old church nun. Your band's image is boring and you need to change it."

"Oh, I see. I guess you would have preferred seeing us wearing pants that were sagging so everybody could see our boxers. And of course Layla should've been wearing something short and tight-fitting, so her ass and tits would be hanging out."

"Terry, you need to wake up and understand that this is a business. You've got a sexy female in your group and you've got to take advantage of that. If your audience sees you as dull and boring, then they will look at your music the same way."

"Obviously, you weren't listening to our band that night. The audience seemed to enjoy our music."

"Don't go patting yourself on the back because you heard a few cheers from that crowd. Some of those people may have cheered for you, but the bottom line is that you came in second place to a group of mediocre rappers. In this business, image is everything. Nobody cares about your family-oriented music or your squeaky-clean image," Caldwell said, standing up from his desk. "Look at these successful artists I've produced over the last five years," he said, pointing to the gold CDs encased in glass frames on his office walls. "Here's Bad News Bruce, King Krunk and Mack Attack. When I signed these guys, they were average rappers. I took them and molded them into money making, successful artists. How did I do it? I turned them into the bad boys that their fans wanted to see. Their fans wanted to hear about the violence, the illegal drugs, and making it out of the ghetto and becoming rich and famous. Terry, listen to what I'm telling you. Don't make a bad decision that you and your band will regret."

"I think I've done a pretty good job making decisions for our band," I said, confidently.

"You think you know the music business better than I do? These people don't want to hear love songs or any of that old school jazz or that softcore R&B. They want to hear about big money, expensive cars, sex and violence, mixed with all the profanity the censors will allow. For most of these people, hardcore rap music is their escape from reality. When they see and listen to these rap artists, they can identify with what they're rapping about. You need to understand that this is the society we live in now. These people want hardcore, we give them hardcore. The music industry is like any other business. It's all about supply and demand. If you can't follow that basic concept, you may as well go back to playing gospel music in your uncle's church."

As I sat back and listened to Caldwell's annoying and nonsensical speech, I realized that he and I were miles apart in our way of thinking.

"Mr. Caldwell, I understand what you're saying, but that's not us. We're not thugs, we're not drug dealers, and we're not gang-bangers. We're not going to be fake and pretend to be something we're not. We want to play music we can be proud of. We just want to keep it real," I said, trying to plead my case.

"Keep it real?" he said with a smirk on his face. "Let me explain something to you. I've been in this music business for sixteen years. I've seen artists like Infinite Noise come and go. The artists that stay on top are the ones that give the people what they want. The artists that fail, are groups like yours that try to keep it real. You want to keep it real, let's keep it real. Infinite Noise is a small-time, local band that has little or no chance of becoming a major success. With my experience, my knowledge, and my connections in the music industry, I can take you to the top.

"You mean by dressing like street thugs and degrading black people in our songs? No, that's not how we want to represent our band."

"No, that's not how *you* want to represent your band," he said, sitting back down at his desk. "I've talked to Warren and Reggie and they totally agree with me about the direction of the band."

"That may be true, but Warren and Reggie don't make the decisions for our band."

"Do you honestly think you have the experience and knowledge to make decisions for everyone in your band?"

"I seem to remember you telling me that every successful band needs a leader. I'm that leader. So, yes, I'm making a decision for everyone in my band," I said, defiantly.

"What exactly is the decision you're making here, Terry?"

"Mr. Caldwell, if we can't negotiate some of the clauses in this contract, I'm going to have to turn it down."

Walter looked at me in disbelief.

"I'm giving you the opportunity to sign a recording contract with one of the most successful record labels in the country and now you want to be an ungrateful ass!"

"Hold up, Mr. Caldwell," I said, interrupting him. Nobody is being ungrateful. Don't act like you bent over backwards to help our band. You came to us, remember? You saw that Infinite Noise had the potential to be successful and, as a smart businessman, you took the opportunity to sign our band."

"Stop fooling yourself," he said, grinning at me. "I've been in this business a long time. I know Infinite Noise was one of the most popular bands in the South two or three years ago. Then, for a year or two, your band faded away and so has your popularity. Infinite Noise is no longer relevant in the music world. Now, you're trying to get back to where you were and you can't do that without me!"

I could feel the anger rising inside of me, but I tried to control it. I knew the reason Infinite Noise "faded away" from the music world, but I wasn't going to waste my time explaining it to this egotistical asshole.

"Okay, Walter. You want to talk business, let's talk business," I said, holding up the contract. "I've carefully gone over this contract with my attorney and we don't think this is a good deal for our band. There are way too many restrictions on our music and I honestly feel we deserve more money than what you're offering."

"You think you deserve more money? Son, you need to wake up and . . ."

"Hey!" I said, cutting him off. "First of all, I'm not your son! I'm not some young punk kid, so don't play mind games with me!" It was pretty obvious that Caldwell and I were not getting anywhere with our negotiations, so I leaned back in my chair and tried to calm the situation. "Mr. Caldwell, we obviously aren't on the same page with the direction of my band. Regardless of what you think about our band, I know we can be successful. We were a good band before we met you and we'll be a good band without you."

"Do you really think you can succeed in this business without me?" he fired back, slamming his fist on his desk. "Let me explain something to you. I can make you or I can break you. Look at you. You're just like these other dumb-ass niggas out there who think they know every damn thing."

"No, that's where you're wrong," I fired back. "I'm not going to be one of your dumb-ass niggas that jumps whenever you say so. You don't own me and you're not going to control me!"

"Who the hell do you think you're talking to!? You want to fuck with me!? I've got major connections in this industry. I'll make sure your little band never gets a recording contract!"

"Oh, you got it like that?" I asked, standing up from my chair.

"You damn right I do! Nobody fucks with Walter Caldwell. Now, get your ass out of my office!

"Here you go!" I said, tossing the contract on his desk. "You and your record label can kiss my black ass!" I said, storming out of his office, making sure I slammed the door behind me.

As I walked out of the Galactic Records building, I felt a sense of satisfaction, knowing that I made the right decision. At the same time, I felt a great sense of loss and disappointment. I thought Infinite Noise was on the verge of signing that elusive big record deal and now that opportunity was gone. Even though I felt that I made the right decision, I wasn't looking forward to explaining to everyone in the band that I turned down a contract offer from a major record label.

Chapter 27

It was Friday, 9:50 a.m. Terry was sitting at his desk at work, poring over a large stack of accounts. Suddenly, he heard a small buzzing sound, glanced up and noticed a message flashing on his computer screen which read, *Department meeting in Conference Room A at 10 am.* A few minutes later, Terry noticed his co-workers rising from their desks and walking to the conference room like a herd of mindless sheep. Any other day, Terry would be following them and dreading another long, boring meeting with Frank Gordon, but this day was different. After his meeting with Walter Caldwell four days ago, he realized that if he was serious about making Infinite Noise a successful band, he was going to need help from someone with experience in the music industry. Terry was so impressed with his meeting with Paul Jefferson, he decided to hire him as the band's business manager. Now that the band had an experienced business manager, he felt energized and confident about the future of Infinite Noise. Hiring a business manager was something he should have done a long time ago. Maybe Damon was right when he told Terry that he had gotten too comfortable at his job and it was preventing him from focusing on the success of the band. Suddenly, the office telephone rang.

"NexTech Solutions . . . this is Terry Freeman."

"Yeah, Freeman, this is Jim Harper."

"Hello, Mr. Harper. What can I do for you?"

"You can tell me why I'm having major problems with that damn accounting software I purchased from you last week. Every time I try to download it, I keep getting this error message about insufficient data space or something like that."

Terry's co-worker, Sandra, walked up and tapped him on the shoulder.

"Don't forget the meeting at ten," she whispered.

Terry nodded his head in acknowledgement as she headed to the conference room.

"Mr. Harper, the problem you're having is not with the software. It's your computer."

"What are you talking about, Freeman? That's a brand new computer I bought from your company three weeks ago," he said angrily.

"I know, Mr. Harper. You bought a Cytrex 2000, which is a fine computer, but it only has 4.0 GB of memory. The spreadsheets, graphs, anti-virus, and the accounting software package you purchased requires 4.5 GB of memory."

"Well, why the hell didn't you tell me that when I bought that computer!"

"Mr. Harper, I did tell you that. I offered the extra memory card as part of the package you purchased and you said you didn't want to pay the extra $300.00."

"Well, I've got a business to run. I need you to send me that damn memory card right away!"

"Okay, Mr. Harper. I'll send the memory card to you by express mail. You should receive it tomorrow morning."

"It better be here tomorrow morning or you'll be hearing from me again!" Before Terry could say another word, he heard the sound of the dial-tone on his phone.

"If his cheap ass would have listened to me, the software he purchased would have worked," he muttered to himself. Terry glanced at his watch which read 10:02 am. "Oh, great. Now, I have to go to this meeting late," he said to himself. He jumped up from his desk and quickly jogged to the conference room which was on the other side of the building. As he reached the conference room, he took a deep breath and opened the door. As he quietly walked into the conference room, fifteen of his co-workers were seated around a long, rectangular table. Frank Gordon was standing in front of an easel, talking about the decline in software sales and the loss of clients in the second quarter. Terry walked over to an empty chair on the other side of the table, but before he could sit down, Mr. Gordon stopped talking and looked at Terry.

"Mr. Freeman, were you not aware this meeting started at ten o'clock? It's now 10:04," he said, looking at his watch.

"I apologize for being late, but I had to handle an important phone call."

"I'm not interested in your excuses, Mr. Freeman. In the future, you need to handle any telephone calls after the meeting," Gordon said, turning back to his easel to continue the meeting.

Any other day, Terry would have ignored a comment like that, but this was not one of those days.

"I wasn't making an excuse."

"What did you say, Mr. Freeman?"

As Terry looked around the room, he could see the stunned look on his co-workers' faces.

"I said, I wasn't making an excuse. My reason for being late was business-related."

"Mr. Freeman, you have already disrupted this meeting with your tardiness. I'm not interested in your excuses or your explanations," Gordon said, looking irritated.

"I'm not trying to disrupt your meeting. I'm trying to add to your meeting by explaining to you why I think we've been losing some of our clients the last two quarters."

"I've heard enough from you, Mr. Freeman," he said, sternly.

"Mr. Gordon, part of the reason we're losing clients is because of our poor customer service. I was on the phone talking to a very unhappy client. I was able to solve his problem on the phone and, hopefully, satisfy a client that has spent approximately $10,000 in the last two months with our company. Isn't that more important than my missing four minutes of your meeting?"

"Mr. Freeman, you are not running this meeting. I am. Now, I suggest you sit down and shut your mouth!"

"And I suggest you stop talking to me like I'm a child!" Terry fired back.

"Mr. Freeman, leave this conference room immediately or I will have you thrown out!" he responded, walking toward Terry.

"Frank, please don't make the mistake of putting your hands on me. I promise you won't like the results," Terry responded, sternly.

Frank Gordon stopped, saw the look in Terry's eyes, and realized he did not want a physical altercation with him.

"Freeman, as of this second, you are suspended indefinitely!"

"Frank, you can't suspend me. As of this second, I quit!"

As Terry walked toward the conference room door, he couldn't help but notice the shocked look on the faces of his co-workers. He calmly opened and closed the conference door behind him. As he walked back to his desk, he could feel the adrenaline rushing through his body. After all the years of pent-up anger and frustration, he finally stood up to Frank Gordon. When Terry reached his work area, he noticed Mike Dawkins, one of the company's security guards, standing at his desk with a large, empty box.

"What's up, Mike?"

"Hey, Terry," Mike replied, looking very uncomfortable. "Look, man. I'm sorry about this, but they told me to bring you this empty box to clean out your desk. Then they told me to escort you out of the building."

"It's cool, Mike," Terry said as he began to empty all of the contents from his office desk into the box.

"Damn, bro, you must have really pissed somebody off," he whispered, looking around to make sure no one could hear him.

"Yeah, it was Frank Gordon."

"Gopher-face Gordon? Man, I hope you told him to kiss your black ass."

"No, but it sure felt great seeing the look on his face when I told him I was quitting," Terry said proudly.

"Well, good luck, my man." Mike said, extending his hand.

"Thanks, Mike."

Terry finished packing his belongings in the box and began to make his final walk out of the building he had worked in for the last ten years. As he left the office building, feeling the warm sunshine on his face, he began to smile. He felt like an old, Negro slave that had just been emancipated. There were no more chains and shackles to hold him down any longer. He felt extremely excited, knowing that quitting his job was the beginning of fulfilling a long-time dream. There were no more excuses, no more job obligations, and no more problems from Frank Gordon. It was time he put his heart and soul into taking Infinite Noise to the top.

Chapter 28

Terry was driving into the parking lot of Gerald's Warehouse to practice with his band and discuss his meeting with Walter Caldwell. The clock on his car's dashboard read 5:58 p.m., but he was not in a hurry to go inside to talk to his family and friends about the contract offer he rejected from Galactic Records. He considered asking Paul to come to this meeting to help explain to the band why the contract offer was turned down, but he decided it was best to do this by himself. As he walked toward the door to the warehouse, he could hear Warren and Reggie, loudly rapping some profanity-laced lyrics into a microphone. He briefly paused at the door entrance, trying to get his thoughts together. As he stood at the door, he realized he couldn't put it off any longer. It was time to let everyone know about his contract meeting with Walter Caldwell. He took a deep breath and entered the warehouse.

"Hey, Terry," Layla said, walking up and giving him a hug.

"What's up, cuz?" said Reggie over the microphone. "We were trying out some new lyrics we wrote."

"Yeah, I could hear you yelling and screaming as I was driving into the parking lot," Terry said.

"Come on, man, you know those lyrics sounded tight," Warren said proudly.

"No, those lyrics sounded foolish," Terry replied.

"Yo, dog, don't hate on our lyrics just because you can't rap like us."

"Reggie, please stop talking like a street thug. You sound ridiculous," Terry replied, causing the group to laugh.

"How are you going to schedule a band practice and arrive ten minutes late?" said Reggie, with an attitude.

"Awww, come on. You two kiss and make up," Damon said, trying to lighten the mood.

"Anyway, he's only three minutes late," he said, looking at his watch.

Terry grabbed a chair, walked over to the group and sat down.

"Okay, everybody have a seat."

Terry could tell by the look on each person's face that they were anxious to hear the news of his meeting with Walter Caldwell. Terry took a deep breath and tried to speak with confidence.

"As I told everyone last week, I've been talking with Walter Caldwell, of Galactic Records, about a contract offer.

"Yeah, yeah, we know all that," Reggie said, impatiently. "So, did we hit the jackpot or not?"

Terry realized that there was no sense in trying to sugar-coat the situation, so he came right out and explained everything to the group.

"Alright, here's the deal. I met with Caldwell earlier this week in his office. After going over the contract and a lot of negotiating, I decided it wasn't in our best interest to sign with Galactic Records."

Everyone began looking at each other with a confused expression on their faces.

"Hold on," Warren said. "What do you mean *you* decided? Don't we all have a voice in this band?"

"Yeah, who the hell died and made you king of the world?" Reggie asked, sarcastically.

"Listen, everyone. Caldwell basically gave us an ultimatum. We do things his way or no deal. So, I said no deal."

"What the hell do you mean, no deal!?" Reggie asked, raising his voice. "How much was he offering us?"

"It was a two year $700,000 offer with a $50,000 signing bonus. I went over the contract with an attorney and he said it wasn't a good contract for us. Another big issue was that the contract offer had some clauses that would allow the record company to control our image and what type of music we play."

"Hold on, let me get this straight." Reggie said, trying to remain calm. "They offered us a $700,000 contract and you turned it down. For that kind of money, I'll dress up as a slave and perform at a Ku Klux Klan party. Just because you got some personal issues with Caldwell, don't fuck up our chances to get paid!"

Terry got up from his chair and walked over to Reggie.

"First of all, you need to lower your voice. Don't talk to me like I'm one of your homeboys from the hood," he said, in a stern voice.

"Okay, everybody, calm down," Damon said, walking in between Terry and Reggie. "We can talk about this without yelling. Let's hear what Terry has to say."

"I heard what he had to say and I don't like what I'm hearing," Warren responded. "How is he going to turn down that much money without talking to us about it?"

"If you were listening, I said that I went over the contract with an attorney and he determined that it wasn't a good contract for us," Terry said, trying to defend himself.

"How is $700,000 dollars not a good contract?" Reggie asked, clearly agitated.

"I know it sounds like a lot of money, but we wouldn't have made a profit in the first year of that contract."

"Who are you to make that decision for all of us?" Reggie asked.

"I did what was best for the band."

"No, you did what was best for you!" Reggie said, angrily.

Even though Terry anticipated some frustration and disappointment from his decision to turn down the contract offer, he didn't think it would escalate to this level of anger.

"In all the years we've been together, I think I've done a damn good job making decisions for this band," Terry said, with confidence.

"Well, maybe it's time we let someone else make the financial decisions for this band," Reggie responded.

"If you don't like the way I handle things around here, you can leave," Terry said, firmly.

"Oh, it's like that, cuz?" Reggie said, walking up to Terry.

"Yeah, it's just like that!"

"That's cool, I'm outta here." Reggie said, walking toward the exit.

"Reggie, wait! Don't leave!" Layla said, standing up from her chair.

Layla walked up to Terry and grabbed his arm.

"Terry, go talk to him," Layla pleaded.

"No, let him go, we don't need him. I'm sick and tired of his whining and complaining."

Reggie stormed out of the warehouse, slamming the door behind him.

"After all I've done for him, how can he just walk out on us like that?" Terry asked, looking at Damon.

"You know, Reggie's got a point," Damon responded.

"What? You're agreeing with Reggie?" Terry asked, sounding surprised.

"For that amount of money, you probably should have talked to all of us before turning down that contract."

"Damon, there was nothing to talk about. The money wasn't right and there were too many restrictions on our band. I know we can get a better contract offer than that," Terry said, trying to plead his case.

"I understand what you're saying, but hear me out. Our band started out almost four years ago. We have performed all over the Southeast and done very well, but times have changed. Maybe we need to consider transitioning to a different style of music if we're going to be successful."

"Are you serious? After all the years we've been doing this together, you're telling me that you want to sellout and start rapping about gangbanging, drug dealing, and pimping women."

"No, what I'm saying is that at some point, we need to decide on the direction of Infinite Noise. We've always talked about signing a deal with a major record label and when the opportunity presented itself, you made the decision to turn it down without consulting with any of us."

"Why are you questioning me about this? I did what was best for the band. After all, I put this band together," Terry said, arrogantly.

"Whoa, buddy. You need to get your facts straight. *We* put this band together. I've been here from day one and I have a right to make any decisions that concerns this band."

"Damon, I can't believe you're making such a big deal about this."

"I'm making a big deal about this because I have a family to think about. It's no big deal to you because you're single with no kids and you have a big-time corporate job to pay your bills. I've got a wife and kid to take care of on my bullshit salary at the post office! Look, Terry, you know I love playing in this band, but I can't keep doing this," Damon said, trying to regain his composure. "I have a wife and son to think about. Either we're going to move forward or I have to leave the band."

Terry was stunned to hear this from his best friend. In all the years they had been together, Damon never expressed that he was unhappy or frustrated with the band.

"Damon, I didn't know you felt that way. Why didn't you say anything?"

"I didn't think I needed to say anything. I thought we were both trying to achieve our dream of making Infinite Noise a big success. I guess you weren't looking at this dream the same way I was." Damon picked up his bass guitar and placed it inside its case. Without saying another word, Damon turned and walked toward the exit.

"Damon, are you walking out on me, too?"

"I think I better leave before we both say something we'll regret," he said as he walked out of the door.

"Way to go, big brother. You put this band together and now you've torn it apart," Warren said, sarcastically.

"Warren, I don't want to hear it," he said in a stern voice.

"No, you need to hear this. You always want to do things your way. For years, me and Reggie have tried to talk you into letting us do some rap lyrics in our shows, but you always ignored us. Come on Terry, think about it. We won the band competition at Club Elite two years ago. This year, we came in second place behind the Thug Lordz, which happens to be a rap group. We've been out of the music game for almost two years. Things have changed. Hip hop music is what people want to hear, not that old school music we play."

"Yeah, I know you and Reggie would love to rap about the life of a street thug and gangbanging," Terry responded.

"Man, you sound just like those old ass, know-it-alls who blame everything bad on rap music. A man robs a bank, blame it on rap music. A young girl gets hooked on drugs, she must have been listening to rap music. A group of teens steal a car, they must be listening to that evil rap music."

Terry looked at his brother with anger in his eyes.

"You made your point . . . now drop it!"

"Look, what happened to Dad was really fucked up, but that was two years ago. You need to move on and let that shit go."

Suddenly, Terry rushed Warren, grabbed him by the front of his shirt and pinned him against the wall.

"I don't care if it was twenty years ago! He was our father! I will never let it go!" he said, getting in Warren's face.

"Get off of me, Terry!" he yelled, struggling to break away from Terry's grip.

"Stop it, you two!" Layla yelled, desperately trying to break them apart.

Finally coming to his senses, Terry released his grip from Warren and walked away from him. Warren glared at his brother with anger in his eyes.

"If you weren't my brother . . ."

"What?" Terry asked, cutting him off. "What are you going to do, tough guy? Come on, Mr. Thug Gangster! Pull out your gun and blow my brains out!"

Warren took a step toward his brother, stopped, and stared at him angrily.

"Please, Warren, let's just go," Layla pleaded, grabbing Warren's arm.

"Yeah, you're right. I don't need to waste my time listening to this bullshit."

As angry as Terry was feeling, he wanted to say more to his brother, but he realized that it wouldn't change anything. Too much had already been said. It had become very obvious that he and his brother had grown apart. As he watched Warren and Layla walk out of the door, he stood there all alone. He felt an empty void inside himself as he realized that this was the end of Infinite Noise and, possibly, his relationship with his brother.

Chapter 29

It was a very humid evening in August. I walked into Variance, a popular, after-work restaurant located in the Virginia-Highland area, about ten minutes from downtown Atlanta. It had been almost two weeks since the huge argument that broke up the band. This night out with Angela was just what I needed to get my mind off the band breaking up. A few weeks ago, I told Angela I quit my job at NexTech to focus more on Infinite Noise. I didn't want her to think I was totally unemployed, which I was, so I hadn't said anything about the band breaking up. I glanced at my watch, which read 5:32 p.m. I smiled to myself wondering how late Angela would arrive for our dinner date. She was the one who suggested meeting here for dinner at 5:30 p.m. since the restaurant was only fifteen minutes away from her law firm. I left work at 4:00 p.m., drove home, showered, got dressed, drove through the city traffic, and I still beat her here. As I entered the restaurant, I was surprised to see so many women sitting together at tables without a man in sight. A young woman in her early twenties approached me and greeted me with a forced smile. Her blond hair was pulled back in an unruly ponytail and her eyes looked strained and tired. I looked at the name tag dangling from the front of her shirt which read, "Casey."

"Good evening, sir. Will you be dining alone?"

"No, someone will be joining me shortly."

"I'm sorry sir, but I won't be able to seat you at a table until everyone in your party arrives," she said with a tired voice.

"It sounds like you've had a very long day, Casey." I said, trying to get a smile out of her.

"Is it that obvious?" she replied.

"Yeah, but you still have that pretty smile working for you."

"Oh, stop it," she said, slightly blushing. "Why don't you wait over at the bar and I'll see what I can do about getting a table for you?"

"Thank you very much, Casey."

I usually don't have a drink before dinner, but I figured it would help pass the time while I waited for Angela to arrive. As I walked to the bar, I noticed two ladies sitting at a table, watching me intently.

"Girl, that nigga is fine is hell," I overheard one of them say as I passed their table. I felt like a walking piece of meat on display, but I accepted her comment as a compliment. After all, I did make a conscious effort to look very suave for my date with Angela. I had just gotten a haircut. The navy blue slacks I was wearing had that nice, crisp crease in the pant legs. The blue silk shirt I was wearing did a great job of showcasing my toned arms and chest. I had heard Angela mention how she likes a well-groomed man, so I spent some extra time at the mirror trimming my mustache and goatee so it would look just right. When I got to the bar, I noticed there were no seats available. After circling the bar a few times, my luck changed as a couple got up and left. I quickly walked over and sat down on one of the empty bar stools. As I looked around the room, I was surprised to see how much this place had changed. I remembered coming here three years ago to celebrate a co-worker's birthday. Back then, it was a quiet Italian restaurant that catered to an upscale, family-oriented clientele. Now, it had evolved into a restaurant that catered to young, business-oriented professionals.

"What can I get you, sir," the bartender asked.

"I'll have a strawberry margarita."

"Okay, coming right up."

As the bartender walked away, I glanced at my watch which read 5:46 p.m. I looked around the restaurant and Angela was nowhere in sight.

"Excuse me," a female voice said from behind me. I turned around and found myself looking up and into the eyes of a very attractive, young woman. She had short, dark hair, exotic green eyes and a honey-brown complexion.

"Is anyone sitting there?" she asked, pointing at the empty bar stool beside me.

"No, it's all yours," I said, pulling the bar stool out for her to sit.

From her accent, I assumed she was from Trinidad, Jamaica or maybe Barbados.

"Thank you. It's nice to see there are still gentlemen around . . . and a handsome gentleman at that," she said with a sensuous smile.

It's funny how certain things happen in your life that you just can't explain. A few months ago, when I wasn't dating anyone, I never was approached by an attractive woman like this. Now that I was dating Angela, it seemed like I was being approached by beautiful women everywhere I go. After several seconds of deliberating, I decided not to give in to this temptation. I looked around the room to see if Angela had arrived. I noticed a couple sitting next to the bar, having dinner. The man was staring so hard at the woman sitting next to me that his female companion reached over and smacked him on the side of his head.

"Ouch, that's going to leave a mark," I said to myself.

The attractive woman sitting next to me began to laugh.

"I was just thinking the same thing," she said, trying to stop laughing.

"I guess I should have kept that comment to myself."

"No, I needed a good laugh." The bartender walked up and placed my drink in front of me.

"Here you are, sir. That will be $7.50," he said, holding his hand out.

"Please, let me take care of that for you," she said, reaching into her purse. "It's the least I can do for such a nice gentleman."

"I've got it, but I appreciate the offer," I said, handing the bartender a ten-dollar bill.

"You surprise me," she said.

"Why do I surprise you?"

"Most men would have accepted an offer like that."

"I'd like to think I'm not like most men."

"No, I can tell you're quite different, Mr. . . .?" she paused, waiting for my response.

"Freeman. Terry Freeman. And you are?"

"Monique Hemsley," she replied, shaking my hand.

"It's nice to meet you, Monique. I notice you have an accent."

"I was born and raised in Barbados, but I'm currently living in Los Angeles."

"What brings you to Atlanta?" I asked.

"I'm a professional dancer. I'm doing a music video with Chad Donovan. Have you heard of him?"

"Yes, he's a local hip-hop artist with Real Deal Records."

"My agent says there are several artists here in the city I might be able to work with."

"He's right," I responded, sipping on my drink. "There's Usher, T.I., Ludacris, Lil' Jon, and Outkast, just to name a few."

"It sounds like you know quite a bit about the Atlanta music scene. Are you from Atlanta?"

"Yes, I was born and raised here," I said proudly.

"I didn't know there were so many handsome men in Atlanta," she said, looking at me with those exotic eyes.

"Is this your first time visiting Atlanta," I asked, trying to change the subject."

"Yes, it is. I hear there is so much to see here. Terry, I hope I'm not being too bold, but if you're not busy this evening, I would appreciate a gentleman like you showing me around your beautiful city."

I looked at this stunningly-attractive woman as one of life's many temptations. It had become very obvious that Monique was flirting with me, but I was determined to not let this temptation get the best of me.

"Unfortunately, I do have plans for the evening. I'm meeting someone here for dinner."

"Your wife?"

"No, my girlfriend."

"That's too bad. I was really enjoying our conversation. It's so nice talking to an intelligent black man who knows how to talk with respect to a woman. Your girlfriend is very fortunate to have a man like you."

"Thank you. I appreciate that. Well, I probably need to give my friend a call and find out why she's so late," I said, as I stood up. "It was nice meeting you, Monique," I said, extending my hand.

"The pleasure was all mine, Terry," she said, walking up to me, gently wrapping her arms around my neck and giving me a hug.

The sweet aroma from her perfume was intoxicating. As I pulled away from her embrace, I noticed a chubby-looking guy in a bright, red suit, staring at me with an envious look on his face. Lord, let me hurry up and get away from this woman, I thought to myself. Suddenly, I looked up and saw Angela standing at the entrance of the restaurant.

"Take care, Monique," I said, as I quickly walked to the front of the restaurant to join Angela. I noticed Casey, the waitress, walking toward me.

"Casey, my friend is finally here."

"Okay, I've got a table for you on the other side of the bar," she said, grabbing two dinner menus.

As I continued walking to the front of the restaurant to join Angela, I noticed a tall, slender guy with dreadlocks walking toward her like a hungry animal stalking its prey. He quickly moved in and began having a conversation with her. Some guys would probably get upset to see another man approach their woman. To me, it's just a natural thing for a man to "hit on" an attractive woman. As usual, Angela was looking very attractive wearing a short, black halter dress, which accentuated her toned, sexy legs. The tall guy talking to Angela noticed me approaching. As we made eye contact, I gave him the "that's my woman" stare and he respectfully walked away.

"Hello, beautiful," I said, giving Angela a kiss on the cheek.

"Sorry I'm late," she replied. "I had to stay late re-writing a deposition for one of the attorneys."

"It's okay. You're looking very sexy in that dress." Angela looked at me and gave me a half smile. "Come on, our table is ready."

As we walked to our table, I could tell something was bothering her. Just before we reached our table, the chubby guy in the bright, red suit I had seen earlier approached me. He noticed me walking with Angela and grinned mischievously.

"Damn, player! You're trying to get all the women, aren't you?" he said, walking past me.

"What was that all about?" Angela asked.

"I'm not sure. I don't even know that guy."

As we got to our table, I pulled Angela's chair out and she sat down without saying another word. Casey walked up and handed us our dinner menus.

"I'll give you two a minute to go over the menu," she said.

"Thank you, Casey," I replied, politely.

Angela was looking intently at her menu. She hadn't said a word since we sat down and I could tell something was definitely bothering her.

"Do you see anything good on the menu?" I asked, trying to start up a conversation.

"Not yet," she replied, still staring at her menu.

"Are you okay?" I asked.

"I'm fine," she replied, not even giving me eye contact.

It was obvious that something was troubling her and she didn't want to talk about it. Now, I was forced to play the guessing game and keep asking questions until I found out what was bothering her.

"Angela, did you have a bad day at the office? Did you break a fingernail?" I asked, jokingly.

"I said I was fine," she said in an agitated tone.

I had never considered myself to be an expert when it comes to understanding the female species, but I did know that I was in a very precarious situation. If I continued to ask Angela what was bothering her, she might become angry because I was invading her privacy. On the other hand, if I didn't continue to ask what was bothering her, she would have assumed that I didn't care. I decided the best course of action was to not press the issue and let her know that I cared.

"I don't know what's bothering you, but when you're ready to talk about it, I'm here to listen."

"Please don't patronize me, Terry."

"I'm not trying to patronize you. I'm just concerned that something is bothering you."

Before she could respond, our waitress walked back to our table, with pen and pad in hand.

"Are you two ready to order?" Casey asked.

"Yes, I think we are," I replied.

"Before I take your order, this is for you," Casey said, placing a bottle of Moet champagne on our table.

"I didn't order any champagne," I said, looking confused.

"I was asked to bring this bottle of champagne to your table as a dinner gift."

"From whom?" I asked. Casey looked uncomfortable as she glanced at Angela, then looked back at me.

"It was from a lady that was sitting at the bar," Casey replied.

I glanced over at the bar, looking for Monique, but I didn't see her.

"She left right after she paid for the champagne," Casey said.

"Well, that was very nice of her," Angela said, giving me a cold stare.

Our waitress noticed the obvious tension between Angela and me and tried to take our dinner orders.

"Ma'am, what would you like to order this evening?" Casey asked.

"All of a sudden, I'm not feeling very hungry," Angela replied, standing up from the table and walking away.

"Angela, wait! Where are you going?" I asked, still sitting at the table, looking bewildered.

"I guess your friend doesn't like Moet," Casey said, sarcastically.

"I guess not," I said, pulling out my wallet and giving her a five-dollar bill for her time.

"Sir, you're forgetting your champagne," Casey said.

"Consider it part of your tip," I replied as I quickly sprinted toward the exit after Angela.

As I rushed out of the restaurant, I saw Angela walking toward the parking lot.

"Angela, wait!" I yelled as I ran to catch up with her. "What is your problem?!" I asked, stepping in front of her.

"My problem is trusting low-down, lying men like you," she said, shoving me in my chest.

"What the hell are you talking about?"

"Don't play dumb with me."

"Angela, I really don't know what you're talking about."

"You and I planned to have a nice dinner tonight and I walk into the restaurant and see my man hugging on some strange woman."

"Is that what this is all about? There's no need to be upset," I said, reaching out to hold her hand.

"Don't touch me!" she said, pulling away. "You know, I actually thought you were different, but you're just like the rest of these no-good, lying men."

"Will you please calm down and give me a chance to explain?"

"Sure, go ahead," she says, folding her arms. "I would love to hear you explain why that cheap-looking tramp was hugging all over you."

"I was sitting at the bar waiting for you. She came over and asked if she could sit in the empty seat next to me. I said, yes, she sat down, and we just talked."

"How long were you talking to this woman?"

"I don't know, maybe twenty minutes. I was just talking to her while I was waiting for you."

"Oh . . . so now you're going to blame this on me?"

"No, I'm not blaming you. I'm not blaming anyone. No one is at fault here."

"And your conversation with her was so intriguing that she felt the urge to hug you," she said, sarcastically. "Now I understand why that guy in the restaurant called you a player. One minute he sees you hugging on that woman at the bar and the next minute he sees you hugging on me."

"Angela, why would I try to come on to that woman knowing you were going to be there?" I asked, trying to reason with her.

"You tell me, Mr. Player!" she said, putting her hand on her hip. "Do you know what really pisses me off? That tramp had the audacity to disrespect me by sending a bottle of champagne to our table."

"The waitress said she sent the champagne as a dinner gift to us," I said, getting frustrated.

"No, it was a dinner gift for you! If this woman approached you, why couldn't you just ignore her? Why were you even talking to her!? Why didn't you just get up and walk away from her?"

"Because I'm a grown-ass man and I can talk to whoever I want to!" I replied, angrily.

Angela looked at me with a stunned look on her face and was unable to speak. As angry as I felt, I didn't want us to continue yelling at each other in the parking lot. I took a deep breath and tried to calm down.

"Angela, this isn't about some female hugging me or buying me a bottle of champagne. This is about your lack of trust in me."

"After what I saw tonight, you made it very clear that I can't trust you," she said, walking away from me.

"You think I'm cheating on you because you saw some woman hugging me? You know what your problem is? You're insecure and you've got serious trust issues!"

"Don't talk to me like that! I'm not a child!"

"Then stop acting like one!" I fired back.

Angela looked at me with anger in her eyes. If looks could kill, I would have been lying dead on that hot, parking lot pavement. She was so upset with me, she couldn't utter another word. For what seemed like minutes, we stood there looking at each other in complete silence. Finally, I tried to calmly talk to her.

"Angela, let's not do this. Let's talk tomorrow after we've both cooled down," I said, wiping perspiration from my forehead.

"There's nothing else we need to talk about," she said, getting into her car and slamming the door.

For a brief moment, I thought about stopping her from leaving, but I realized it would be a waste of time. Too many hurtful words had been spoken that couldn't be taken back. As she drove away, I was left standing in that hot parking lot, feeling angry, frustrated, and very confused.

* * *

Terry walked out of his bathroom, feeling invigorated after taking a nice, hot shower. He threw on a t-shirt and some shorts as he tried to relax for the rest of the evening. As he walked into his living room, he glanced at the clock on the wall which read 11:14 p.m. He thought jogging around the apartment complex would help relieve some of the frustration he was feeling since his argument with Angela earlier that evening, but it didn't. As he paced around the room, he still couldn't believe Angela had made such a big deal about Monique giving him a friendly hug. Did it really look that bad? He wondered if he should have ignored Monique when she approached him. Maybe he should have just walked away from her. No, that would have been absolutely ridiculous. He knew he didn't do anything wrong and he wasn't going to blame himself for Angela's insecurities. Maybe it was for the best that they had this argument. He quit his job at NexTech a few weeks ago and his band had broken up. The last thing he needed in his life was a moody, insecure woman. He walked into his den, picked up his guitar and began playing. After playing a few chords, he stopped and leaned the guitar against a chair. No matter how hard he tried, he couldn't get the argument with Angela out of his mind. He walked into the kitchen, opened the refrigerator and pulled out a chilled bottle of Chardonnay. After pouring himself a full glass of wine, he took the bottle and the glass with him into the den. He took a few more sips from his glass and began searching through his collection of compact discs. He came across a CD that he hoped would soothe his mind and relieve his frustrations. After putting the CD in the player, he laid back in his recliner and began to slowly drink his wine. Seconds later, the smooth, melodic sound of Sade's voice filled the room. As he closed his eyes and listened to the song, the lyrics seemed so appropriate for the current situation. *"Is it a crime, is it a crime, that I still want you and I want you to want me, too?"* As he took another sip of wine, he wondered how he could have been so wrong about their relationship? He really thought they had something special between them. After all these months together, he realized that she never cared about him and obviously she never trusted him. He decided he wasn't going to worry about it anymore. He finished his glass of wine, leaned back in his recliner, and closed his eyes as the music slowly lulled him to sleep. Thirty-two minutes later, Terry was awakened by the sound of soft knocking at his door. He glanced at the clock on his wall which read 11:53 p.m.

"Who could be knocking at my door at this hour?" he muttered to himself.

He hoped it wasn't his cousin, Reggie, dropping by to borrow money or looking for a place to stay. As he peered through the peep-hole, he was very surprised to see Angela standing on the other side of the door. When he opened the door, he immediately noticed that her eyes were red and slightly puffy. She had obviously been crying quite a bit.

"Can I come in?" she asked softly. Without saying a word, Terry stepped aside as she walked into his apartment. "I'm sorry to drop by on you like this. I know I should have called, but I was afraid you wouldn't answer the phone."

"Or maybe you dropped by to see if I had a female over here," he said, sarcastically.

"Okay, I guess I deserved that." Angela began to nervously pace around the room. She turned and faced Terry, hoping he would say something, anything, to ease the tremendous tension she was feeling. "I know you're angry with me, but I wanted to at least explain my actions at the restaurant."

"Please, sit down," he said, trying to make her feel more comfortable.

For several minutes, Angela sat quietly, trying to find the right words to express her feelings to Terry. As Terry looked into her eyes, he could tell that Angela was feeling very emotional and extremely upset. He walked over and sat next to her.

"I'm listening," he said in a comforting voice.

Angela wiped the tears from her eyes and took a deep breath.

"You were right about what you said earlier," she said, softly. "I do have some trust issues. I wasn't always like this. There was a time when I was a very trusting person. Then I met Kenya's father, Preston. We dated for a while and I let him know I was focused on my goal of becoming a lawyer and didn't want a relationship. In the two months we dated, I was never intimate with him. We went out one night to a club and he convinced me to try a few drinks. I guess I drank too much because I didn't remember anything else that night. The next morning, I woke up in his bed with him lying next to me. I was so angry that he took advantage of me that I stopped seeing him. Then a month later, I found out I was pregnant."

Angela stopped talking as tears began to roll down her face. Terry got up, grabbed a tissue and handed it to her.

"Thank you," she said, wiping the tears from her eyes. "I thought about having an abortion, but I just couldn't go through with it. I was young, confused, and scared. I didn't know what to do. I eventually told him I was pregnant. He told me he loved me and begged me to have the baby. He promised he would take care of me and the baby. I believed him. I trusted him, and he did nothing but lie and cheat on me," she said, as the tears continued to flow down her face.

"Angela, if you were so unhappy, why didn't you just leave him?"

"My mother and father divorced when I was ten-years old. It was so hard for me growing up without a father. For six years, I put up with Preston's lies and cheating because I didn't want Kenya to grow up without a father in her life like I did."

As Angela continued to open up to Terry about her painful past, he began to understand that she had gone through some serious abandonment and trust issues. Her situation was a little different, but he could definitely understand the hurt and pain of losing a father.

"Terry, I am so sorry about the way I acted at the restaurant. I've let my anger and bitterness toward Preston change me into this cold, untrusting person. I don't want to be that person anymore. I love you and I don't want to lose you. Please don't give up on me," she said as she broke down crying.

Terry reached over and gently wiped the tears from her face.

"I'm not giving up on you," he said as he put his arms around her and held her closely.

Terry could tell that Angela was tired and emotionally drained. He picked her up, carried her to his room and gently laid her on his bed. No words were spoken as he began to softly stroke her hair. Moments later, she fell asleep. Terry smiled as he noticed how peaceful and beautiful she looked as she slept.

"Sleep well," he whispered as he gave her a gentle kiss on her cheek.

He walked out of the room and silently closed the door behind him.

* * *

When Angela woke up later that morning, she quickly sat up, realizing she wasn't in her own bed. As she tried to shake the sleepiness from her head, she remembered coming over to see Terry. She looked over at the empty space in the bed next to her and smiled. She recalled how Terry treated her with so much kindness and compassion even after she had treated him so badly at the restaurant. As she got out of the bed, she could hear the faint sounds of a piano playing outside of the closed bedroom door. She walked out of the bedroom and followed the sound of the music. As she approached the den area, she peeked around the corner and saw Terry sitting in front of a keyboard, playing a very moving, romantic song. Not wanting to disturb his playing, she stood quietly at a distance so she could enjoy listening to the beautiful song. She watched in amazement as he smoothly and flawlessly played the song with no sheet music in front of him. When he played the last note of the song, she quietly walked into the room.

"That was beautiful. Did you write that?" she asked.

"No, my father did. It was one of the first songs he wrote with his band."

"In what band did he play?" she asked, trying to remember.

Terry got up and walked over to a shelf in the corner of the room. He slowly pulled out a sealed record album and handed it to Angela.

"The Jazzy Gents," she said, looking at the album cover. "I remember them. My mother used to listen to these guys when I was in junior high."

As Angela continued looking at the album, she noticed a name that caught her attention.

"Your father was Bobby Free?"

"Yes," he answered softly.

"I never made the connection since your last name is Freeman."

"My father always used the last name, Free, because he never wanted my brother and I to be caught up in his celebrity status. He didn't want anyone treating us differently because he was a famous musician. From elementary school to high school, no one knew that Bobby Free was my father. He came to a few of my school events, but none of my classmates knew who he was. I'll never forget when he came to my talent show my senior year. Some of the parents at the show recognized him and it got a little chaotic when they swarmed him, asking for his autograph. He finally had to leave his seat and watch the talent show from the back of the stage.

"What was it like growing up with a famous dad?"

"It was pretty cool watching him perform with the Jazzy Gents, but there was also the down side. There were several weeks out of the year we didn't see him because he was traveling and performing all over the country. But, after he finished his tours, he tried his best to make up that time with me, my brother, and my mom."

Terry looked up and noticed Angela looking at a gold CD encased in a glass frame on his wall.

"*In memory of Bobby Freeman. Your music will live on in our hearts forever,*" she read aloud. "This was your father's CD?"

"No, it was Infinite Noise's first CD. We dedicated it to my father," he said, gently touching the glass frame.

"When did he die?" she asked, almost wishing she could take back the question after seeing the painful look on his face.

"Next Thursday will be two years."

"Terry, I am so sorry. I shouldn't have asked."

"No, it's okay." Terry walked over to the sofa and sat down. For several moments, he didn't say anything, as if he was deep in thought. Suddenly, he began to speak. "Two years ago, our band was performing downtown at the Regal Ballroom. It was the first major performance for our band and we were so excited. About an hour before we went onstage, I discovered that my guitar amplifier wasn't working. My father was backstage with us at the time and I asked him if he could drive home and get my spare amplifier. My father left, but he didn't make it back in time for the start of the show. I had to borrow an amplifier from another band that was performing after us. Anyway, we put on such a good performance, we were asked to do an encore performance. After the show was over, I didn't see my father anywhere. I just couldn't believe that he never returned to watch us perform. As our band was leaving the building, two police officers walked up and asked to speak to me and my brother. Before they said another word, I knew. My father would have never missed seeing us perform unless he wasn't able to make it. The police officers said my father was robbed, shot, and his car stolen in a parking lot one block from where we were performing. An hour later, two teens were arrested driving my father's car. In the back seat of my father's car was my spare guitar amplifier . . . the same amplifier I asked him to get for me."

Angela walked over and sat next to Terry, gently holding his hand.

"It wasn't your fault, Terry."

"Yes, it was. I was the one who asked him to get that damn amplifier," he said, getting up and walking away from her. "I actually had the audacity to be disappointed in him for missing our show and, all along, he was lying in a dark, parking lot, dying," he said as the tears flowed down his face.

"It's okay, Terry," she said softly.

Angela stood up and walked over to Terry. She gently put her arms around his waist and held him closely, wanting him to know that she was there for him. She softly caressed his face, then kissed his lips. Not able to hold back his desires any longer, Terry pulled her close to his body and kissed her passionately. Her first impulse was to push him away, but she felt her hands gently touching his warm chest. As he continued to kiss her warm, soft lips, she could feel her heart racing.

"Terry, maybe we should stop," she whispered, trying to fight the urges building within her.

She gasped as he slowly started to glide his warm, moist tongue all over her smooth neck. She could feel her heart pounding as his warm lips pressed against hers, unleashing a passion she thought she would never experience again. In all the years she was involved with Preston, she had never imagined being with another man. She couldn't fathom the thought of loving another man the way she had loved him. But, as Angela felt the warmth of Terry's probing tongue and his soft lips all over her neck and face, she felt a desire inside of her she thought was lost. He reached behind her and unzipped her dress, which effortlessly, fell from her body and to the floor. With one quick motion, Terry pulled his t-shirt from his body. He lifted Angela in his arms and gently laid her nude body on the sofa. Her body stiffened as he began to softly slide his tongue down the front of her neck to the warm cleavage between her supple breasts. Her body began to tremble as his lips gently brushed against her hardened nipples. She closed her eyes as he softly kissed her from her breasts down to her warm, taut belly. "Terry, no . . . maybe we should slow down," she whispered. Terry heard her faint pleas, but her protests only made him more determined to please her. A low moan escaped her lips as his gentle hands and lips worked in harmony all over her quivering body. Her body arched as he slowly moved downward and glided his warm tongue on the inner part of her thighs. "Terry, please . . . wait," she moaned, breathing heavily.

"No more waiting," he whispered in her ear.

No longer able to resist the burning desires within her any longer, she reached down with both hands and held his head in place, not wanting him to stop. Suddenly, without warning, she gently grabbed his arms and pulled him on top of her quivering body.

"Go slow, please. It's been a very long time," she whispered.

"Of course," he said softly, stroking her long, dark hair.

As he gazed deeply into her eyes, he could feel the intense passion burning inside of her. She no longer tried to hold back her desires. All of her inhibitions were gone and she totally submitted to her sexual desires. He then made love to her with a passion she only thought possible in those romantic novels she had read as a young teenager. She moved her hips in unison with him, matching each of his powerful, rhythmic thrusts. Terry could feel a wave of energy building within him, creating a surge of excitement and anticipation. He groaned deeply as he continued to pump and grind his hips into her, enjoying the sensation of pleasure coursing throughout his body. Her breathing quickened and her heart raced as she was totally caught up in the heat of this special moment. Suddenly, she arched her back as her nails dug lightly into his bare, sweaty back. She wrapped her arms and legs around him tightly, holding him closely, as if never wanting to let him go. They shuddered together in a powerful climax that left them breathless and drained. For several minutes, not a word was said. As the powerful sensations slowly subsided from her trembling body, Angela rolled over and laid her head on Terry's chest.

"Okay, now I'm impressed," she whispered, softly rubbing his chest.

Without a word, he leaned over and gave her a long passionate kiss. As they gazed into each other's eyes, Terry smiled, knowing that their relationship had just become very, very special.

Chapter 30

It had been over a year since Damon played a full court game of basketball and the throbbing pain in his knees was reminding him of that. After a long, stressful week at work, he decided he would get up early and spend his Saturday morning playing some hoops at a neighborhood park. Before he got into music, basketball was always Damon's favorite pastime. Even though his whole body was tired and aching, he felt very good about his performance on the court. At six feet, one hundred and eighty pounds, he more than held his own playing against guys who were ten to fifteen years younger than himself. The first two games he felt fine, but the third game and the ninety three degree heat, took everything out of him. As he sat down under a tree, with a towel draped over his sweaty head, he noticed a large group of new players walking toward the basketball court. "Man, I'm glad I got here early," he muttered to himself. He closed his eyes and laid his head back against the shaded tree as tried to summon the energy to get up and walk home. Damon's brief rest was interrupted by a loud voice.

"Hey, man! What were you doing out there on the court?"

Damon opened his eyes and saw a slender teenager, wearing a Miami Heat jersey, walking toward him.

"Are you talking to me?" Damon asked, looking puzzled.

"Yeah, I'm talking to you. You scored a lot of points on me. I don't like being disrespected on the basketball court," the teenager said, angrily.

"Look, I was just out there playing some ball. I wasn't trying to disrespect anyone," Damon replied.

"Nigga, you ain't that damn good. You just got lucky," the teen responded.

"Are you seriously giving me attitude because I scored some points on you in a basketball game?" Damon asked, sounding irritated.

"Don't ever disrespect me like that again," the teen said, with a scowl on his face.

Being a veteran of the streets, Damon knew he had to turn into the aggressor or the teen would walk all over him.

"Who the fuck do you think you're talking to, youngster?" Damon said, standing up and getting in the teen's face.

The teen was momentarily surprised, not expecting Damon to stand up to him.

"Nigga, you better back off! You don't know me! I've been to prison, I'll fuck you up!" he said, trying to sound tough.

Damon could see the look of fear in the teen's eyes. With all of his tough talk and idle threats, he knew the teen didn't want to fight him. Suddenly, the teen pulled up his Miami Heat jersey to reveal the handle of a gun, protruding from his shorts.

"Oh, that's how it is?" Damon said, standing his ground.

"Yeah, nigga, that's how it is," the teen replied, arrogantly.

Damon realized it would be crazy for him to continue this confrontation when he knew he was at a distinct disadvantage. Even though Damon wanted to teach this teenage punk a lesson, he knew he had to keep his pride in check. He had a wife and son at home to think about and he understood that his common sense needed to prevail in this situation.

"I don't have time for this," Damon said as he turned and walked away from the teen.

"Yeah, that's right, nigga!" the teen yelled, arrogantly. "You better take your old ass home before I fuck you up!"

Damon continued to walk away, ignoring the teen's taunts. He realized he would rather go home with a bruised ego than to be shot and killed by a young punk trying to prove his manhood over a meaningless basketball game.

Chapter 31

I was sitting in Angela's apartment, clicking on the cable remote, trying to find something good on TV to watch. Angela's regular babysitter had an unexpected emergency, so I told her I would come over to watch Kenya while she was at class. It seemed like she was beginning to feel more comfortable with me watching her daughter because Kenya and I had started developing a good relationship. Since it was a school night, I made sure Kenya was in her bed at 8:15 p.m. As I flipped through the TV channels, I came across a baseball game between the Atlanta Braves and the New York Mets. The score was tied 2-2 in the bottom of the fifth inning. Angela would be home from her class in about thirty minutes, so I figured the game should keep me occupied until she arrived. I was feeling a little hungry, so I got up to go into the kitchen to find something to snack on. Before I reached the kitchen, I decided to check on Kenya. As I slowly opened her bedroom door, I saw flashing lights from the darkness of her room. Kenya was sitting on her bed playing a hand held video game.

"Kenya, what are you doing up?" I said turning on her bedroom lights. "It's 8:52." I said, looking at the small, digital clock on her night stand. "You know your bedtime is at 8:15."

"I've got one more level to beat to get a high score," she replied, not taking her eyes off the video game.

"Kenya, you know you have to go to school in the morning. Please turn the game off and go to bed," I said in calm voice.

"If I turn the game off, I'll have to start back from the beginning again. Just let me finish this last level."

"Look, your mom is going to kill both of us if she comes home and you're still awake. Turn the game off, please."

"Just give me ten more minutes."

"No, Kenya. Turn the game off or I'm going to take it from you," I said in a stern voice.

"Yeah, whatever," she said, not taking her eyes off the video game.

"Whatever?" I asked in a stunned voice. "Kenya, turn that game off right now and go to bed."

"You don't tell me what to do. You're not my father!" she replied in a defiant tone.

I stood there in silence, looking at Kenya in disbelief. I couldn't believe she opened her mouth and said that to me. Kenya saw the stunned look on my face and without saying another word, she turned the game off and put it on her night stand. Neither one of us said anything as I turned out the lights and walked out of her bedroom. I was feeling disappointed and slightly angry, but then I realized that I was feeling more hurt than anything else. After all, she was only telling the truth. I wasn't her father. As I walked back into the den, I sat back down and tried to watch the rest of the baseball game, but the only thing I could think about was Kenya's angry comment ringing in my head. Kenya's outburst really bothered me, especially since I thought she and I were getting along so well the past few months. My thoughts were interrupted as I heard the sound of keys opening the front door. I got up and greeted Angela as she walked inside.

"Hey, how did everything go?" she asked.

"Fine," I said, trying to force a smile.

"I hope she didn't give you a hard time going to bed."

"No, everything went well. How was your class?" I said, trying to change the subject.

"It was long and very boring. I thought that instructor would never stop talking. Let me check on Kenya and make sure she's asleep and then we can spend some alone time together," she said, putting her arms around my neck.

"Can I get a rain check on that?" I have to get up very early for a job interview."

"Okay," she replied, looking slightly puzzled. "Thank you again for watching Kenya for me," she said, giving me a big hug. "I'm so happy you two are getting along so well. She really likes you."

I like her, too," I replied, trying to sound upbeat. "I'll give you a call tomorrow."

"Okay. Good luck on your interview. Goodnight, Terry."

As Angela closed the door behind me, my mind began to wander as I walked into the humid night air. All these months I've spent with Kenya, I honestly thought she and I had developed a very close bond. Obviously, I was wrong. The fact that Kenya felt it necessary to throw in my face that I wasn't her father made it clear that we hadn't developed a friendship at all. I needed to accept the fact that this was a major problem. How would I be able to develop a serious relationship with Angela if I couldn't develop a good relationship with her daughter?

Chapter 32

Angela and Kenya were quickly walking into the Epic Community Center, a large auditorium located in the city of Stone Mountain. It was Simon Volkoff's annual piano recital, a very popular event that music lovers from around the city made a point to attend. The piano recital was scheduled to start at 11:00 a.m. and Mr. Volkoff requested that all of the performers arrive at the center no later than 10:30 a.m. Of course Angela was arriving late.

"Hurry up, Kenya, we're running a little late," she said, looking at her watch. Angela noticed that Kenya had been very quiet most of the morning and she knew that something was bothering her daughter.

"Sweetheart, I know you're a little nervous, but you're going to do fine," Angela said, putting her arm around her daughter's shoulder.

"Okay," Kenya replied, meekly.

As they continued walking into the auditorium, Angela noticed a sign with a big arrow, pointing to a closed door.

"There's the room where you need to meet with the other performers. You go ahead and join them while I find a couple of seats for me and Terry."

"I don't think he's coming," Kenya said in a quiet voice.

"Of course he's coming. You know Terry wouldn't miss your piano recital."

Kenya looked at her mother with a sad look on her face.

"Mom, I know he's not coming."

"What are talking about?"

"The other night, when Terry was watching me, he told me to go to bed and I said something very mean to him."

"What did you say?"

"I told him I didn't have to listen to him because he's not my father."

"Why did you . . ." Angela stopped talking when she saw the tears in her daughter's eyes. "Kenya, that wasn't a nice thing to say."

"I know, mom. Now he hates me."

"He doesn't hate you, sweetheart," Angela said, wiping the tears streaming down Kenya's face. "It's okay. Please stop crying. Go ahead and join the others and we'll talk later."

"Okay, mom," she said, slowly walking away.

"I know you're going to play that song very well. Good luck. I love you," Angela said, as she watched her daughter walk to the dressing room.

For a brief moment, she stood motionless, still reeling from her daughter's confession.

"Can everyone please be seated?" a woman's voice is heard on the auditorium speakers. "We are about to begin our program."

Angela walked down the congested aisles, pushing her way through the crowd of people looking for vacant seats. She walked over to three vacant seats in the second row, wondering if she should save one of the seats for Terry. That option became moot when a young couple, hurriedly sat down in the two vacant seats next to her.

"I told you we should have gotten here earlier," the woman said to her male companion.

"Stop complaining, dear. Just be happy we don't have to sit in the balcony."

Suddenly, the lights in the auditorium dimmed and a tall, gray-haired gentleman in a white suit walked to the center of the stage.

"Good morning, ladies and gentlemen. I would like to welcome all of you to the Young & Gifted Academy's eighth annual piano recital. My name is Simon Volkoff. I am the instructor of these talented young people that will be performing for you today." He paused as he received a light applause from the audience. "These young people have worked extremely hard to put on a wonderful show for you. We request that you refrain from taking pictures until each performance is completed. Our first performer is Wendell Livingston, playing "Minuet in G," a popular selection from Ludwig van Beethoven."

The crowd applauded as a young boy came walking across the stage and sat down at the piano. For the next forty minutes, one by one, the performers came out to the stage and played a selected piece of music for the audience. Angela glanced at her watch, wondering when Kenya was going to perform. Moments later, Simon Volkoff walked onto the stage to introduce the next performer.

"Ladies and gentlemen, our final performer will be Miss Kenya Greer, playing "Requiem in D Minor" by Wolfgang Amadeus Mozart.

The crowd applauded as Kenya slowly walked to the piano wearing a pretty pink dress with a matching bow in her hair. Kenya looked out into the audience and saw her mother sitting in the second row, who was giving her a big smile for encouragement. Kenya sat down at the piano and stared at the music sheet in front of her. She was noticeably nervous as she placed her trembling hands on the piano keys. She began to play and after the first line of the song, struck the wrong keys. She stopped playing and removed her hands from the piano keys. The crowd began to murmur loudly as Kenya sat motionless, staring at the music sheet.

"Come on, baby, you can do it," Angela said in a low voice. As Kenya looked out into the crowd, she felt like the entire audience was focused on her every move. After all the years of piano lessons and the long hours of practice, Kenya realized that she was too nervous to play. Not only did she feel nervous, she felt totally embarrassed. She decided the best thing to do was to get up and walk off the stage.

"Espressivo!" a voice yelled from the back of the crowded auditorium.

Kenya smiled as she recognized the voice. She was suddenly filled with confidence knowing that *he* was in the audience giving her the encouragement to play her best. Even though she was still nervous, she knew that he was watching her and she didn't want to let him down. She placed her hands back on the piano keys and began to play. As she continued to play, she surprised herself at how effortlessly her fingers glided across the piano keys. When she came to the most difficult part of the song, she did her best to put "expression" into her playing. At the end of the song, the crowd applauded loudly. Kenya stood up from the piano seat, bowed, and walked off the stage, happy and proud that she played so well. Simon Volkoff greeted her at the side of the stage.

"Young lady, you played beautifully. I am so very proud of you," he said, giving Kenya a big hug. Simon Volkoff walked to the center of the stage to address the audience.

"Ladies and gentlemen, this concludes our piano recital. Thank you all for coming."

As the audience began to disperse, Angela rushed to the stage area to greet Kenya.

"Come here, baby. I am so proud of you," she said, hugging Kenya tightly.

"Where is he?" Kenya asked, looking into the crowd.

"Where is who?" Angela asked, looking bewildered.

"Terry," she replied, still looking around the dispersing crowd.

"I don't think he's here, sweetheart."

"Mom, didn't you hear that guy yell out something? That was Terry."

"Are you sure it was him? It could have been someone else."

"No, mom. I know it was him."

Suddenly, Terry pushed his way through a crowd of people and walked up behind Angela and Kenya.

"Congratulations, Kenya," he said, extending a dozen roses to her.

"Terry!" she yelled, excitedly. "I'm so glad you came," she said, hugging him tightly, not wanting to let him go. "I'm so sorry for what I said," she said with tears in her eyes.

"Hey, don't cry. It's okay," he said, softly stroking her hair.

"Thank you for coming," Angela said, giving him a kiss on the cheek.

"There's no way I would have missed this piano recital. Kenya, you were magnificent."

"No, I wasn't," she said, looking very bashful. I was so nervous I thought I was going to throw up on that piano."

"Well, I'm glad you didn't. I don't think anyone in the auditorium wanted to see what you ate for breakfast," he said, as they all started laughing. "According to my watch, it's 12:37. If it's okay with you beautiful ladies, I would like to take you out to lunch and celebrate Kenya's fine piano performance."

"Can we, mom? Please?" Kenya asked, pleading to her mother. Angela looked at Terry with a big smile on her face.

"We would love to go out and celebrate with you, Mr. Freeman."

Kenya reached out and gently grabbed Terry's hand, feeling extremely happy that her friend was back in her life.

Chapter 33

It was Tuesday evening and I was standing in Angela's kitchen cooking dinner. It was the third week that I had been watching Kenya while Angela attended her law classes and everything had been going smoothly. The last few months had been very hectic for me. It had been over a month since our band broke up, but I still couldn't accept that it happened. After all the time and effort we put into Infinite Noise, it was hard to believe that it was over. I quit my job at NexTech, the band that I worked so hard to make a success of had broken up and now I'm unemployed. Anyway, it wasn't going to do me any good to worry about all of that now. At least things were going well with my relationship with Angela and Kenya. I glanced at the clock on the kitchen wall, which read 6:51 p.m. Angela usually got home from her Tuesday night class around 7:30 p.m., so I thought I would surprise her and have a nice dinner ready. I wanted to cook something easy to prepare, so I decided to go with baked pork chops, macaroni and cheese, and green beans. After putting the pork chops in the oven, I decided to check on Kenya. I brought her a gymnastics DVD to watch, hoping it would keep her occupied until I finished dinner. As I walked to the den, I could hear the volume on the TV turned up very loud. I entered the den and noticed that Kenya had changed into a bright yellow skirt and white top and was dancing in front of the TV.

"Hey, little lady, what are you doing?" I said loudly, so she could hear me over the TV.

"I'm working on my gymnastics moves," she said, dancing around the room.

"Alright, but please be careful," I said, turning the volume down with the remote control.

"Your mom will have a cow if you break her big-screen TV." I walked over to the center of the room and pulled a glass table away from where she was dancing. "Okay, now you have plenty of room to do your gymnastics."

"Thanks, Terry," she said, as I walked back into the kitchen.

As soon as I entered the kitchen, I opened the oven to check on the pork chops.

"Angela is going to love this dinner," I said to myself. Suddenly, I heard a loud crash coming from the den. I raced into the room and found Kenya lying in a pile of broken glass.

"Kenya, are you alright?" I asked frantically, picking her up from the floor.

"My neck hurts really bad," she said, crying, with both hands pressed against the side of her neck.

"Let me see your neck, Kenya." I said, trying to pull her hands away.

"No, no, don't touch it! It hurts!" she cried.

"Okay, Kenya, I won't touch it. Stay right here. I'll be right back."

I rushed into the bathroom and grabbed a towel. When I ran back into the den, Kenya was sitting up, holding her neck. I could see a stream of blood oozing through her fingers.

"Here, keep this towel pressed against your neck," I said.

My first thought was to call 911, but I decided it would be quicker to drive her to the hospital myself than to wait for the paramedics to arrive. I ran into the kitchen, turned off the oven, and ran back into the room to get Kenya.

"You're going to be alright, sweetheart." I said, picking her up and carrying her outside to my car.

I drove down the road trying my best to keep close to the speed limit. After a twenty-five minute drive, I turned down the street leading to the hospital, thankful that traffic wasn't too congested. I reached for my cell phone to call Angela. After four rings, it went to her voice mail. I didn't want to leave a message that would upset her, so I disconnected the call.

"Terry, it hurts so bad," Kenya cried, tightly pressing the towel against her bloody neck.

"I know, sweetheart. It's going to be alright, I promise. You're going to be alright," I said, trying to keep her and myself calm.

As I finally reached the hospital, the emergency room parking lot was full. Not wanting to waste any more time, I parked on the side of the street across from the hospital. My heart was pounding as I got out of the car and ran to the passenger side. I opened the door and lifted Kenya into my arms. The towel she was holding to her neck was drenched with blood. A hospital security guard, sitting in an outside booth, walked outside and started yelling at me. "Hey, you! You can't park there! Move that car!" he shouted as I continued running to the emergency room entrance.

"I have an emergency here!" I yelled back at him.

After running about fifty yards, I finally reached the emergency room entrance where a group of people were blocking my way. "Excuse me! Get out of the way, please!" I yelled, pushing my way through the crowd with Kenya in my arms. I frantically looked around for a nurse, doctor, or anyone that looked like they could help me. As I reached the front desk, a young woman, who I assumed to be the receptionist, was sitting there, typing on a computer. "Excuse me, I need some help!" I said, breathing heavily.

"Sir, you need to calm down," she said, nonchalantly. "What happened to her?"

"She fell and cut her neck on some glass," I said, trying to catch my breath.

"I'm going to need you to fill out some paperwork," she said, handing me a clipboard with hospital forms. "Have a seat in the waiting room. We'll have someone with you shortly."

"Shortly? She's bleeding. Someone needs to see her right now!" I said, raising my voice.

"Sir, I'm going to need you to calm down."

"Terry, I'm scared," Kenya said, with tears in her eyes.

"It's okay, you're going to be fine," I said, trying to ease her fears.

As I held her in my arms, I suddenly realized how attached I had gotten to this little girl. I honestly felt like I was going through the same pain she was feeling. I realized I needed to keep a cool head if I was going to get some help for Kenya. I glanced down at the receptionist's name tag on her uniform.

"Please, Ms. Nolley, can you have someone see her right now?" I asked, pleading with her.

The receptionist looked up at me holding little Kenya in my arms. She then picked up the phone on her desk.

"I need an orderly at the front desk right away," she said.

"Thank you very much, Ms. Nolley." Moments later, a male orderly came from the back room pushing a gurney. I softly placed Kenya on the gurney as she continued to hold onto me.

"Don't leave me, Terry. Please don't leave me," Kenya said, sobbing.

"Sir, I'm sorry, but you can't go back there right now," the male orderly said.

"I need to be with her," I replied. "Can't you see she's upset?"

"I'm sorry, but it's hospital policy. If you could take a seat in the waiting room, someone will be out to give you an update on her condition."

I didn't want to create a scene in front of Kenya, so I tried to calm down. I reached over and softly caressed Kenya's blood-soaked hand.

"It's okay, baby, you'll be fine. These nice people will take good care of you. I promise I'll be with you as soon as I can."

"Okay," Kenya said, with tears streaming down her face.

Tears began to form in my eyes as the male orderly transported Kenya to the back room.

"Excuse me, sir," Ms. Nolley said. "I need to get some information from you.

There was nothing more I could do for Kenya, so I walked back over to the receptionist's desk.

"What's the little girl's name?" Ms. Nolley asked.

"Kenya Greer," I replied, trying to regain my composure.

"Are you her father?"

"No, I'm a very close friend."

"Have her parents been notified?" she asked.

"Well . . . no, I didn't have time to call. I mean, everything happened so fast."

"Sir, her parents need to be notified in case we need their consent for any treatment. We're going to need information about medical records and insurance."

"Okay, I understand. I'll call her mother right now," I said, reaching for my cell phone attached to my belt.

My stress level increased as I realized that in my haste to get Kenya to the hospital, I left my cell phone in the car.

"There are some pay phones down the hall," Ms. Nolley said.

"Thank you. I'll be right back."

I glanced at my watch to check the time. It was 7:24 p.m. so I assumed Angela would be driving home from her class. I walked into the waiting area, picked up the receiver at a pay phone, and nervously dialed Angela's cell phone number. After a few rings, Angela answered the phone.

"Hello?" she said on the other end of the line.

"Angela, this is Terry, I said, trying to talk calmly.

"Did you change your cell phone number?" she asked.

"No, I'm calling from a pay phone. I'm at the hospital. Angela, there was an . . . accident," I said, trying to get the words out.

"What happened?" she asked with fear in her voice.

"Kenya fell and cut herself on the neck."

"Oh God, is she alright?!"

"They're looking at her now, but they say she's going to be fine," I lied, trying to reassure her. "We're at Saint Paulding Memorial Hospital on Forsyth Street."

"Okay, I'll be there as soon as possible!"

After hanging up the phone, I walked into the men's bathroom and began washing Kenya's blood off my arms and hands. A wave of guilt began to envelop me as I stood in front of the sink, staring at myself in the mirror. How could this have happened? One minute Kenya was dancing around and the next she was screaming and lying in a pool of blood. I closed my eyes and said a prayer for Kenya. "Heavenly Father, please let her be okay," I said to myself over and over. After finishing my prayer, I dried my hands and walked back outside to the waiting room. Twenty-three minutes went by as I paced up and down the hospital floor waiting for Angela to arrive. Moments later, I heard the sound of the elevator doors opening. Angela stepped out from the elevator and sprinted toward me.

"Where's Kenya? Is she okay?" she asked, frantically.

I placed my hands on her shoulders and tried to calm her down.

"The doctor is looking at her now."

"Oh my God! Is that her blood on your shirt?"

"Yes, I carried her to the emergency room.

"Terry, what happened? How did she cut herself?" Angela asked, with tears flowing down her face.

"She was dancing around in the den. I guess she must have tripped and fallen on that glass table. I'm not really sure. I was in the kitchen. Everything happened so fast. I am so sorry."

"Okay, I need to see my daughter," she said, turning and walking to the nurse's station. "I'm Angela Greer," she said to a female intern. "I'm here to see my daughter, Kenya Greer."

The nurse looked at her computer screen.

"The doctor is seeing her right now," the nurse responded.

"Where is she?" Angela asked in a stern voice.

"Ma'am, she's with the doctor right now. The doctor will see you, shortly," she replied.

"I want to see my daughter right now!" Angela said, raising her voice.

"Angela, please," I said, putting my hand on her shoulder. "I know you're upset, but please try to calm down."

"Calm down?! I need to see my baby girl!"

"I know Angela, I know. She's going to be fine," I said, giving her a consoling hug.

For the next fifteen minutes, Angela and I nervously sat in the waiting room area. Suddenly, a tall man in a business suit walked into the waiting room.

"Angela, I got here as soon as I got your message," the man said, putting his arm around Angela. "How is Kenya?" he asked.

"I don't know. I'm still waiting to see her doctor," she replied.

"What happened to her?" the man asked.

Angela tried to respond, but she was so upset, she couldn't speak.

"Kenya fell on a glass table and cut herself," I said, answering his question. The man in the business suit looked at me with a cold stare, then looked at Angela.

"Who the hell is this guy?" he asked, sounding annoyed.

"Preston, this is my friend, Terry Freeman," she replied. "Terry, this is Preston Seymour, Kenya's father."

"I'm not here for social introductions," he said, glaring coldly at me. "Is that my daughter's blood all over your shirt?" he asked, angrily.

"Preston, please lower your voice. This isn't the time for this," Angela said, trying to calm him down.

"I've already spoken to one of the nurses and she assured me that Kenya is going to be fine," I said, trying to ease the tension.

"Look, man, I don't need you giving me medical updates about my daughter. Why am I even talking to this guy?" he said, turning away from me to confront Angela. "Angela, where the hell were you when all this was going on?"

"Preston, please calm down and lower your voice."

"Calm down? My daughter is in the hospital and I want to know why. For all I know, you were neglecting my daughter while you were with this guy," he said in a stern voice.

"You have a lot of nerve accusing me of neglecting our daughter when you haven't been in her life all these years!"

Angela was obviously upset, so I tried to shift the entire accident on myself.

"This is not her fault. Angela was in class and I was watching Kenya."

"I don't believe this," Preston said, glaring at Angela. "You left our daughter with this incompetent negro?" he asked, angrily.

"Look, I understand you're upset, but, you need to calm down," I said, firmly.

"Do you think you're man enough to calm me down?" he replied, walking toward me.

"Will you two please stop!" Angela said, stepping in between us. Preston and I stared at each other for what seemed like minutes, when suddenly a nurse walked into the waiting room.

"Miss Greer, the doctor will see you now," the nurse said.

Preston and I put our anger on hold as we all followed the nurse. As we reached Kenya's room, a doctor greeted us at the door.

"Hello, I'm Doctor Anderson," he said, shaking Angela's hand.

"I'm Angela Greer, Kenya's mother. How is she?"

"She had a nasty little cut on the side of her neck that required about four stitches and some other minor little cuts, but she's going to be fine." the doctor said, smiling. "I gave her a mild sedative to help calm her down, so she's a little sleepy right now."

"Can I see her?" Angela asked, with a look of relief on her face.

"Yes, but not too long. I want her to get some rest. She's been asking for someone named Terry," the doctor said.

"That's me." I said, walking up to the doctor.

"Are you her father?" the doctor asked.

"No, he's not her father!" Preston said firmly. "Doctor Anderson, my name is Preston Seymour. I'm Kenya's father. I would like to see my daughter," he said in an assertive voice.

"Okay, but let's limit it to two visitors at a time."

"Thank you, doctor," Angela said, trying to force a smile.

As the doctor walked away, Preston turned toward me.

"You might as well leave because I don't want you around my daughter. You're the reason she's here in the first place."

Before I could reply, Angela reached out and touched my hand.

"Terry, do you mind . . . ?" Before she could finish her request, I cut her off.

"No, that's fine. I'll head on home," I said, trying to hide my disappointment.

"Thank you. I'll call you later and let you know how she's doing," she said as she followed Preston into Kenya's room.

I continued to watch as Preston and Angela entered Kenya's room and closed the door behind them. It had become very clear to me that my relationship with Angela was not as strong as I thought. After all the time we had spent together, how could she so easily decide to let Preston see Kenya instead of me? Who was I kidding? I already knew why she asked me to leave. Preston was Kenya's father and I wasn't. As I stood outside of that closed door, I couldn't help but notice the obvious metaphor of my current situation. Angela, Preston, and Kenya would always have a bond together and I would always be the man on the outside of the door looking in.

***

The knock at her door sent a numbing chill throughout Angela's body. Even though she knew Preston was coming over to her apartment to talk, she wasn't looking forward to their conversation. Last night, she was able to avoid talking to Preston because she was busy taking care of Kenya after leaving the hospital. When he called earlier this morning, he insisted on coming over to see their daughter in person. Kenya was his daughter, so it was hard to tell him no. She had known Preston long enough to know that there was more to his visit than just to check on Kenya. Whatever his reasons, she was sure it couldn't be anything good. When she opened the door, she was somewhat surprised to see that Preston wasn't wearing a suit. Instead, he was wearing blue jeans and a Chicago Bulls t-shirt holding a small gift-wrapped box, with a white bow. She could also tell by the stubbles of hair on his face, that he hadn't shaved this morning. In the years that they were together, Preston had always taken great pride in his appearance and attire. If he wasn't wearing a suit, he was wearing designer clothing such as Sean John, Ralph Laurent, or Tommy Hilfiger.

"Are you going to invite me in this time?" he asked, sarcastically.

"Come in." she replied. "I'm making some coffee. Would you like some?" she asked walking to the kitchen.

"No, thank you. I had breakfast at the hotel," he said, sitting down on her sofa. "How is Kenya doing?"

"She's in her room watching TV. The doctor recommended she rest in bed for a few days to make sure her cuts heal properly."

"I was so upset about what happened to Kenya, I don't think I slept at all last night," he said, rubbing his eyes. "Is it okay, if I go to her room and give her this gift?"

"It's the first room on the right."

Preston walked to Kenya's room and knocked softy on her door.

"Come in," Kenya said. Preston entered her room, concealing the gift behind his back.

"Hey, baby, how are you feeling?"

"It stings a little bit, but I'm okay," she said, touching the bandage on her neck.

Preston walked over to her bed and sat next to her.

"Here you go," he said, pulling the gift from behind his back.

"Is that for me?" she asked.

It sure is. Go ahead and open it."

Kenya hurriedly tore the gift paper from the box.

"Oh, wow! It's a cell phone!" she said, excitedly.

"That's right, baby. It's your very own phone. Now, you can call your daddy anytime you want. Plus, you can download a lot of fun games to play."

"This is so cool. Thank you, daddy," she said, giving him a hug.

"Be careful, don't hug too tight. We don't want to pop those stitches on your neck. Hey, I need to talk to mommy, so why don't you play with your phone and I'll be back a little later to check on you."

"Okay, daddy. Thanks again for my cell phone."

"You're very welcome, baby."

Preston walked out of Kenya's room, closing the door behind him. When Preston entered the living room area, Angela was in the kitchen, pouring herself a cup of coffee.

"I think she really likes her gift," he said.

"I'm glad to hear that," Angela replied, stirring her coffee.

"It's a $300 dollar cell phone. I've got a warranty on it, so if she breaks or loses it, I can get it replaced."

"Okay," she replied, sounding disinterested."

"Could you please come over here and sit down?" he asked.

Angela reluctantly walked into the living room and sat on the sofa next to Preston.

"As I mentioned on the phone, I was hoping we could talk," he said, sliding a little closer to her.

"What do we need to talk about?"

"Listen, I know I've made some mistakes in the past, but I'm hoping you'll give me a chance to prove to you that I'm a changed man."

"Preston, we've been over this before. I've already given you several chances and several years of my life. I'm not going through that anymore."

"We have a daughter to think about. Have you thought about how this could possibly affect her? You know how much it hurt you growing up without your father."

"Don't go there. That's pretty low, even for you, to bring that up," she said, standing up and walking away from him. Preston got up, walked over to Angela and tried to put his arm around her.

"Don't touch me!" she said, pulling away from him.

"I'm sorry. I shouldn't have said that," he said, backing away from her. "You have to understand that I love you and Kenya very much. The two years you've been away has been torture for me. When I told you I was here in Atlanta on a business trip, I lied. I came here to see you and my daughter. I've changed. I can make you happy if you just give me a chance."

"Preston, what you don't understand is that I'm already happy. I'm in law school, I have an internship with a reputable law firm and I'm taking care of my daughter. I'm very happy with my life."

"I guess you're also happy with that negligent, little punk?"

"His name is Terry."

"I know who he is. I did a little research on this guy. He's nothing but a small-time musician, playing in a small-time band. He's probably on drugs and screwing every female groupie he meets."

"You're wrong about him. He's nothing like that," she said defensively.

"Do you really know this guy? Look what happened when you left him alone with our daughter. He obviously isn't a responsible person."

"Stop it. You don't even know him."

"I know he was watching our daughter when she nearly bled to death," he fired back.

Angela could feel herself becoming angry, but she didn't respond, wondering if there was a bit of truth in what Preston was saying. She turned her back to him, not wanting to face his piercing stare. Preston noticed that Angela had become very quiet. He felt confident that he had planted a seed of doubt in her mind about Terry.

"Angela, please. Let's not argue. This isn't about you, me, or that guy, Terry. This is about our daughter. We need to think about what's best for her." Preston walked over to Angela and gently put his hand on her shoulder. "I really think you should move back to Chicago."

"One of the main reasons I moved here was to get away from you," she said, turning around to face him. "I moved here to be on my own, to stand on my own two feet."

"I truly understand what you're saying. You moved to Atlanta to prove that you could make it on your own and you've done that. Now, it's time for you to come back home. I miss you and your family misses you. I stopped by your mother's house last week to check on her and all she talked about was how much she misses her daughter and granddaughter. I'm very concerned about her."

"Don't play head games with me, Preston. I talk to my mother two to three times a week, so I know how she's doing."

"Do you really think your mother is going to tell you how much she misses you and how lonely she feels without seeing you and Kenya?"

Angela could feel herself becoming emotional so she turned away and walked into the kitchen.

"Even if I wanted to, I can't just pack up and move back to Chicago. I'm finishing my second year of law school, I have my internship at the law firm, and Kenya is in a very good school."

"Angela, I truly admire you for all of your accomplishments since you moved here, but this isn't your home. Everything you know and love is back in Chicago. Here's my suggestion. After you finish your semester here, you move back to Chicago and transfer to John Marshal, Loyola, Depaul, or any other law school you choose. I'll pay for your tuition so you won't have to work so you can totally focus on your classes."

"I can't just leave like that. I worked hard to get my internship at the law firm and I don't want to give that up."

"You know my dad is a senior manager at one of the largest accounting firms in Chicago. He has major connections and I know he can get you an internship with just about any law firm in the city." Preston walked toward Angela, reached out and gently touched her hand. "Please, Angela. Come back home. I need you. Your mother needs you."

Angela stood quietly with her head down, giving Preston the confidence he needed to continue pressuring her.

"I know you're still angry with me and you have every right to be. Listen, don't do it for me. Do it for yourself. Do it for your mother. Most of all, do it for Kenya. She deserves to be with a father who will love and protect her," he said, trying to sound sincere.

"I don't know, Preston. I have to think about it," she said, looking down at the floor, not wanting to make eye contact with him.

"Okay, I understand. I know this is a lot to process right now. Please, just think about it. I'm flying back to Chicago in a few hours, but I'll be back here sometime in October. That should give you plenty of time to think about this."

"Okay," she whispered.

"Before I go, I'd like to say good-bye to Kenya, if that's okay with you?"

"Yes, that's fine"

"Thank you, Angela. As he walked away, he suddenly stopped, turned around and faced Angela.

"I know you'll make the right decision," he said as he turned and walked toward Kenya's room with a devious smile on his face.

Chapter 34

It had been eight days since Kenya's terrible accident. I had called Angela several times the night of the accident to check on Kenya, but she never returned my calls. After calling and leaving numerous voice messages, she finally called me back the next day. We didn't talk very long and she made it very clear that she was still upset about what happened to Kenya. She said she didn't blame me for the accident, but she thought it was best for us to take a break from each other for awhile. As much as I wanted to see her and Kenya, I reluctantly agreed with her suggestion. Maybe she was right. Maybe we did need a little break from each other to get past all of the emotional turmoil of Kenya's accident. It had been so hard on me going through all those days without seeing them. I never realized how much Angela and Kenya had become an important part of my life until that tragic incident. I had never been through anything quite like that before. When I lost my father, it felt like a part of me was lost, too. All the sorrow and pain I went through was difficult, but my mother and Uncle Henry were always there to give me their strength and support. This was so much different. It seemed like I had lost so much in such a short period of time. I lost my job with NexTech, even though I technically quit. I lost an opportunity to sign with a major record label for our band. I had most likely lost my relationship with my brother. Now, I had apparently lost my relationship with Angela and Kenya. I might as well be honest with myself and admit something I had known for a few years. I had also lost my faith. There was a time when I felt that prayer could get me through anything, but I just didn't believe that anymore. For the past two days, I had been sitting in my apartment, not calling anyone and not caring if anyone called me. I felt like I had fallen into a deep, dark pit with no way to get out. I had been sitting in my room feeling sad, angry, helpless and all alone. I had not eaten in almost two days, but for some strange reason, I didn't feel hungry. I glanced up at the clock on my night stand which read 2:41 am. My eyes were tired and my body felt drained, but no matter how hard I tried, I just couldn't fall asleep. I thought drinking a fifth of Hennessy would help ease my mind or at least numb me from my depressive state of mind. Unfortunately, the only thing the Hennessy did was make me sick to my stomach. I often wondered why people committed suicide. How could anyone take their own life? As I quietly sat alone in my apartment, I finally understood. If someone felt lost, helpless, unwanted, all alone, with little or no faith, what would be the reason to continue living? Then it finally happened. I got that nauseous feeling that let me know that everything in my stomach was about to come up. I got up, ran to the bathroom, and knelt over the toilet as a torrent of liquor and everything else in my stomach came gushing out of my mouth. For what seemed like hours, I hovered over the toilet throwing up, thinking a quick death would be better than the agony I was going through. As I sat on the bathroom floor, leaning against the toilet, I felt like I had finally hit rock bottom. I had failed my family, my friends, and myself. Images of my father began to form in my head. It felt like he was in the room with me, standing over me, with a disappointed look on his face. Maybe it was good that my father wasn't around to see what a mess I had made of my life and my musical career. He would be so ashamed of me. No, that wouldn't be true. If my father was with me, he would have told me to get my ass off the bathroom floor and stop feeling sorry for myself. There I was, sitting on that hard bathroom tile. I felt so tired. All I wanted to do was sleep. My head was pounding and my stomach felt like it was twisted in knots. I tried to get up and walk to my bedroom, but I just didn't have the strength. I laid down on the bathroom floor, praying that this emotional and physical pain would just go away long enough for me to sleep. "Oh, God, please help me." I pleaded, as another torrent of vomit started spewing from my mouth. Forty five minutes went by and I finally started feeling a little better. I didn't even think about standing up.

I continued to lay on that cold bathroom floor until I finally fell asleep. After what seemed like days, I woke up, shielding my eyes from the bright, sunlight beaming through my bathroom window. I slowly tried to sit up, not wanting to upset my queasy stomach. As

I slowly stood on my feet and cautiously walked to my bedroom, I felt relieved that other than feeling a little nauseous with a minor headache, I was feeling pretty good. I picked up my cell phone from the night stand and checked the time, which read 5:18 p.m. My cell phone indicated that I had three missed calls. One missed call from my Uncle Henry and two from my mother. I immediately called my mother and let her know that I was fine and was just too tired to answer the phone. She told me that I was on her mind so she called to see how I was doing. I convinced my mother that I was okay and promised to come by and see her over the weekend. There's nothing quite like a mother's love. A smile came across my face as I realized that I wasn't as alone as I thought. Suddenly I felt strong, invigorated and confident. More important, I felt my faith was renewed. Whatever demons were inside of me were now gone. It was time for me to stop feeling sorry for myself and to move on with my life. I was determined to get my life back on track and not doubt myself anymore. As I walked to my closet to get some clean clothes, I noticed the calendar on my night stand with a big, red circle around the date of September 12. On that date, I had written a note which read *WRPP at 7:00 am.* Suddenly, I remembered. I was scheduled to be on a panel tomorrow morning at WRPP radio station. I already knew I was going to catch hell debating my views on a rap radio station, but I wasn't going to back down. I realized that when I got on that radio show, I was going to be representing my family, friends, and my music. For several weeks I had been reading numerous articles, magazines and books to prepare myself for the radio debate and I felt very confident. My Uncle Henry was right. As long as I believed in what I was saying, I had nothing to fear. I felt like my faith and my confidence had been restored. I didn't care how many obstacles blocked my way, I would never give up and I would never lose my faith again. Thank you, Lord. You opened my eyes and allowed me to see the light.

Chapter 35

It was early Friday morning as I walked into the lobby of WRPP 101, the city's number one rap radio station. I wanted to feel as comfortable as possible, so I decided to wear my new jeans, an Atlanta Falcons jersey, and my new Air Jordans. I looked at the large clock on the lobby wall which read 6:34 am. As I walked up to the receptionist's desk, I was greeted by a young woman, with very long braids, who appeared to be around nineteen-years old.

"Good morning, I'm Terry Freeman. I'm here to see Brenda Thornton." The receptionist picked up the phone and called Miss Thornton.

"She'll be right with you," she said, with a friendly smile.

"Thank you," I said, already feeling the nervousness building in my stomach.

As I looked around the lobby, I noticed several framed awards on the walls that the station had received over the years. WRPP 101 was one of the most popular radio stations in the city, with a listening audience of 1.3 million between the ages of eighteen to thirty-five. The radio station's format was hip-hop music and they played it all day and night. The morning show talk host was the very popular, Thurman Payne. Payne was a former rap artist back in the early nineties and had been the voice of rap music for WRPP for over a decade. When the morning show producer invited me to talk about the pros and cons of today's rap music, I thought it would be a great opportunity to voice my point of view. Now that I was at the radio station, I started to feel like I might be making a big mistake. After all, I was going to be explaining my issues with hardcore rap music on a radio station that plays nothing but hardcore rap music. Even with all the reading and research I had done over the last few weeks, I still didn't feel very comfortable with this radio debate. Suddenly, a black woman, dressed in a dark blue business suit approached me.

"Good morning, Mr. Freeman. I'm Brenda Thornton, the morning show producer," she said, extending her hand. Thank you again for being part of our panel."

"Thank you for inviting me, Brenda."

"Follow me, I'll take you to the studio," she said.

Brenda escorted me to the studio, where I saw Thurman Payne sitting at a table, reading over some paperwork.

"Thurman, this is Terry Freeman." Thurman got up from the table to greet me.

"Nice to meet you, Terry," he said, shaking my hand. "This is my first time meeting you in person, but I saw you and your band perform at Jazz Fest a few years ago. You guys were the bomb."

"Thank you, Thurman," I said, feeling a little more comfortable.

"I hope we didn't get you up too early."

"No, I'm good," I replied, wishing I could go home and crawl back into my bed.

"Are you a fan of our show, Terry?"

"I've listened to your show at times."

As I sat down at the studio table, a young woman, around eighteen-years old, approached me with a headset.

"Terry, this is one of our interns, Keishia Griffin. She'll get you prepared for the show. I'll be right back. I need to get our other guest speaker," he said as he walked out of the studio.

Keishia handed me a headset and placed a microphone in front of me.

"Mr. Freeman, I heard that you're in some sort of band," Keishia said, adjusting my headset.

"Yes, I'm in the band, Infinite Noise." Keishia stood there looking at me with a blank look on her face. "I know you've heard the songs, "Heat Beat, Party Night, or Dark Whispers?"

"No, I don't think I've heard any of those songs."

"A few years ago, we won the Battle of the Bands competition. We've played in all of the local nightclubs in the city.

"Sorry, I'm just seventeen. I'm not old enough to get into most of the nightclubs."

All of a sudden, this intern was making me feel very old. Just then, the door to the studio opened and Thurman Payne walked in with someone behind him.

"Terry, this is Marcus Jones," Thurman said. "He's going to be the other member on our panel this morning."

I could not believe it. Of all the rap artists in the city, they had to pick that arrogant, big-mouthed, fool.

"What's up, dog?" Marcus said, extending his fist toward me.

"I'm good, Marcus," I said, leaning over to tap my fist against his.

"My producer tells me that you two were in a talent competition at Club Elite," Thurman said, already trying to create some friction between me and Marcus.

"Yeah, I don't mean to brag, but we did come in first place," Marcus said arrogantly. "By the way, when we're on the air, y'all can call me Grill. That's my street name."

"Okay, Grill, I'll try to remember that," Thurman said, reading over his notes for the show.

The studio door opened again and Brenda Thornton entered the room.

"Okay, everybody, we'll be on the air in ten minutes," she said. "Could all of you please sit down so we can do a mike check?"

After watching Brenda in action, I could see why she was the producer of one of the top radio stations in the city. Brenda checked the microphone levels, printed out information from her computer, and went over the show's format with those present to make sure the show would run smoothly. Ten minutes later, the morning show was ready to go on air.

"Okay, guys, just relax and be yourselves and we'll have a great show," Thurman said, adjusting his headset and microphone.

As I heard the theme song for the morning show play, I started getting that queasy, nervous feeling in my stomach. The "on the air" light came on and Thurman Payne went into action.

"Good morning, Atlanta! You're listening to WRPP 101 on your radio dial. Welcome to the Thurman Payne Morning Show. I'm your host, Thurman Payne. Today is hot topic Friday. Our topic this morning is very hot and very controversial. Does hardcore or gangster rap music have a negative influence on our young people? We're going to start our show this morning with two gentlemen who are members of two successful, but very different bands. Joining me this morning are Marcus "Grill" Taylor of the Thug Lordz, who won this year's Shining Star competition at Club Elite and Terry Freeman from the group, Infinite Noise. I'll start with you, Terry. Tell us a little bit about yourself and how you got started in the music industry," Thurman said, turning to me.

"Good morning, everyone." I said, trying not to sound nervous. "I started getting into music around the age of six. My father taught me to play the piano, saxophone, and guitar."

"I'm reading here that your father was a professional musician," Thurman said, glancing at his notes.

"Yes, my father played the saxophone and guitar for a band called the Jazzy Gents."

"When did you first start performing, Terry?"

"At eight-years old, I started singing and playing gospel music in the youth choir. When I was ten, I started getting into jazz and R&B."

"Are you talking about the jazz music that my daddy would listen to like Duke Ellington and Louis Armstrong?" Thurman asked, jokingly.

"Those two were great jazz musicians, but my influences were artists like Herbie Hancock, Kenny G and Ramsey Lewis, just to name a few."

"Can you tell us about the members of Infinite Noise?"

I paused for a moment to think. I guess I could have told Thurman that Infinite Noise had broken up, but that's not what he asked me.

"Infinite Noise consists of my brother, Warren, who plays the keyboard, my cousin, Reggie, plays the drums, and my best friend, Damon Thompson, plays the bass guitar and helps write a lot of our songs. Our newest member is Layla Simmons, who plays the violin and does a lot of our lead vocals."

"Terry, what music category would you say your band falls into?"

"That's a difficult question to answer. We play R&B, jazz, hip-hop, reggae, and a little bit of rock and roll."

"It sounds like your band doesn't limit itself into one musical category," he responded.

"That's true," I said proudly. "I feel it's important to have diversity in our music so it won't get too stale or boring."

"I was doing a little research and I found that Infinite Noise was one of the hottest bands in the South a few years ago. Then, your band suddenly disappeared from the music scene. Can you tell our listeners what happened to Infinite Noise?"

For a brief moment, my mind went blank. I remembered Paul telling me months ago, that this question could come up about our band, but I was still caught off-guard. I cleared my throat and tried to answer his question.

"Our band . . . was on a very hectic schedule. There were some . . . unexpected things that happened and . . . we needed a break," I stuttered, trying to get the words out.

Suddenly, Brenda Thornton walked into the studio, waved at Thurman, then pointed to her watch.

"My producer is telling me we need to take a short break," Thurman said, looking bewildered. "We'll be right back to the Thurman Payne Morning Show."

As the sound of a commercial played on the air, Thurman took off his headset and turned to Brenda.

"Hey, what was that all about?" he asked, looking slightly annoyed. "We weren't scheduled for a commercial break," he said, glancing over the show's morning format.

"We're on a very tight schedule," Brenda said, sternly. "I need you to stick with the questions on the show's script. When we get back from the break, we need to open with Marcus," she said, walking back to the control center. After the final commercial, Brenda gave Thurman the signal that the show was back on the air.

"Good morning and welcome back to the Thurman Payne Morning Show. If you're just joining us, our topic this morning is about hardcore rap music and its possible negative impact on young listeners. My next guest is Marcus "Grill" Taylor, a rapper from the group, Thug Lordz. Marcus, tell our listening audience a little bit about you and the Thug Lordz."

"Wuzzup, ATL, this is ya boy, Grill, up in this bitch!"

"Okay, Grill, I know you're excited to be here this morning, but I'm going to need you to watch your language."

"Come on, dog. I know you can bleep that stuff out."

"That's true, but it won't be much of an interview if we have to bleep out every other word coming out of your mouth."

"Okay . . . my bad."

"No problem, Marcus. Okay, you were about to tell us about the Thug Lordz."

"Well, first of all, everybody calls me Grill," he said, smiling widely to show his teeth.

"For all our radio listeners out there, Grill has a mouth full of gold teeth," Thurman said.

"That's right, cuz' all the lyrics that come out of my mouth are golden," he said, laughing at his own joke. "I guess you could say I'm the lead rapper of the group. We also got my home boys, "Lizard" Lou Jenkins, Jake "The Player" Miller, and Teddy "Too Crunk" Watson."

"Grill, do you play any musical instruments in your band?"

"No, I'm not into playing any instruments. I write lyrics and I rap. I be rappin' about my homies, my females, makin' money, and survivin' in the streets."

"Grill, I'm reading here that the Thug Lordz have recorded a new CD," Thurman said.

"Yeah, we just finished recording a new CD and it's off the chain. So, all my dogs and she-dogs, y'all be lookin' out for our new CD at your local gas stations and liquor stores," he said proudly.

"Thank you for sharing that information with us, Grill," Thurman said, trying hard not to laugh.

"Okay, I hope I won't have the FCC coming down on me, but we're going to try to get to the bottom of the use of the word, "nigger." For years, there has been an ongoing controversy with many black comedians, actors and rap artists, using the word nigger. Terry, does your band use the word nigger in your performances?"

"No, we don't. It's historically a cruel and degrading word and our band doesn't use it in any of our performances when referring to black people," I replied.

"Grill, do you use the word nigger in any of your group's performances?" Thurman asked, already knowing Grill's answer to his question.

"Yeah, of course we do," Grill said, proudly. "We use words in our rap songs that people can relate to. Come on, let's keep it real. White folks have been calling black people niggers since way back in the slave days. We just took the word nigger and re-made it into our own vocabulary."

"Okay, we have our first caller who wants to make a comment on our topic this morning. Good morning, caller, what's your name and what's your comment?"

"Yeah, this is Eddie callin' from East Point. I don't see nothin' wrong with black folks using the word nigga. That dude, Terry, don't know what he's talkin' bout. Nigga is just a word we use in the black community. It's like part of our black culture."

"Thank you, Eddie," Thurman said. "Our producer, Brenda, is telling me our phone lines are full. Let's get to another caller. What's your name and what's your comment?"

"Hi, Thurman. This is Jasmine, calling from Decatur. I don't think there's anything wrong with rappers or comedians using the word nigger. Don't we have freedom of speech in this country?"

"That's right, sweetheart," Grill said, with confidence. "I'm a musical artist and I should have the right to express myself. Isn't that part of my rights as an American to have freedom of speech?"

Suddenly, Brenda raised her hand and flashed a signal to Thurman.

"Hold that thought, everybody. We have to take a short break. You are listening to the Thurman Payne Morning Show on WRPP 101." Thurman took off his headset while the show went into a commercial. "Our show is hot this morning!" Thurman said, excitedly. "Brenda, are we still getting a lot of calls?"

"The phone lines have been full since we started the show," she said, glancing at the telephone call board.

"You hear those callers?" Marcus asked, taking off his headset. "The people love me!" he said, grinning at me.

The radio debate was not going well. I had been sitting in the studio listening to Marcus and a few callers condoning the use of the word nigger, and I actually heard a caller use the United States Constitution as a defense. I felt like I was on an island all by myself. I honestly felt in my heart that Marcus and the callers were wrong, but I just didn't know what I could say to get my point across. Suddenly, Brenda walked back into the room.

"Marcus, I need you to put your headset back on and sit down. We're going back on the air in thirty seconds," Brenda said, sounding slightly annoyed.

"Sure, sweetheart," Marcus replied, flashing his gold teeth.

The morning show's theme music began to play, then transitioned to the sound of a rapper's voice played loudly in the studio.

"Met this bitch in the club, now it's time to get laid. Niggas jealous of me, cuz they know I get paid." The music faded and Thurman continued the show.

"Good morning, Atlanta. Welcome back to the Thurman Payne Morning Show. This morning we are talking about the controversial topic of hardcore rap music and the possible negative influence on young listeners. We have with us Marcus "Grill" Taylor of the rap group, Thug Lordz and Terry Freeman of the group, Infinite Noise. Grill, we just heard a cut from your new song, "Nigga Like Me." What do you say to those people who say the lyrics might be a little too strong?"

"Hey, I'm just rappin' about the life of a player," Grill said proudly. Part of being a player is hookin' up with sexy females and makin' money. It's what I do."

"Okay, we have another caller on line three," Thurman said. "Caller, what's your name and what's your comment?"

"Hello, hello? Am I on the radio?" the caller asked.

"Yes, caller, you're on the air," Thurman replied, shaking his head.

"Okay, cool. It seems like every time a black rapper like Tupac or Biggie Smalls becomes successful, other black people try to bring them down. Why can't we as black people support our black rappers and black entertainers?"

"See, that's what I'm talkin' bout!" Grill said with excitement. "As a rapper, I should be able to express myself. I'm just a hard workin' brotha' tryin' to get paid. It's a shame that you got some black folks tryin' to keep a brotha' down."

"Terry, how would you respond to what the caller and Grill are saying?" Thurman asked, anxious to hear my response.

As I looked around the studio room, all eyes were focused on me. My mind suddenly went blank as I realized that most of the city was probably listening, waiting for my response. For a few seconds, I remained silent, not knowing what to say. I closed my eyes and said a prayer to myself. "Lord, be with me. Please help me and show me the way." I opened my eyes and then it happened. All my doubts and fears began to fade away. My mind cleared and I was engulfed with this feeling of calmness. My nervousness and fears were replaced with a powerful feeling of confidence. Suddenly, I knew what I needed to say.

"Terry, do you have a response?" Thurman asked, trying to break me out of my silence.

"Yes, I have a response. Why do we as black people continue to make excuses for disrespecting each other? I enjoy listening to music from Hispanic artists like Carlos Santana and Asian artists like Hiroshima. When I listen to some of these musical artists from different ethnic backgrounds, I don't hear the racial name-calling and disrespect in their music. Yes, I do have an issue with hardcore or gangster rap music. When these so-called gangster rap artists continuously glorify violence, selling illegal drugs, and disrespecting black women, it perpetuates the mind-set that black men have to be hard and ruthless to be viewed as real men."

"Come on, man," Grill said, cutting in. "Gangsta rap is so popular, even white folks listen to it."

"You're right," I responded. "A lot of white people listen to gangster rap music and that's another major problem. When white people listen to some of the lyrics in many of these songs, it creates and reinforces negative, racial stereotypes about black people."

I could tell by the look on Thurman's face that this discussion on rap music was starting to go my way, so he tried to shift gears by slightly changing the subject.

"Terry, it's not just gangster rap music that's causing a lot of criticism in the black community. What do you say about the many successful comedians like Eddie Murphy and Chris Rock who use the word nigger in their comedy shows?" Thurman asked.

"Eddie and Chris are very successful comedians," I responded. "They both have given credit for some of their success to the late Richard Pryor, one of the funniest comedians of all time. Richard Pryor took a cruel and demeaning word like nigger and turned it into a common and acceptable word among black people."

"Yeah, I remember listening to my daddy's Richard Pryor albums when I was a little boy," Marcus chimed in. "Let's keep it real. Richard Pryor used the word nigga all the time and he became famous."

"That's true, but did you know that after taking a trip to Africa and spending time with the people there, Pryor vowed to never use the word nigger again in his comedy performances?" I asked in response.

"Man, that's bull. I ain't never heard that before," Marcus replied.

Thurman motioned to Brenda and she began typing on the computer in front of her.

"I've got our show's producer pulling up some information from our computer. Do you have anything, Brenda?" Thurman asked.

"It's coming up now," she said, reading from her computer screen. "It says here that in 1979, Richard Pryor took a trip to Kenya, Africa to deal with some personal issues. After spending time among the African people, it opened his eyes and made him realize that the word nigger was a hateful, degrading word, and vowed he would never use that word again in his comedy shows."

"There it is, Atlanta!" Thurman said, excitedly. "You always learn something new on the Thurman Payne Morning Show."

"First of all, I don't even say nigger, I say nigga," Marcus said, cutting in. "When I call someone a nigga, it's like I'm callin' him my homey or my buddy."

"Saying nigga instead of nigger doesn't change the meaning or intent of the word," I said, feeling embarrassed by Marcus' ignorant comment.

"Let me ask you this, Grill," Thurman said, leaning back in his chair. "Would it be okay if a white person called you a nigga?"

"Man, if a white person called me a nigga, they would get a beat down, for real!" Grill responded, trying to sound tough.

"Is it okay for Asian, Hispanic or Indian people to use the word nigga?" Thurman asked.

"Hell, no! Only black people can call each other nigga," Marcus replied.

"Terry, how do you respond to that?"

"That doesn't make any sense to me," I said. "How is it okay for black people to call each other nigger, but it's wrong for any other race to use that same word?"

"Man, it's not just me. All the famous hip-hop artists say nigga in their songs," Marcus said, trying to defend himself. "You need to know your music, dog."

"And you need to know your history, my brother. "The word nigger wasn't created by some old school hip-hop artist. The word nigger was created from hate, racism and ignorance. The word nigger has been used so frequently within the black community that most black people have become desensitized to the word. The bottom line is that the word nigger is a very demeaning and hateful word that we as black people need to stop using in our vocabulary," I said with passion.

Thurman could tell that Marcus was losing momentum in the debate so he tried to add more fuel to the fire.

"Let me get this straight, Terry," Thurman said. "If a major record label offered your band a lucrative contract to record a song using the word nigger, you would turn them down?"

As I looked at Thurman, I could tell he thought he had me pushed into a corner. I looked him straight in his eyes to answer the question.

"Thurman, I made a stand. Infinite Noise made a stand. We will never bow down to any record label that wants us to sing or rap about songs degrading black people or any other race."

"Man, that's a bunch of bull!" Marcus said, cutting in. "Me and the Thug Lordz keep it real, ya know what I'm sayin'? People want to hear what we rap about, ya know what I'm sayin'? We represent the people in the hood, ya know what I'm sayin'?"

"No, I really don't know what you're saying, Marcus," I replied. "Let me explain some things to you. I'm quite a bit older than you and yes, I *am* from the old school. I was listening to hip-hop music when you were still learning your alphabets on Sesame Street. I want to make this very clear to everyone. I don't think all rap music is bad. I grew up listening to rappers like N.W.A., Public Enemy and, Run D MC, just to name a few. Some of these rappers talked about life on the streets and living in the hood, but they also rapped about social issues in our society."

"Hey, I got nothin' but love and respect for those old school rappers, but times have changed," Marcus responded. "Rap music has changed a lot since those folks were around. That's why you can't relate to today's rappers. You're still livin' in the past, dog."

"Let me jump in for a second, gentlemen," Thurman said. "I'd like to read some of the lyrics from a rap song Grill wrote called "Cold Thug. *"I robbed this old nigga, then stole his fine bitch, then took all his money, now I'm feelin' rich."* You have to admit, those lyrics are pretty strong."

"Hey, I'm just keepin' it real, dog," Marcus replied. "When you grow up poor in the hood, you've gotta take what you want to survive. Ya feel me?"

I had to give it to Thurman. He definitely knew how to play the role of radio host. One minute he was defending Marcus, then he would turn around and agree with my point of view.

"Terry, how do you feel about the lyrics to this song?" Thurman asked.

"Rap songs like "Cold Thug" are part of the problem I have with rappers like Marcus. In this one, short lyric, he disrespects a black man, a black woman and then he basically encourages black-on-black crime."

"Man, that's just lyrics to a song. Ain't nobody takin' any of that stuff serious," Marcus responded.

"That's where you're wrong. Unfortunately, there are some people out there who hear the lyrics to these songs and they do take it seriously . . . and it's not just music. Some people can be influenced by what they see on television, video games, what they read in books and magazines and yes, even what they hear on the radio. You mentioned earlier about your rights to have freedom of speech. Do you know how many black men and women fought and died for your right to have freedom of speech? Then rappers like you show your appreciation for their sacrifices by disrespecting black men and women in your rap songs."

"Man, I ain't disrespectin' black people. I'm just rappin' about life in the hood," Marcus replied, angrily.

"Terry, wouldn't you say that Marcus has a right to rap about his experiences growing up in the hood?"

"Sure, he has that right, but there's more to life in the hood than gangbanging, selling illegal drugs, and pimping women," I responded.

"Man, you ain't nothin' but a sellout," Marcus fired back. "Instead of hatin' on a brotha, you should be supportin' a brotha. You sound just like those white folks who want to keep the black man down."

As I listened to Marcus, I could tell he was becoming very upset. For the first time since the show started, Marcus was beginning to feel like he was on the hot seat instead of me. I decided to press the issue and stay on the offense.

"When you're constantly using the word nigger in your rap songs, *you* are part of the problem of keeping the black man down. Yes, you have the right to say whatever you want to say, but keep in mind, you need to be accountable for what you say or rap about. The bottom line is that a lot of our black music artists are getting paid millions of dollars by record companies to constantly disrespect our black men and women. You and rappers like you are the real sellouts. At some point, we as black people have to say "no" and stop supporting these music artists who constantly disrespect black people in their music. It would be great if some of these successful rap artists would take a stance like the late Richard Pryor and say, no, I'm not going to call black people niggas anymore."

Marcus leaned back in his chair and looked at me with a sneer on his face.

"Man, you sound crazy. If a record company is going to pay me big money, then I'm going to rap about whatever they want me to rap about. I think you just hatin' on me and my crew cuz we gettin' paid. The Thug Lordz aint no lame band like Infinite Noise," he said, raising his voice. Y'all probably only play at those uppity white clubs, but the Thug Lordz perform at clubs in the hood. We keep it real, dog. Ya feel me?"

By the tone in his voice, I could tell that Marcus was angry and trying to provoke me into an argument. I didn't want to argue with him but, at the same time, I wasn't going to let him insult the people I consider my family.

"Why are you calling Infinite Noise a lame band?" Is it because we don't perform songs that glorify drug dealers, gangbanging, or degrading our black women? Let me explain something to you, Marcus. Infinite Noise is a complete band. We write most of our songs and we play all our instruments. We don't get on stage yelling and screaming profanity into a microphone with pre-recorded music playing in the background. Most important, we don't let record company executives tell us what type of music we're going to play, especially if it means degrading black people. Now, do you feel *me*?" I asked, giving him a taste of his own medicine.

"Man, you need to stop living in the past. Rap music is what the people want to hear and you don't want to accept that. I'll give you your props. Your band was good a long time ago, but it's time to step aside and let the new generation of music take over!" Marcus said in a stern voice.

Thurman must have noticed that Marcus was losing his temper, so he decided to jump into the conversation.

"Gentlemen, the tenth annual Battle of the Bands is going to be at Phillips Arena next month. Some of the top bands from around the country will be performing. Will your two bands be participating?" Thurman asked, excitedly.

"Yeah, you better believe the Thug Lordz will be there doing what we do best."

"Terry, will Infinite Noise be part of the Battle of the Bands?" Thurman asked.

Before I could answer, Marcus interrupted.

"Nobody wants to hear no boring, lame music at a hip-hop concert," Marcus said, with a smug look on his face. In case everyone out there in radio land don't know, the Thug Lordz came in first place in a talent show competition at Club Elite earlier this year. Infinite Noise came in a distant second. Believe me, Infinite Noise don't want no part of the Thug Lordz."

"Wow, Terry, that sounds like a challenge to me!" Thurman responded.

Even though I knew Thurman was trying to goad me into a war of words with Marcus, I let my ego get the best of me.

"Infinite Noise will be at the Battle of the Bands and we'll see which band will be holding up that first place trophy," I said with confidence.

"There you have it, Atlanta! It's official!" Thurman said, sounding like a boxing promoter. "The Thug Lordz and Infinite Noise will be competing in this year's Atlanta Battle of the Bands, on Saturday, October 15th, at Phillips Arena. Okay, our phones lines are still full. We're going to get back to your calls so we can hear from all you listeners out there. "Okay, we're going to grab one more call before we take a short break. Hello, caller, welcome to the Thurman Payne Morning Show."

"Good morning, Thurman. My name is Jean. I used to listen to your radio show every morning while driving my kids to school. Unfortunately, I stopped listening to your radio station when you started playing a lot of that vulgar, profanity-filled, rap music. A friend called me this morning and told me about your morning show topic, so I decided to tune in and listen. Terry, I just want to say thank you. I think it's wonderful that somebody is finally speaking up for black people. Don't let those callers get you down. You keep on doing what you're doing."

"Thank you, Jean," I said, feeling a sense of pride.

"Jean, thank you for calling and being part of the Thurman Payne Morning Show. We're going to take a short break, but we'll be right back and continue today's hot topic."

For the next hour, several people called into the radio station to express their views on rap music. As I listened to the callers, it became very obvious that the younger callers condoned the profanity and degrading lyrics in rap music. Several of the young callers expressed that I was too old and "out of touch" with the new hip-hop culture. Most of the older callers didn't like the profanity-laced rap music because of the negative impact they felt it had on young people. After two hours of intense conversation and debating, the show finally came to an end. Brenda signaled to Thurman to wind up the show and the ending theme song began to play.

"We've come to the end of another exciting show. I'd like to thank our guests on today's show, Terry Freeman, of Infinite Noise and Marcus "Grill" Taylor of the Thug Lordz. Be sure to join us

Monday morning on WRPP 101. I'm Thurman Payne, have a great weekend." Once the show was over, Thurman took off his headset and leaned back in his seat. "Now that's what I call a great morning talk show!" he said, proudly.

Brenda walked into the studio with a big smile on her face.

"Great show, everybody. Our phone lines are still lit up." "You guys did a fantastic job. Thank you again for coming."

As Brenda walked out of the studio, Thurman stood up and walked toward me and Marcus.

"Hey, guys, thanks again for being on our show today," Thurman said.

"No problem," I said shaking Thurman's hand.

"Okay, Grill, you stay cool, my brother," Thurman said, giving Marcus a high five and a hug.

"You know I will, dog. I'm gonna do my thing no matter what the haters say about me," he responded, glaring at me.

I really didn't feel like dealing with Marcus and his big mouth anymore, so I decided to quickly leave the studio. Just as I walked out of the studio, I heard someone call my name.

"Terry, can I talk to you for a second?" I turned around and saw Brenda walking toward me with a concerned look on her face.

"Sure, Brenda. What's on your mind?" I asked.

"Terry, before you go, I wanted to apologize to you. We had a list of questions for the talk show and Thurman added a question that wasn't on the script. I honestly didn't know Thurman was going to ask you any questions that would make you feel uncomfortable."

It's okay, don't worry about it."

"No, it's not okay."

Brenda looked around to make sure no one could hear our conversation.

"Two years ago, I was a reporter for this station and I remembered doing a story on your father. It was so tragic," she said quietly. "That's why I came into the studio and interrupted the interview. I wasn't going to let Thurman take you down that road again. I know why Infinite Noise disappeared from the music scene and I'm very sorry Thurman brought that up," she said, sincerely.

"Thank you, Brenda," I said, giving her a warm hug.

"Thanks, I needed that," she replied.

"After listening to some of those callers, I hope I'll be able to show my face around this city," I said, jokingly.

"I know most of the callers had a lot of negative things to say to you, but you handled it like a professional."

"Thurman definitely did his part to keep things heated up," I responded.

"Please don't take it personal. Thurman was just playing his role to stir up the listeners. Our viewers love it when we have a controversial topic on our show. As the host of one of the top radio stations in the country, in a city of 4.3 million people, he has to keep our viewers involved and entertained."

"I understand, Brenda. It keeps your ratings high and I'm sure that makes your advertisers very happy."

"You got that right!" she said, raising her hand and giving me a high five. "You may not believe this, but I'm sure you earned a lot of supporters today. You've definitely given me something to think about. I've been the producer for this radio station for almost two years. After listening to Marcus and some of those callers, I felt embarrassed to be associated with this radio station. I know I will run into a lot of opposition, but I'm going to do a better job of screening some of the negative music that's played on our morning show."

"Good for you, Brenda."

"I hate to run," she said, looking at her watch, "but I've got to get things ready for the next show. It was a pleasure meeting you, Terry. Good luck at the Battle of the Bands. I'm expecting great things from you and Infinite Noise."

"Thank you." I replied.

As I walked out of the WRPP radio station, I felt rejuvenated and full of confidence. I walked into the lion's den and I survived. Now that the debate was over, I was focused on getting ready for the Battle of the Bands next month and I knew exactly what I needed to do. It was time for me to bring my family and friends back together. It was time for me to re-unite Infinite Noise.

Chapter 36

When Terry called his best friend, Damon, a few hours ago, he wanted to make sure they could talk in person. It was going to be a conversation of great magnitude and he didn't want to discuss it over the telephone. He had been sitting in his car, outside of Damon's apartment for the last fifteen minutes, trying to get his thoughts together. He glanced at his watch which read 5:23 p.m.

"Okay, let's do this," he said to himself. As Terry walked up to the apartment door, he could hear Damon's son, Darius, laughing and running around inside. He took a deep breath and knocked on the door. The door opened and Damon's wife, Gail, greeted him with an annoyed look on her face.

"Hello, Gail."

"I'll get him," she said coldly.

In all the years Terry had known her, Gail never tried to hide the fact that she didn't like his friendship with Damon. She always felt like Terry was responsible for her husband's obsession with Infinite Noise.

"Uncle Terry!" Darius yelled, jumping into Terry's arms.

"Hey, Darius. Wow, you're getting so big," Terry said, gently putting him down on the floor.

"I'm big cuz I eat a lot of food," he said, patting his belly.

Moments later, Damon walked into the room.

"What's going on, T?" Damon said, walking up to Terry and giving him a hug."

"I'm good. I'm just amazed at how big Darius has gotten since the last time I saw him."

"Yeah, he's one of the biggest kids in his first-grade class."

"No, I'm the biggest kid, daddy," Darius said, tugging on Damon's arm.

"Okay, okay. I believe you, son. Hey, Gail, can you come in here for a second?" Moments later,

Gail walked into the room with an irritated look on her face. "Hey, baby, can you take Darius to his room so Terry and I can talk?"

"Why, so Terry can talk you into getting back into the band?" she said sarcastically.

"We'll talk about this later."

"Talk later? Why? It's not going to change anything. You're still going to listen to him instead of your own wife."

"Gail, you need to chill out," Damon said, slightly raising his voice.

"Don't tell me to chill out. I'm your wife and I have a right to speak my mind when it involves this family!"

"And I'm your husband and you need to respect that!" he said in a stern voice. "Now, can you please take our son to his room," he said, trying to regain his composure.

"Yeah, whatever!" she responded, picking up Darius and carrying him to his room.

"Hey, man, I'm really sorry about that," Damon said, feeling somewhat embarrassed.

"No need to apologize. As a matter of fact, I'm here to apologize to you. I've had a lot of time to think about what you said at the warehouse and you were right. When we started Infinite Noise, we both had a goal of becoming a great and successful band. You never stopped trying to reach that goal, but I did. I was so wrapped up in my own personal problems that I forgot that you and the others had a life outside of our band. I held us back from reaching our goals and I'm sorry for that."

"No, you didn't hold us back, Terry."

"Yes, I did. After what happened to my father, I lost my focus. It took me almost two years to get myself back together. It wasn't fair to you and it wasn't fair to everyone else in the band."

Damon walked over and sat in a chair across from Terry.

"Hey, listen to me. You didn't hold us back. We all had personal issues going on in our lives that side- tracked us. Two years ago we were one of the hottest bands in the South. We were writing songs and performing all over the country in front of sellout crowds. "When we lost your dad, everything changed for me, too. You know I grew up without a father. My father left me and my mom when I was four-years old. I never told you this, but it really bothered me that I didn't have a father to come to my baseball games or to the school talent shows to watch me perform like your father did. Your dad was always there for you." As Terry listened to his best friend, he could hear the hurt in his voice. "After I got to know your dad, he was always there for me. He treated me like I was his own son."

"That's because my dad looked at you like you were one of his sons," Terry said, proudly.

"When you and Warren lost your father, I felt like I lost my father, too." After your dad's funeral, I didn't call or come by to see you for several weeks. I kept telling myself you needed time to yourself. I never told you this, but I stayed away because it was too hard being around you. Being around you was a constant reminder that your father was gone and I didn't know how to deal with that. I'm the one who owes you an apology. You're my best friend and I should have been there for you, but I wasn't. You lost your father. You needed time to heal. We all needed time to heal. You didn't hold us back," Damon said, trying to suppress his tears.

Just hearing his best friend say those words, brought a great sense of relief to Terry.

"By the way, you're not my best friend. You're more like my brother," Terry said, sincerely.

"Thanks, that means a lot to me," Damon replied. "Okay, okay. Enough of this sad talk," Damon said, wiping his eyes with his shirt sleeve. "I heard you on the radio last week. Man, you sounded great."

"Are you serious?" Terry asked, laughing. "I was nervous as hell."

"If I was there, I probably would have knocked the gold teeth out of Grill's big mouth."

"Believe me, I was very tempted."

"Did you really mean what you said? Do you really think Infinite Noise can win the Battle of the Bands?"

"Of course I do," Terry said with confidence. "There's no way I would say that on the radio, if I didn't believe it. That's another reason I came by to see you. I want Infinite Noise to perform at the Battle of the Bands next month. I want to prove to everyone that we're still one of the best bands on this planet."

Damon didn't respond. Instead, he got up and started walking around the room. Then he began to speak.

"Terry, you know I've always had your back. When I was younger and single, I felt like we could accomplish anything we wanted. When we started performing together in high school, I was seventeen-years old, with no kids and no responsibilities. Now, I'm thirty-two years old. I have a wife and a little boy to take care of. As much as I love traveling and performing in front of those crowds, I have to put my family ahead of my personal goals and dreams. I'm trying to save up enough money to move out of this small apartment and into a house. I want Darius to have a back yard where he can safely play. In order for me to do that, I need a steady, full-time job. It's hard to do that if I'm traveling all over the country performing with the band."

Terry stood up and walked over to his friend.

"I hear what you're saying and I totally respect that. All I'm asking is for you to help me get Infinite Noise back together one last time. You know this is a nationally-recognized event. There are going to be talent scouts, promoters, and record company executives from all over the country. When we win that first-prize trophy, that will put us in a great position to land a major recording contract. Plus, we'll be right here in Atlanta so Gail won't have to worry about you traveling out of town."

"Have you talked to Warren, Reggie, and Layla about this?" Damon asked.

"No, I haven't. I wanted to talk to you first. If you don't come back, Infinite Noise won't win the Battle of the Bands."

"I don't know, Terry. We haven't practiced or performed together in over a month."

"We have about three weeks to get ready," I replied.

"Three weeks? Do you think that's enough time to get everyone ready for the Battle of the Bands?"

"I don't know about the other guys, but I know you'll be ready. You're a very talented musician."

"Look, I already know I'm good," Damon said, smiling. "I don't need you to stroke my ego."

"Seriously, I know Infinite Noise can win this competition."

"And if we lose?" Damon asked.

Terry walked up to Damon and looked at his friend with a serious look on his face.

"Losing is not an option." Damon didn't reply. Instead, he just walked over to a window and gazed out into the darkness of the night. "Damon, I can't do this without you." For several minutes, Damon continued to stare out of the window. Suddenly, he turned around and faced his long-time friend.

"Alright, Terry. I'm in, but after the Battle of the Bands, I can't make any promises about staying in the band."

"I understand. Thanks, Damon. I knew I could count on you," he said, giving his friend a hug.

"Okay, I've got to run. I've got one more stop to make," Terry said glancing at his watch.

"Hey, I just thought of something. Isn't there a deadline to enter the Battle of the Bands?" Damon asked.

"Yeah, the deadline was yesterday, but I already signed us up two days ago," Terry said, as he walked to the door to leave."

"You already signed us up?" he asked, surprised by Terry's arrogance. "You're a very confident bastard, aren't you? You'd be looking real stupid right now if I had said, no."

"You're right. I'd be looking stupid and disappointed, but I knew my best friend wouldn't let me down," Terry said, grinning, as he walked out of the apartment.

* * *

After convincing Damon to rejoin the band, I drove over to Smitty's Music Store to see if I could have the same success with my brother, Warren. As I walked into the store, I noticed Smitty talking to some customers on the other side of the room. Melvin "Smitty" Smith was the owner of one the oldest music stores in the city. Smitty was a feisty, old guy, in his late fifties who started his own music store about twenty years ago. He started out selling vinyl records and cassette tapes; then he expanded his business and began selling musical instruments. Smitty tried to convince everyone he was a mean, grumpy old man, but once you got to know him, you realized that he had a heart of gold. When Warren and I started learning how to play musical instruments, our father would bring us here to Smitty's store. My dad and Smitty were really good friends and he would let us come into his music store and practice. The more we played in his store, the better we got. Warren and I always thought Smitty was a pretty cool guy for letting two young kids play all of the instruments in his store, even though he was trying to run a business. Any time our father wanted to buy an album or a cassette, he would buy it from Smitty's store. He said it was his way of helping to support his friend's business. Once we got home, our father would play those albums on his turntable with the volume turned all the way up on his stereo system. Our father enjoyed listening to a wide range of music. Sometimes he would start off by listening to Miles Davis, then switch to some James Brown, then jump into some Kool and the Gang. My father bought my first guitar from Smitty's on my tenth birthday. When Warren began learning to play the keyboard, he would come along with me into Smitty's store to practice and play. Smitty wasn't too happy that Warren would always try to play on the most expensive keyboards in his store. Of course, I would grab one of the more expensive guitars from his wall display and play on them. He would always remind us that "if you break it, you pay for it." Smitty would constantly complain to me and my brother about playing on his expensive merchandise but, surprisingly, he never got mad and he never threw us out of his store. Over the years, as Warren and I became very good musicians, he didn't mind us coming into his store and playing his instruments. As a matter of fact, Smitty looked forward to the two of us coming around. I would play the lead guitar, Warren would play on the keyboard and we would have all the customers in his store dancing and singing. I noticed the clock on Smitty's wall read 6:35 p.m., which gave me about twenty-five minutes to find and talk to Warren before the store closed. If my brother was in here, I knew I would be able to find him where the keyboard synthesizers were located. As I continued to walk around the store, I was feeling very up-beat and energetic after my conversation with Damon. Getting Damon to rejoin the band was a huge step in bringing everyone back together again. I just got off my cell phone with Layla and she was excited to hear that I was trying to reunite Infinite Noise. If I could just convince my brother to come back, Infinite Noise would have a great chance to win the Battle of the Bands next month. I wasn't able to reach Reggie, but I didn't think he would turn me down if

Warren rejoined the band. We had always been a very close family and I honestly felt he would be there if I needed him.

"Terrence Freeman!" a gravel-sounding voice yelled out from behind me. I turned around and saw my old friend, Melvin Smith, walking toward me with a huge smile on his face. How's it going, young fella?" he asked, giving me a hug.

"I'm doing good, Smitty."

"I guess you and your band are so big-time that you don't have the time to come by and see an old man."

"No, it's not like that. I just can't afford to buy anything in your store anymore," I said, jokingly.

"Hey, I heard you on the radio the other day. You sure put that young punk in his place. It sure felt good to hear an intelligent black man speak up and tell it like it is. Your daddy would have been so proud of you," he said, patting me on the back.

"Thanks, Smitty."

As I looked around the store, I saw my brother over in the keyboard section.

"Yeah, your brother has been in here over an hour messing around with that new synthesizer that came in a few months ago. He's been playing the hell out of that thing. It's amazing what he can do on that keyboard."

"Well, what did you expect? I helped teach him how to play," I said proudly.

"I don't know, Terrence. It's very possible that the student might be better than the teacher."

While I continued my conversation with Smitty, I noticed some new guitars hanging on the wall display.

"Hey, Smitty, do you mind if I try out one of those new guitars on the wall?"

"Try it out? You know damn well you ain't gonna buy any of those guitars," he said, laughing. I walked over to the guitars on the wall and began reaching for a vintage, 1969, gold, Gibson Les Paul electric guitar.

"Oh hell, no!" Smitty exclaimed. "You can't play around with that one!"

"Eighteen thousand dollars, Smitty?" I asked, looking at the price tag.

"Hey, if you want the best, you gotta pay for the best."

Smitty began to frown as I reached up and grabbed the Gibson Les Paul guitar from the wall display.

"Why do you always have to play around with my expensive merchandise?" he asked.

"Calm down, Smitty. I'm not going to damage your precious guitar."

"Just remember my store policy; you break it, you pay for it."

"Yeah, yeah, I know." As I looked around to find an amplifier to plug the guitar into, I noticed some very new merchandise Smitty had on sale. "Hey, Smitty, when did you get these new amplifiers?"

"They came in a few weeks ago. You know I've got to keep up with my competition. Plug that guitar into that new Omega Pro amplifier. I think you'll really like how it sounds."

After plugging the guitar into the amplifier, I began playing a musical scale to warm up.

"Oh, yeah, this amp sounds great," I said as I tried out all the amplifier's features.

"Are you ready to trade in that old guitar you got at home and get this musical masterpiece?" Smitty asked, sounding like a typical salesman.

"I really like the weight and the balance of this guitar," I said, inspecting the guitar.

"Just listen to that clear, crisp sound," Smitty said, grinning. "Doesn't it sound great?"

"If I spend eighteen grand on a guitar, it better sound great." As we continued to talk, I noticed a brand new, all-black Fender Telecaster on the wall display.

"Here you go, Smitty," I said, handing him the Les Paul guitar. I walked over and took the black guitar from the wall and walked back over to Smitty.

"Hey, be careful, I just got that guitar delivered here yesterday."

"This is a beautiful-looking guitar," I said as I began to tune up the strings.

"It's a great guitar and it's probably more in your price range. That guitar is listed at $12,000, but for you, I'll let you have it for $9,500," he said, gently putting the gold Les Paul guitar back on the wall display.

I plugged the guitar into the amplifier and began playing various songs. Some of the customers in the store began to slowly walk toward the guitar section to hear me play. After some adjustments on the amplifier, I began playing "Sampa Pa Ti" by Carlos Santana. Then I smoothly switched to playing "Love Ballad" by LTD.

"So, what do you think?" Smitty asked with a big grin on his face.

"Not bad. I have to admit, I really like this guitar. It feels and sounds as nice as that $18,000 Les Paul guitar."

"Why don't you go over there and play with Warren so you can really get the feel of that guitar?"

"I think I'll do that, Smitty."

I unplugged the guitar and walked over to the other side of the store to listen to Warren play. As I walked into the keyboard section, I noticed my brother was playing on the Spectrum 2000. It was the same keyboard my brother had been begging me for months to buy with the band's instrument account. When Infinite Noise started performing and making money, each member agreed to put a small percentage of their earnings into a special account to pay for any of our damaged music equipment or other expenses related to the band. There was about $3,400 in our band's account. The price tag for the Spectrum 2000 was $2,995. I had played on that keyboard a few times and I discovered it was an awesome instrument. The Spectrum 2000 keyboard featured eighty-eight keys, twenty-eight simultaneous oscillators, and a complete multi-interface 128MB memory sequencer. Even though it was a great-sounding instrument, I didn't think it was wise to spend most of the band's money on a very expensive keyboard when the one Warren played at our performances sounded just fine. Most of the customers in the store were standing around my brother, listening to him play some song with a funky beat. When we were younger, Warren and I would compete with each other, in Smitty's store, to see who could play a song better. Competing against each other was fun, but entertaining the customers was what we enjoyed the most. As Warren continued to play, he glanced over in my direction, but decided to ignore me. I assumed he was still pissed off at me.

"Do you want me to show you how to play that thing?" I said, walking up to him.

"I suggest you go back over there with that guitar and leave the keyboard playing to an expert," he responded, without looking up at me.

"That sounds like a challenge to me," I said as I set my guitar down next to an available keyboard.

I remembered when I started teaching Warren how to play the piano. My brother never wanted to take the time to learn how to read music. He was one of those gifted players who could play by ear. He could listen to any song and, five minutes later, he could play that song with ease. As I listened to him play, I felt proud knowing what a great keyboardist he had become. I sat down at a keyboard next to him and turned up the volume. I began playing, "Prelude #3," a symphonic fusion piece, recorded by David Sancious and Tone. Warren turned up the volume on his keyboard and began playing, "Get It Up," by Morris Day and the Time.

"Not bad," I said as I started playing, "Let's Go Crazy," by Prince.

We continued doing this for several minutes until every customer in the music store was surrounding us and cheering us on. Usually this back-and-forth competition put a smile on Warren's face, but he still had not made eye contact with me. I realized the only way to get my brother to open up was to play a song he wrote last year called, "Dazzle." This was a song with a very funky, new fusion sound that gave Warren a chance to showcase his keyboard skills. I walked over and picked up the Fender guitar I had brought over and plugged it into an amplifier. I then began playing the introduction of the song, Dazzle. As I continued to play, I noticed my brother had a grin on his face. Warren made a few adjustments on his keyboard and began playing along with me. The customers in the store began cheering loudly as the sounds of my guitar and Warren's keyboard reverberated throughout the entire building. When we completed the song, the customers erupted with cheers and applause.

"Damn, you guys sounded great!" a guy from the crowd yelled.

Suddenly, the sound of Smitty's voice was heard on the store's intercom speakers.

"I hope everyone enjoyed listening to those two talented young men. They buy all their music supplies from Smitty's Music Store and our prices can't be beat!" Smitty said, trying to get some free advertising for his store. "Okay, everybody, it's closing time!"

As the customers began to exit the store, Warren sat quietly at the keyboard, acting as if I wasn't there. When the last customer left, I tried to start up a conversation with Warren.

"I guess we've still got it," I said.

"We never lost it," he said in response.

For several moments, neither one of us said anything. It was almost as if we were worried about saying something that might cause an argument between us. Neither one of us could find the words to break the awkward silence.

"Hey, you guys sounded fantastic," Smitty said, walking toward us.

"Did you expect anything less from the Freeman brothers?" Warren said, sounding extremely cocky.

"I'm getting ready to lock up in five minutes so you guys be sure to turn off that expensive keyboard and that brand-new amplifier," Smitty said, walking back to his office.

As my brother stood up to leave, I decided it was my best opportunity to talk with him.

"Hey, Warren, before you go, I wanted to play something for you."

I sat down at the keyboard I was playing on earlier and began playing a song called, "Lost Without You." The song was a slow, instrumental piece with a cool, hip-hop beat, that Warren started writing several months ago. He got the beats down and a nice piano bass line, but he just couldn't find the right melody to complete the song. For the last few months, I had been helping him by trying different piano arrangements, with no success. Finally, with the help of a little girl, I found the right arrangement that I felt would make his song very special. With all the chaos going on in my life the last few months, I didn't have a chance to sit down with Warren and let him hear what I added to his song. I made a few adjustments on the keyboard to change the electronic effects and began playing the song. After I played the first chorus, Warren looked at me with a grin on his face.

"Okay, that's not bad, but let me show you how to really play this song," he said, pushing a few buttons on his keyboard. Seconds later, the keyboard began playing a mellow, hip hop drum beat.

"Oh, yeah, I like that," I said, bobbing my head up and down to the beat. "The built-in drum machine in that keyboard sounds great," I said, excitedly.

"I told you this keyboard was the bomb," he responded.

I gave my brother a short count-down and we started playing the song together. When we reached the middle of the song, I began to play the new arrangement I had been working on for the last few weeks. Warren stopped playing and looked at me in disbelief as I played a melody that flowed very smoothly with the bass line of his song. When I finished playing, Warren looked at me with a stunned look on his face.

"When did you come up with that arrangement?" he asked.

"I've been working on it for awhile. I hope you like it."

"Like it? Man, I love it! Can you save that arrangement for me on a disk or a flash drive so I can mix it with my original song?"

"Here you go. I already took care of that for you," I said, handing him a USB flash drive I pulled from my pocket.

"Thanks for doing that for me."

"Hey, you're my brother. You know I've always got your back." For what seemed like several minutes, neither one of us said a word. Finally, Warren began to speak.

"I haven't had a chance to talk to you, but I met with Walter Caldwell a few weeks ago. He offered me a contract to join Galactic Records."

"What did you tell him?" I asked.

"I thought about what you said about being in control of my own music, so I turned him down."

"Good for you," I said proudly. "You're too talented to let anyone control what you should do with your music."

"You think I'm talented?" he asked. "Come on, man. You think I'm a big disappointment."

"What? I never said anything like that."

"Aren't you the same guy that's constantly telling me how lazy I am when it comes to music?"

"Warren, you don't read or write music, but you are an incredible keyboardist. You have the ability to play music by ear, but you can be so much better. I constantly stay on you about your music because I want you to take it more seriously. I don't care how well you play the keyboard, nobody is going to accept you as a serious songwriter if you can't read or write music. You have a God-given talent when it comes to music. If you take advantage of that talent, the sky's the limit for you. You might even become a better musician than me."

"Damn, I never thought I would hear that come out of your mouth," he said, as we both started laughing.

"Whoa, slow down, little brother. I said you *might* become a better musician."

As we continued to laugh and joke with each other, I felt a sense of relief knowing that Warren and I were back on speaking terms again.

"By the way, I heard you on the radio the other day talking to that asshole, Grill. Man, I couldn't believe he was disrespecting our band like that. That was cool how you stood up for us."

"I wasn't going to let that loud-mouth jerk put my family and friends down like that," I said, proudly. Warren turned off his keyboard and stood up as if he was ready to leave.

"Terry?"

"Yeah?"

"I would love to be a part of Infinite Noise blowing Grill and the Thug Lordz off the stage at the Battle of the Bands," he said with a grin. "Unless you've found someone else to replace me."

"Replace you?" I asked. "Infinite Noise would not be the same great band without you. I've been trying to reach you the last few days."

"Yeah, Layla called me and said you were trying to get the band back together."

"You big dummy!" If you knew I was trying to re-unite the band, why didn't you call me?"

"I wanted you to hunt me down and beg me to come back," he said, with a smug look on his face.

"Beg you? I think you've lost your damn mind," I said, as we both start laughing.

"I guess we better get out of here before Smitty throws us out," Warren said.

"Yeah, I better put his precious guitar back on the wall display before he has a stroke."

"After all the years we've been coming in here, you would think that cheap bastard would give us a discount on these instruments."

I picked up the Fender Telecaster guitar I was playing earlier and stared at it with admiration.

"Even with a discount, I can't see myself spending that much money on a guitar."

"Hey, you two!" Smitty yelled, walking up to us.

"Okay, we're leaving!" Warren yelled back.

"Hold on. I need to talk to both of you before I throw you out."

"Calm down, Smitty. I'm putting your precious guitar back on the wall," I said, gently holding the guitar.

"No, leave it right there," Smitty said. "Have a seat. I need to talk to both of you."

As Warren and I sat down, I was thinking that Smitty had finally gotten tired of us coming into his store and playing on his equipment. Smitty walked over and stood in front of us.

"Are you guys really going to be playing at the Battle of the Bands next month?"

"Yeah, we'll be there." Warren responded, looking at me with a grin.

Suddenly, Smitty got very quiet and he seemed like he was at a loss for words.

"What's on your mind, Smitty?" I asked.

"I've known you two for over twenty years. I remember when you were little boys running around in my store, trying to play every instrument you could get your hands on. Over the years, I watched both of you grow into very talented musicians. When you compete in the Battle of the Bands next month, I want you to play your best and make me proud."

"We'll do our best, Smitty," I responded.

"I know you will."

Smitty walked over and unplugged the Spectrum 2000 keyboard that Warren was playing on earlier. He then picked up the keyboard and gently slid it into a padded box.

"A musician can only be as good as the instrument he plays. When you perform at the Battle of the Bands next month, I want you to play with the best instruments possible. Here, Warren. This is yours now," Smitty said, handing him the box containing the Spectrum 2000 keyboard.

"What? Are you serious?" Warren asked, jumping out of his seat.

"Yes, I'm very serious."

Before Warren could utter another word, Smitty walked over and picked up the new Fender Telecaster guitar I was playing on earlier. Instead of taking the guitar back to the wall display, he turned and looked at me with a serious look on his face.

"Terry, every time you come in my store, you have to play around with my most expensive guitars. Here you go," he said, handing me the Fender Telecaster guitar. "Maybe if I give you this one, you'll leave my other guitars alone."

Now, it was my turn to have the shocked look on my face. I reached out to take the guitar from him, but I suddenly came to my senses and pulled my hand back.

"Smitty, there's no way I can afford this guitar."

"Hey, I didn't say I was selling you this guitar, I said I was *giving* you this guitar. Now, take it," he said, handing the guitar to me. As much as I wanted that beautiful guitar, I just couldn't bring myself to accept it.

"I really appreciate it, but there's no way I can just take this expensive guitar from you."

"I'll accept my keyboard!" Warren said, finally coming out of his shocked state.

"Will you two sit back down for a second? I want to tell you a story."

Smitty grabbed a chair and sat down next to us. For several seconds, he didn't say anything as if he was collecting his thoughts. Warren and I looked at each other in bewilderment wondering what was on Smitty's mind. Suddenly, he began to speak.

"Twenty-five years ago, I had a dream to start my own music store. I had the knowledge, the desire, and the game plan to make my dream a reality. The only thing I was missing was the money to get my business started. I was struggling back then. I was working two, sometimes three jobs, trying to take care of my wife and son. My family had no money to help me out. All the banks turned me down for a loan. I called an old friend I'd known since I was twelve-years old and told him about my financial situation. I told him I needed about $7,000 to get my music store up and going. Two days later, that friend was knocking on my door. He handed me a check for $7,500. That friend was your father, Bobby Freeman. With that money he loaned me, I was able to open this music store. It took me eighteen months, but I was able to pay him back. Thanks to your father's generosity, I was able to start my business, take care of my family, and provide a service to this community."

As I sat there listening to Smitty talk about his friendship with my father, I was filled with great pride. In all the years I had been coming into this music store, I never knew my father had helped Smitty get his business started. I had always known Smitty to be a tough, hard-nosed, business man. As I listened to him talk about his business and my father, I began to see a kind and caring side of him I had never seen before.

"My dad must have thought you were a very good friend to loan you that money," Warren said.

"Your dad was a very generous and a very humble man. He asked me to never tell anyone that he loaned me that $7,500. He never wanted to take credit for the success of this store. The only reason I'm telling you now is because I want you both to accept these instruments without feeling like you owe me anything in return. Without your father's generosity, I don't know what I . . ." Smitty stopped talking and put his head down. It was obvious that he was feeling very emotional talking about his friendship with my father.

"Thanks for sharing that with us," I said, walking over to Smitty and giving him a hug.

"Anyway, it's time for me to lock up the store," he said, looking at his watch. "Now, both of you get out of here before I change my mind and take those instruments back," he said, reverting back to his "tough guy" image.

"You don't have to tell me twice," Warren said, getting up and grabbing his keyboard.

"Thanks again, Smitty," I said, picking up my new guitar and following Warren out of the store.

As we got to the store's parking lot, I tried to start up another conversation with my brother.

"That was really cool of Smitty to hook us up with these instruments," I said.

"Hell, yeah! I still can't believe he did that."

As I got to my car, I opened the back door and laid my new guitar on the back seat. I looked up to see Warren gently sliding his boxed keyboard on the passenger side seat and securing it with the seat belt.

"Oh, my God, Warren. You're treating that keyboard like it's a newborn baby," I said laughing.

"As much as I love this keyboard, it *is* my baby."

After what seemed like minutes, he and I stood in that parking lot. Neither one of us said a word. I had hoped we could resolve the argument we had a few weeks ago, but I just couldn't seem to find the right words to say. Maybe it wasn't the right time.

"Okay, I guess I'll call you about our next practice," I said, walking to the driver's side of my car.

"Terry, can I talk to you for a second?"

"Sure, what's up?"

Warren walked over and leaned on the hood of my car.

"The last time we talked, I said some things." Warren stopped talking for a moment as if he was trying to collect his thoughts. "I just want to say that I'm sorry for what I said about dad," he said, sounding very remorseful. "You know how I am. Sometimes I open my mouth and say some really stupid shit."

"Hey, don't worry about it," I replied. "We both said some stupid shit."

"No, I was dead wrong for saying that. What happened to dad was really fucked up.

I know I try to act like it doesn't bother me, but it does. I think about him all the time." Warren said, sadly. "Some days I feel sad and other days I feel angry as hell."

I walked over to my brother and put my hand on his shoulder.

"Believe me, I understand how you feel. Let's put all of this behind us and move on. Are we good?" I said, extending my balled fist.

"Yeah, we're good." he replied, tapping his fist against mine.

For several moments, Warren became very quiet. As I looked at my brother, I could see the hurt and sorrow in his eyes. I could tell there was something on his mind and he wanted to talk, but he just stood there, deep in thought. It was getting late, it was dark, and I was extremely tired but I was willing to stand in that dimly-lit parking lot all night if my brother needed to talk. Suddenly, he began to speak .

"Do you remember that day dad found out I stole that candy bar from the gift shop downtown?"

"Of course I remember. It was on my thirteenth birthday. You told dad you stole that candy so you could give it to me as my birthday present."

"Man, I thought dad had lost his mind," Warren said, laughing. "He pulled out that old, black belt and tore my ass up. I remember you kept yelling, "daddy don't kill him, daddy don't kill him!"

"Hey, you were my only brother. I didn't want to grow up as a single child," I said, laughing with him. "I remember that black, leather belt very well. He almost tore my ass up for not telling him you stole that candy bar."

I couldn't remember the last time Warren and I laughed so hard and so long. After a few minutes of laughing, Warren became very quiet again.

"I still remember him taking me back to that store and making me apologize to the store manager. I guess dad knew what he was doing because I never stole another candy bar after that day. Damn, just look at me getting all emotional like a little girl," Warren said, turning away so I couldn't see the tears in his eyes.

As I stood there listening to my brother, I could hear the sadness in his voice. After we lost dad, Warren's personality had become somewhat cold and very distant. Now, I could see that my brother had been hurting inside and trying to hide it from everyone. Warren looked at me with tears in his eyes.

"You know, I use to think our dad was the meanest man in the world, but now, I would give anything to have him back. He was a good man and a great father. He didn't deserve to go out like that!" he said, letting out all the pent-up hurt and anger he had been holding inside. "I miss him so much."

I walked over to my brother and put my arm around his shoulder.

"It's okay, little brother. I miss him, too."

For the first time since our father's death, my brother and I hugged each other and we cried.

Chapter 37

I was nervously pacing the floor at Coretta Byrd's Dance Studio, patiently waiting for the arrival of my family and friends. I glanced at my watch which read, 6:24 p.m. This was going to be the first meeting we had since our band broke up almost seven weeks ago. As the leader of Infinite Noise, I realized that I made some mistakes in the past, but I was determined to correct them. Looking back over the past few years, I saw that I was so immersed in my own personal issues that I didn't take the time to notice the other people around me I truly cared about. I'm sure my fellow band members were curious as to why I asked them to meet me at Corretta Byrd's Dance Studio. If things worked out as I planned, I was hoping we would be meeting here more often. My thoughts were broken by the sound of the front door opening.

"What's up, T?" Damon said, walking into the studio.

"Hey, I'm glad you could make it," I said, shaking his hand.

"No problem. It feels strange not meeting at the warehouse," Damon said, looking around the studio.

"Yeah, I know. I'm not even sure everyone will show up tonight."

Right on cue, the front door opened and Layla walked in, closely followed by Warren.

"Hey, guys. It's so good to see you," Layla said.

"It's good to see you too, pretty lady," I said giving her a warm hug.

I walked over to my brother who extended his hand.

"Come here, man." I said, grabbing him and giving him a hug. "Thanks for coming."

"No problem, big brother." Warren responded.

"Have you heard from Reggie?" I asked.

"I called him earlier and left him a message," Warren replied.

"It's 6:37," I said, glancing at my watch. "If everyone will have a seat, I'll go ahead and get started." Everyone sat down and looked at me intently, waiting to hear what I had to say. "As I said when I called each of you, this won't take very long. First of all, I'd like to thank everyone for coming. I'm sure you all have other things you could be doing."

Suddenly, the front door opened and Reggie came walking into the studio.

"You just had to make your grand entrance, didn't you?" Warren asked, sarcastically.

"Hey, the text message I got said, 6:30. I'm only . . .," he paused to look at his cell phone. "Okay, I'm a little late. Sorry about that," he said, grinning.

In the past, I would have chastised anyone for coming late to a band meeting but, tonight I had more important things to talk about.

"Don't worry about it, Reggie," I said. "We were just getting started."

For several seconds, I stood there, looking at everyone in front of me, trying to collect my thoughts. I finally decided to stop procrastinating and just speak from my heart.

"The last time we were all together, things didn't end very well. Even though we all left feeling angry or disappointed, I think it was important that it happened. I consider everyone in this room my family and I feel like I let my family down. When Damon and I started Infinite Noise, we had a goal to become one of the best bands ever. For the first year or two, we were on our way to fulfilling that goal. When we lost my father, I lost focus on our goals, and for that I'd like to apologize to everyone in this room."

"Terry, you don't owe any of us an apology," Layla said. "We were all in pain. We all understood."

"Please, let me finish." I said, cutting her off. "Not only did I lose focus on our goals, I also lost track of the people I love, right here in this room. I'm ready to get back on track and focus on making Infinite Noise the great band that I know it can be. I understand that everyone has important things going on in their lives. If you decide you want to move on and not be a part of Infinite Noise, I will totally understand."

I stopped talking and looked at everyone, patiently waiting for their response. Layla stood up with tears in her eyes.

"All of you are my family. I want our family to be back together," she said, walking up to me and giving me a hug.

Damon got up and walked up to me.

"You already know where I stand," he said, giving me a hug.

Warren and Reggie were sitting in the chairs talking to each other. Moments later, Warren stood up to speak.

"Terry, you know I've been thinking about doing my own thing for awhile. Like I told you the other night, I'm back with Infinite Noise for the Battle of the Bands. After that, I'm probably moving on."

"Okay, I understand," I said, giving my brother a hug.

Finally, Reggie stood up to address everyone.

"Well, I guess I'm the only one jumping this ship. Sorry guys, but I've got to do what's best for me."

"Are you sure you want to leave the band, Reggie?" I asked.

"Yeah, it's time I moved on. I'm sure it won't be hard for you to find another drummer. Take care, you guys," Reggie said, as he walked toward the exit. Suddenly he stopped, turned around, and started laughing. "Hey, I was just joking. You know I would never leave you guys," he said walking back toward us.

"Man, you're so full of shit," Damon said, lightly punching Warren in the arm. "I have to admit that you had me fooled. I thought you were serious about leaving the band."

"Me leave the band? Come on, Damon. Who else would put up with my lazy ass?"

After we all got a good laugh from Reggie's comment, I tried to get everyone's attention again.

"Okay, listen up, guys and lady. If we're going to make this thing work, we need to make a few changes with Infinite Noise."

"Please don't tell me we're going to start playing country and western music," Reggie said, jokingly.

"Reggie, I think you'll like these changes. Damon suggested that we need to make a few changes to Infinite Noise. We're going to incorporate a little more hip-hop into our performances. That means you and Warren will be writing the lyrics to our rap songs. I only ask that you keep the lyrics respectable. Do you think you two can handle that?"

"Hell yeah, we can do that!" Warren said, giving Reggie a high five.

"There's one more change we'd like to make. I want to get back to the way we use to perform when we first started this band. We're going to do more dancing on stage. We're going to sound good and look good on stage. That's why I wanted to meet here tonight. Miss Byrd has agreed to let us practice here at her dance studio. She closes at 6 p.m., so we're going to meet here at 6:15. Layla, you're going to have a big role in choreographing a lot of our dancing. Do you think you can handle that?"

"Yes, yes, yes!" she replied, excitedly.

Layla, Reggie, and Warren began dancing in front of the large mirrors in the dance studio. Damon looked at me with a big grin on his face.

"I think they're a little excited." Damon said, walking to the center of the floor. "Okay, everybody. Listen up!" he yelled. "We have three weeks and four days to get ready for the Battle of the Bands at Phillips Arena. We're going to practice here Monday through Thursday at 6:15, sharp. For the next three weeks, Terry and I are going to be pushing you guys really hard. We're going to win that first-prize trophy at the Battle of the Bands and show everybody that Infinite Noise is back and better than ever!" he said, firing up everyone.

As I looked around the room, I felt good knowing that everyone was excited, motivated, and happy to be back together as a band. The next few weeks were going to be hard, intense and a lot of fun.

Chapter 38

Preparing for the Battle of the Bands had made the last three weeks very hectic, but it had given me a chance to get my mind off Angela and Kenya. Even though I had talked to both of them on the phone, I hadn't seen them in over a month. I knew Kenya's accident really upset Angela, but I didn't think we would go that long without seeing each other. I tried to call her a few times earlier today, but I kept getting her voice mail. I was somewhat puzzled as to why she hadn't returned any of my calls. It was only 8:06 p.m. and I was very tempted to drive over to her place, but decided it was probably best to give her some space to deal with everything. Anyway, it had been a long day and I just wanted to go home and get some sleep. We had just finished an intense two-hour band practice at Coretta Byrd's Dance Studio and I was feeling really good. The songs we were practicing sounded absolutely incredible. Layla had done a fantastic job in choreographing our dance moves to our songs. Everyone had worked extremely hard the past three weeks and I was very confident that Infinite Noise was going to put on a fantastic performance at the Battle of the Bands this Saturday. Suddenly, my cell phone rang. I glanced at the phone and saw Angela's name on the caller ID.

"Angela, I've been trying to call you all day."

"Hey, Terry. It's me, Kenya."

"Hey, pretty girl. It's good to hear from you."

"Can you come over right now?" she asked in a low voice.

"What's wrong, Kenya? Why are you whispering?"

"I've got to go. Please come over," she said, disconnecting the call.

I tried to call her back, but Angela's voice mail immediately came on. Something was not right over there, I thought to myself. I quickly turned my car around and got on Interstate 285 North, leading to Angela's place. Twenty minutes later, I was parked in front of Angela's apartment building. I noticed there were several lights on inside her apartment, which was a good sign that Angela was still awake. I got out of my car and sprinted to her door. I felt a little awkward dropping by on Angela without calling but, under the circumstances, I thought it was necessary. I knocked on the door, not knowing what to expect. The door opened slightly and Angela looked at me with a very surprised look on her face.

"Terry, what are you doing here?"

"Thanks for the warm greeting," I said, sarcastically.

"I'm sorry, it's just that I had a long day and I was just getting ready to turn in for bed."

"I tried to call you, but your voice mail kept coming on," I said.

"I've been very busy with my classes so I haven't been answering my phone lately," she said, looking somewhat uncomfortable.

"Is there something going on you need to tell me?"

"No. Why did you ask me that?"

"I haven't seen you and Kenya in almost a month and now I'm standing here outside your front door wondering why you haven't invited me inside."

"Terry, it's late, I'm very tired and Kenya's already asleep."

"Kenya called me about twenty minutes ago and asked me to come over."

Angela didn't respond. She just looked at me with a surprised look on her face.

"Mommy, is that Terry?" Kenya's little voice asked from the back room.

"Kenya, I told you to go to bed."

The next few moments, Angela and I just looked at each other without saying a word. Then I finally broke the silence.

"Angela, will you please tell me what's going on?" Angela didn't say a word. She stepped back and opened the door widely, allowing me to come inside. As I walked into her apartment, I noticed that most of her living room furniture was gone and several packing boxes were all over the floor.

"You're moving?" I asked

"Yes," she replied in a soft voice.

"Where are you moving?" Angela looked down at the floor, trying to avoid eye contact with me.

"I'm moving back to Chicago," she replied.

"What!? Are you seriously moving back to Chicago to get back together with Preston?"

"No, it's not like that. I don't want to be with him. Preston wants to become more involved in Kenya's life and that's going to be difficult if we live so far apart."

"When are you leaving?"

"If I get everything packed, we'll be leaving on Tuesday."

"This coming Tuesday?" I asked in amazement. "I don't believe this. When were you going to tell me about all of this? Or were you even going to tell me at all?"

Angela looked up at me, then put her head back down.

"I just didn't know how to tell you," she said, not even able to look me in my eyes. "I just told Kenya earlier today. I'm sorry she called you."

"I'm glad she called," I said, feeling very irritated. "At least I know *she* cares about me."

"Terry, I do care about you."

"No, you don't. If you really cared about me, you wouldn't just move to Chicago without talking to me first."

"This was a very difficult decision," she said, as she started putting various items in a packing box.

"What about law school?" I asked.

"I'm going to transfer to a law school in Chicago."

"You've got this all planned out, don't you?"

"I know you and your band have been busy getting ready for that big concert this Saturday. I know how important this concert is to you and I didn't want to cause you any distractions."

"What are you talking about?" I asked, raising my voice. "You have never been a distraction to me. I already have two reserved seats in the front row for you and Kenya because I wanted you to be there. I want you to be involved in my musical career. I want you and Kenya to be a part of my life."

"Terry, please don't do this. You don't know how hard this is for me. This is why I didn't want to tell you I was leaving. I didn't want to have this conversation with you. I love you, but I have to leave."

"You love me? How can you stand there and tell me you love me when you're moving to Chicago to be with Preston . . . and don't tell me you're doing this for Kenya. You've said out of your own mouth that Preston hasn't been a good father to her."

"That's not entirely true. He has taken care of her financially."

"Okay, Preston pays you child support. So what? That's his daughter. That's what he's supposed to do. There's more to being a good father than sending a check each month."

"He says he wants to be a part of Kenya's life and I can't deprive him of that."

"Preston hasn't been a part of Kenya's life for two years. Why all of a sudden does he want to play daddy now?"

Angela turned away from me and began packing kitchen items into a box.

"Maybe his conscience was bothering him." she responded. "Maybe he's finally grown up. I really don't know."

I walked up to her, grabbed her hand and pulled her toward me.

"All this time we've been spending together, I thought we had something special. I love you and I thought you loved me."

"Terry, you just don't understand."

"Then talk to me and help me understand."

Angela looked at me, turned away, and walked into her living room.

"If I continue to see you, it will cause me a lot of problems."

"Problems?" I asked. "What kind of problems?"

"Can we just drop it? I really don't feel like talking about this."

"No, we're going to talk about this," I said. "If I mean anything to you, you owe me some kind of explanation." I felt myself becoming angry as Angela continued to pack items into a large box. "Will you please stop packing that damn box and talk to me?" I said, raising my voice.

Angela turned toward me with tears in her eyes.

"Terry, I do love you, but I have to think about what's best for me and my daughter. I'm sure you've wondered how I can afford this place while going to school. Preston has been supporting me and Kenya the last two years. He sends me enough money each month to pay my rent, my tuition, and to take care of Kenya's expenses. Even though he hasn't been in her life physically, he has been there financially. He wants us to work things out and he's made it very clear that if I continue to see you, he'll cut me off financially. There's no way I'll be able to pay my rent, pay for law school, and take care of Kenya without his financial help."

"It sounds like he's controlling you with his money."

"It's not like that!" she fired back. "Terry, please try to understand. My dad left me and my mother when I was nine-years old. I know how hard it was for me growing up without my father. I don't want Kenya to go through that. I know Preston hasn't been a good father figure for Kenya, but I think he's honestly changed and wants to be a part of her life now."

"What about us?" I asked. "Doesn't our relationship mean anything to you?"

"You are so close to fulfilling your dream. Infinite Noise is on the verge of becoming a very successful band. In time you'll be traveling all over the country, performing in front of thousands of people. It's just a matter of time before you sign a lucrative contract with a major record label. The future looks bright for you and Infinite Noise. I have to think about me and my daughter . . . and our future."

"I was hoping you and Kenya would be an important part of *my* future," I said.

"I think it's best for me to go back to Chicago. Kenya and I would just slow you down."

"Don't do this, Angela. I know we can work this out," I said, pleading with her.

Angela reached out and held my hand.

"Please don't make this any harder for me. I'm sorry, but I'm moving back to Chicago."

As I looked into her teary eyes, it was very clear to me that she had made her decision and there was nothing I could say or do that would change her mind. Even though I was feeling angry and very hurt, I tried to compose myself.

"Okay, fine. I guess you've made your decision. If this is what you want to do, then go," I said, turning and walking to the door.

As I opened the door to leave, I stopped momentarily. "Will you please tell Kenya I said good-bye?"

"Yes, I'll tell her," she said softly.

For a brief moment, I stood there, looking at her as the tears flowed down her pretty face. Without saying another word, I walked out of Angela's door and out of her life.

Chapter 39

I was quietly sitting in a backstage dressing room at Phillips Arena with the rest of Infinite Noise. This large, domed facility, located in downtown Atlanta, served as the home field for the Atlanta Falcons football team and other entertainment and corporate events. Tonight, it would be the venue for a huge musical extravaganza. A large symphonic stage had been built inside this spacious arena to accommodate the various musical artists that had come to perform at this annual event. Twenty of the top bands from all over the country, not signed by a major record company, were invited to perform at this all day event. Our band won this event two years ago, but the word on the street was that a west coast rap group called the Bayside Boyz was favored to win this year's competition. It was 6:23 p.m. and on stage performing was a four-man group known as The Hard Times Homies, a gangster rap group out of Brooklyn, New York. They couldn't sing, couldn't play a single instrument, but their hardcore rap lyrics had made them famous all over the east coast. Even in our secluded dressing room, I could hear the muffled sounds of the group rapping in sync with the loud music. The crowd was really enjoying their performance as they screamed their approval. Suddenly, there was a knock at the door. The event stage manager stuck his head into our dressing room.

"Infinite Noise, you are scheduled to go onstage in about twenty five minutes," he informed us, before quickly leaving. I tried to look confident as my stomach began to churn. I reached for my guitar and began to tune the strings for the tenth time. As I looked around the room, each member of the band was preparing themselves in their own unique way. Damon was wiping his bass guitar with a white cloth. Warren was reclined in a chair with his headphones on, listening to music. Reggie was walking around tapping his drum sticks on anything in the room that would make noise. Layla was peering into a mirror making sure her hair and makeup were looking good. I could tell that everyone was nervous, but excited about performing in front of the large, sell-out crowd. The room was extremely quiet except for the constant tapping of Reggie's drumsticks.

"Relax, Reggie," I said. "Save some of that energy for the show."

"This is not good, Terry," he said, nervously.

"What are you talking about?" I asked.

"Listen to that crowd," Reggie replied.

"Do we have to come out after these guys? A hardcore rap group? That crowd is going to boo us off the stage."

"What's going on?" Warren asked, taking off his headphones.

"Reggie thinks we're going to get booed off the stage." I responded, walking toward everyone. "Is that how you all feel?" I asked. "We've performed in front of big crowds before. We know what we have to do. In case any of you forgot, we won this competition two years ago. We've been on the cover of Hotlanta Magazine for best new artists. We've performed in front of large crowds at the Atlanta Jazz festival, the Civic Center, Turner Field, and the Fox Theatre. Those other bands out there are good, but we have something those other bands don't have. We are a complete band. We can play jazz, R&B, rock and roll, gospel, and hip-hop. We could play some country and western if we wanted to," I said, sarcastically.

"Yee hah! You tell'em, buckaroo!" Warren said in a country and western accent.

Everyone began laughing which seemed to help settle our nerves a bit. Suddenly, there was another knock at the door. The door opened slightly and a security guard stuck his head in.

"Terry Freeman, there's a young lady here to see you," he said.

Everyone in the room stopped what they were doing and looked at me.

"Check you out, big brother. We haven't even performed yet and you already have the ladies tracking you down," Warren said, jokingly.

For a brief second, I wondered if it could be Angela, but after our conversation the other night, I didn't think it would be her.

"Could you please tell the young lady I can talk to her after the show?" I asked.

"Mr. Freeman, I think you might want to talk to her now," the security guard replied.

"Okay, I'll talk to her outside," I said, wondering who this mystery person could be.

As I walked outside the door of our dressing room, Kenya was standing there with a big smile on her face. Before I could say a word, she ran up to me and gave me a big hug. For several seconds, I hugged Kenya tightly, not wanting to let her go. After what seemed like minutes, we finally pulled apart.

"Kenya, what are you doing here?" I said, getting down on one knee so I could talk to her face-to-face.

"I came to see you and Infinite Noise perform," she replied with a big smile on her face.

"Where is your mother?"

"She's visiting my dad."

"Why aren't you with them?"

"I was with them and now I'm here with you."

"Kenya, please don't do this. This is a serious matter."

Kenya looked at me with those big, brown eyes and she could tell that I wasn't in the mood for games.

"Okay, will you promise not to get mad at me?" she asked.

"Yes, I promise. Please tell me what's going on."

"Mommy took me to see my daddy at this big hotel downtown. Since we were close by, I asked her if I could see you and the band perform tonight, but she and my daddy said no. So, I kind of snuck out and came here by myself."

"What?! Kenya, you shouldn't have done that!" I said, scolding her.

You came to my piano recital to see me perform, so I wanted to come here to see you perform. I'm sorry. I thought you would be happy to see me," she said with a sad look on her face.

"Sweetheart, of course I'm happy to see you, but you shouldn't have come down here by yourself without your mother's permission. How did you get here?"

"I got on the MARTA bus, then I just kinda followed the crowd. It wasn't hard to find," she said, proudly.

"Kenya, you're a smart little girl, but you shouldn't have come here all by yourself."

"I made it here, didn't I?" she said, with a mischievous smile.

I gritted my teeth, trying my best not to smile at her cute little comment.

"I need to call your mother. Come inside with me and wait until she gets here," I said, gently grabbing her hand.

"Hey, everybody!" Kenya yelled as we entered the dressing room.

"Kenya! It's so good to see you!" Layla said, giving her a big hug.

"You look so pretty, Layla. I just love your dress," Kenya said with her cute little voice.

As the rest of the band members greeted Kenya, I reached into my travel bag to retrieve my cell phone. As happy as I was to see Kenya, I knew I needed to contact Angela and let her know what was going on. After two rings, Angela answered the phone.

"Terry, I can't talk right now! Kenya is missing!" she said, frantically.

"Angela, calm down. Kenya is here with me at Phillips Arena. She's fine," I said, reassuring her.

"Thank God! I was about to lose my mind. I'm leaving now to come get her."

"When you get here, come to the security gate and I'll have them bring you directly here to our dressing room.

"Thank you, Terry. I'm already downtown, so I'll be there in fifteen minutes."

I walked up to Kenya who was surrounded by everyone in the band.

"Kenya, I just spoke with your mom. She'll be here in about fifteen minutes."

"Awww, man," she whined.

"I'm sorry, but I had to call her and let her know you're okay. I'm sure she's been worried sick about you."

"Will I be able to stay and watch you guys perform?" she asked.

"I don't know, sweetheart," I replied. "Your mother sounded pretty upset."

"Will you talk to her and ask if I can stay?"

I could tell that Kenya was happy and very excited to be with us, but I didn't want to get her hopes up that she could stay for our show.

"Hey everyone, I need to talk to Kenya for a second," I said, putting my arm around her shoulder.

As we walked to the other side of the room, Kenya put her arm around my waist.

"I missed you so much." she said, looking up at me with her gorgeous smile.

"I missed you, too."

"If you missed me, why haven't you come by to see me?"

"I wanted to see you, but your mother thought I shouldn't come by for a while after your accident."

"I told her it wasn't your fault that I got hurt. I told my dad, too, but I guess they didn't believe me. You're not mad at me, are you?"

"Of course not, but you shouldn't have come here by yourself," I said, trying to look serious. "But, now that you're here, I am so happy to see you," I said giving her a big hug.

For the next fifteen minutes, Kenya walked around the dressing room, playfully interacting with everyone in the band. I think Kenya's unexpected visit was just what we all needed. Talking and joking with Kenya seemed to have helped everyone relax. I looked at my watch and began to worry. Our band was scheduled to go onstage to perform in eight minutes and Angela hadn't arrived yet. I decided the best thing to do was to ask one of the security guards to stay with Kenya in our dressing room until Angela arrived. Suddenly, the dressing room door opened as Angela and Preston came rushing into the room.

"Kenya, thank God you're alright," Angela said, hugging Kenya tightly. "Why would you do something like this?"

"I'm sorry, mommy. I didn't want to miss their show."

Reggie noticed the clean cut, well-dressed man standing next to Angela.

"Who's Mr. Pretty Boy?" Reggie whispered to me.

"That's Kenya's father," I replied, quietly.

"Awww, shit. It's getting ready to get real ugly up in here," Reggie said, snickering.

Preston walked up and put his arm around Kenya.

"Young lady, I can't believe you would worry me and your mother like this," Preston said, angrily.

"I'm sorry, daddy. I just wanted to see my friends perform. Can I please stay?"

"After this little stunt you pulled, I don't think so!" Preston replied, sternly.

Kenya reached up and grabbed Angela's hand.

"Please, mommy, can I stay?"

"Angela, I can get VIP seats for the three of you. You're already here, you may as well stay for the show," I said.

"I'm not sure," Angela said, contemplating. "Maybe we can stay for . . ."

"Absolutely not!" Preston said, cutting Angela off. "Kenya needs to learn that she can't just sneak away whenever she wants to.

"Daddy, I'm sorry for sneaking away, but I really wanted to see my friends perform. Please let me stay."

"No, Kenya, we're leaving!" he said, grabbing Kenya by the arm.

I tried to remain calm, but the sight of Preston grabbing Kenya's arm was more that I could take.

"Hey, is that really necessary?" I asked, walking toward Preston.

"Angela, take our daughter to the car. I need to talk to your friend."

"Preston, let's just go," Angela said, grabbing Preston's arm.

"Please take Kenya to the car!" he said, firmly.

Angela put her arm around Kenya and walked her toward the door. Kenya stopped, turned and looked at me with a sadness that melted my heart.

"I'm sorry, Terry," she said with tears in her eyes.

"It's okay, Kenya," I said as Angela escorted her out of the dressing room.

Once Angela and Kenya left the room and the door closed behind them, Reggie wasn't able to contain his temper any longer.

"What's your problem, man? Why can't she stay for the show?"

"Why can't you mind your own business?" Preston replied, arrogantly.

"Why don't you make me mind my own business?" Reggie fired back, walking toward Preston.

"Reggie, back off!" I said, stepping in front of him to block his way.

"Who does this high yellow negro think he is, walking in here like he's all that?"

"I've got this, Reggie." I said, turning to face Preston. "If you've got something to say to me, say it and leave."

"Freeman, you need to stay away from my daughter. You're lucky I don't call the police and press charges against you."

"Press charges for what?" I asked, looking bewildered.

"For persuading an eight-year-old to come down here to this concert by herself!"

"First of all, she's nine-years-old," I said, correcting him. "Second, I didn't persuade Kenya to come down here. But you're right, Kenya shouldn't have come down here by herself. She made a mistake and I hope you won't come down too hard on her."

"I don't need you to tell me how to discipline my daughter! This is the second time you've put my daughter in a dangerous situation. You need to stay the hell away from my daughter. Do we understand each other?" he asked, trying to talk tough.

I had tried my best to control my anger, but he finally pushed me too far. I walked up to Preston and got directly in his face.

"The only thing I understand is that you're a whining, little, bitch, and a sorry excuse for a father."

I could see the anger in Preston's eyes, but he knew he didn't want to get into a physical confrontation with me, especially with Warren and Reggie standing a few feet away, just itching to kick his ass.

"You and your small-time band are not worth my time, Freeman," he said with disdain in his voice.

Preston turned and walked toward the door to leave. As he opened the door, he stopped to throw one more verbal jab at me.

"You had your little fun with Angela and you got your chance to play pretend daddy with Kenya, but that's all over now. Angela and Kenya are coming back to Chicago to be with me. Whatever bond you think you developed with them . . . it's over. Don't ever forget one important fact. Angela and I have a daughter together and that's a bond you can never break," he said, arrogantly.

Before I could say anything, he walked out of the dressing room, slamming the door behind him. My first impulse was to go after him and punch him in his arrogant face, but I reminded myself that I was getting ready for a very important performance. For several seconds everyone in the room was quiet, not knowing what to say. Finally, Reggie broke the silence.

"You should have kicked his ass, Terry."

Layla walked up to me and gave me a hug.

"Are you okay?" she asked.

"Yeah, I'm fine," I said, trying to force a smile. "As a matter of fact, I feel great. I can't wait to go out there and prove to Preston and other assholes like him that Infinite Noise is the real deal."

The dressing room door opened and a concert employee stuck his head inside.

"Infinite Noise, you're up in five minutes," he said, closing the door behind him.

I turned around and looked into the faces of my family and friends. I could tell that everyone was upset about the incident that just took place. I'm sure they were all concerned about how it was going to affect me. This was going to be a very important night for us and I wanted them to know that I was focused and ready to put on a great show. Before each performance, one of us is chosen to lead a prayer. I wanted everyone to know that the incident had not shaken me, so I decided to lead the prayer. I smiled as I looked at everyone and began to speak with a confident tone in my voice.

"Let's bow our heads and pray," I said as everyone joined hands. "Dear Lord, thank you for giving us this opportunity to display our talents in front of this large crowd this evening. Please be with us tonight and help us to perform to the best of our abilities. In your name we pray, amen."

"Amen!" everyone said in unison.

As I looked into the eyes of everyone standing around me, I could sense their nervousness. As I picked up my guitar, I could feel my hands trembling. The insides of my stomach felt like they were twisting into knots. This was arguably the most important performance of our careers. We were all aware that talent scouts, producers, and music recording executives from around the country would be watching. However, I wasn't worried. This was a proud and talented group of people and I knew they would perform at their best. As each band member started walking out of the dressing room, I decided to give the group a quick pep talk.

"Hey!" I yelled loudly. Everyone stopped, turned, and looked at me. "Let's go out there and put on a show these people will never forget!"

"Hell, yeah!" Warren responded.

As we walked closer to the main stage, we were greeted by Jerome Bradley, the concert organizer and MC of this show.

"Are you guys ready?" Jerome asked.

"Damn right, we're ready!" Reggie said, excitedly.

"Remember, you get thirty minutes to perform and that includes the time it takes for you to set up on stage. Please try to stay within that time frame. Good luck," he said, walking out to the center of the main stage.

Jerome walked up to a microphone stand and began to pump up the crowd.

"What's up, Atlanta?! I told you we were going to tear the roof off this arena tonight! Are you ready for more music?!" The crowd cheered loudly in response. "Alright, we've got three more bands to go, people! The next group performing tonight is straight out of the ATL. They've been voted "best new artists" by Top Music Magazine. They are former winners of the Battle of the Bands. Please show some love for . . . Infinite Noise!"

The roar of the crowd was deafening as we walked out to the main stage. I looked out into the crowd and saw what appeared to be thousands of people spread out all over the arena. The bright flashing lights from cameras and the cheering of the crowd was almost overwhelming. As I put my guitar strap around my neck, I felt that queasy feeling in the pit of my stomach I always get before a big performance. On the right side of the stage, I saw Gary Reed, the concert sound engineer, signaling to us to play our instruments, so he could adjust the volume on his sound board. After a few seconds, he gave us the "thumbs up" sign, letting us know we could begin our performance. I knew there were several music producers, promoters, and music reporters in the building watching us, but I really didn't care. All I wanted was for us to put on a great show and entertain the audience. As I listened to the loud, frenzied crowd, I could feel their passion and energy. The louder the crowd yelled, the more it motivated and inspired me. All my nervousness and doubts had faded away and was replaced with confidence and positive energy. The time had come. It was time to show everyone that Infinite Noise was one of the most musically-talented and entertaining bands of this generation. I looked around the stage and saw that everyone was ready to perform. I turned my back to the audience so I could make eye contact with everyone in the band.

"Let's do this!" I said, loudly.

I took a deep breath, nodded my head, and we began to play. For the next thirty minutes, our band put on a performance that had the entire crowd dancing, singing, and cheering throughout the entire arena. The energy and emotion that we put into our music and the positive feedback we got back from the crowd was absolutely exhilarating. After finishing our final song, I felt a great sense of accomplishment, knowing that all of the hard work, the long hours of practice, and all of our sacrifices had finally paid off. We wanted to put on a great performance and the deafening sound of the cheering crowd confirmed that we had succeeded. Infinite Noise was back!

The Decision

It was a chilly Friday evening. Paul and I were sitting at an office desk, reading over a contract proposal inside of an old office building I leased two months ago. After our recent success at the Battle of the Bands, I decided it would be advantageous for Infinite Noise to have its own office building to handle all of our business affairs. Forty-five minutes earlier, Paul and I were involved in an intense meeting with two producers from Rise Up Records, a local record company located in the business district of Buckhead.

"So, what do you think, Paul?"

"It looks good." Paul replied, skimming through the contract pages.

"I don't know," I said leaning back in my new office chair. "I'm not sure it's the best offer.

"It's a three year contract for $6.2 million. In the second year of the contract, you'll be doing a twenty one city tour, twenty thousand dollars appearance fee, and one percent of the total gate revenue. By the end of the contract, . . ." he paused to tap the figures on his calculator. "Each of you could earn roughly $1.4 million before taxes. Rise Up Records is by far the best offer we've received in the last two months."

Paul obviously noticed the apprehensive look on my face. "Alright, what's wrong?"

"There are a few things in the contract I'm not sure about," I replied.

"Let me guess . . . page sixteen, paragraph five, *"Artist agrees to fully cooperate with the Company, in good faith, in the production of the Recording. Artist also agrees to assign to the Company all of his/her rights and interest to the songs, artist's performance of the songs, and the title of the Recording."*

"I'm just not comfortable with that." I said.

"The next best offer is Peach State Records," Paul said, putting on his reading glasses.

"They're offering a two-year $5.4 million contract. They have some pretty good perks, like the ten-percent in royalties."

"And if we go with Peach State, we'll have more control of our music," I chimed in.

"That's true, but let's compare." Paul said, scanning over the paperwork. "At the end of the contract, each band member will earn about $576,000 dollars with Rise Up Records," If you sign with Peach State Records, each member will earn roughly $207,000. Come on, you do the math."

"I've already done the math," I replied.

"I know you don't want to give up the rights to your music to any record company, but you have to understand that this is a multi-million dollar business. Record companies want as much control as possible to maximize their chances of making a profit."

"I do understand. Infinite Noise can make more money with Rise Up Records, but lose the ownership rights on our music. If the record company wants our band to put out some musical garbage that degrades black people, we have to do it because we're getting paid a lot of money to follow and obey. Believe me, I have a very good understanding."

Paul began putting all the contractual paperwork into his briefcase. I understood what he was trying to explain to me, but I just wasn't ready to give up control of our music.

"Terry, it's been two months since you guys won the Battle of the Bands. Infinite Noise is very hot right now, but we can't keep turning down contract offers. We need to take advantage of the band's popularity while you're still in the spotlight. As your business manager, it's my job to get you the best deal possible. However, as your friend, I think you need to go with the offer that feels right for you. I don't want you to have any doubts or regrets. Of course, there are four other people in this equation you have to consider."

"Yeah, you're right. I already know Warren and Reggie will want to sign with Rise Up Records. I'm not sure what Damon and Layla will decide."

"Whatever you decide, I'll back you all the way," Paul said.

"Thanks, I appreciate that. Okay, before we make any decisions, let me talk to the rest of the group and let them know what's going on," I said, leaning back in my chair and rubbing my eyes.

"You look exhausted," Paul said, sounding concerned. "You need to go home and get some rest. I'll call everyone and let them know about the contract proposals."

"I'll be fine as soon as this kicks in," I said, opening up an energy drink.

"You can't continue at this pace drinking coffee and energy drinks."

"I'm also taking multi-vitamins," I replied, trying to be humorous.

"You won't think it's funny when you end up in the hospital from exhaustion. You need to slow down."

"Slow down? I've got too many important things to do."

"I'm serious about this. For the past two months, you and the band have been performing all over the Southeast. You've done around sixty radio and TV interviews in twenty-three different cities, and now you're planning to use this office building to open up a youth community center. Don't get me wrong, I think it's great you want to give back to the community and help under- privileged kids, but why did you pick this part of town?"

"I know this area has a bad reputation, but that's why the youth center needs to be here. These kids need a safe and positive place they can go to instead of hanging out on the streets," I said, still rubbing my tired eyes.

"Just look at you. You can barely keep your eyes open. You need to go home and . . ."

"I said I'll be fine!" I said, cutting him off.

"Terry, as your business manager and, even more important, your friend, I'm asking you to ease up. You hired me to help you with some of these projects. You don't have to do all of this on your own. Let me do my job."

I was tempted to argue with Paul, but I felt so tired, I just leaned back in my chair and closed my eyes.

"Okay, maybe you're right," I said, barely able to keep my eyes open. I guess I'm so used to handling all of Infinite Noise's business affairs that it's hard for me to let go."

"I understand. I just want you to know that I'm here if you need me."

Paul's words truly touched me and warmed my heart because I knew he was being sincere.

"I want to thank you for all of your hard work and dedication to our band. You've been a good business manager and a good friend."

"No, I should be the one thanking you. You could have hired any attorney in this city, but you chose me and I appreciate that."

"Well, you did come highly-recommended," I said, reminding him of how we met.

I could tell by the look on Paul's face that my comment caught him completely off-guard. It had been months since the subject of Angela Greer had come up in our conversations.

"Have you spoken to her since she moved back to Chicago?"

"No, I haven't."

"Maybe you should call her. It's been over two months. Maybe things have changed."

"Why should I call her? She's the one who moved back to Chicago to get back together with Kenya's father. Damn her!"

For a few moments, I was feeling angry and frustrated. Then I realized that I was taking my anger out on the wrong person. Paul was not the person that had filled me with so much anger and frustration.

"I'm sorry about that, Paul."

"It's okay. I understand. I've been there before."

"I still can't believe she left me like that."

"Hey, it's her loss. You and Infinite Noise are getting ready to get paid big-time. If it was me, I would call her just to rub her nose in all the money I was getting ready to make."

"I'd like to think I wouldn't lower myself to that level of immaturity," I said, looking very serious. "Let me stop lying. I've seriously thought about it," I said, as we both started laughing.

"I know what we can do. When we update the Infinite Noise website, you should let me put how much money you and the band will make on the next tour. That would really stick it to her.

"Wow, Paul. I never realized you were so devious. Remind me to never get on your bad side."

The two of us laughed for several minutes, which is exactly what we needed after two months of intense contract negotiations and numerous business meetings.

"By the way, Terry, I talked with Jericho Promotions yesterday and they want to talk about Infinite Noise doing a twenty-five city tour starting around May or June of next year."

"What did you tell them?"

"I told them I'd let them know something after I talked with all of you guys. I didn't think you wanted to do too much touring during those months with Warren and Layla getting married next spring."

"That was very thoughtful of you, Paul."

"In case you're interested, Jericho Promotions is offering a $75,000 appearance fee and one percent of the total gate at each venue where you perform. I've done the calculations, if you're interested."

"No, that's it for me. If I hear about any more numbers tonight, my head will explode."

"I understand. One more thing. If you decide you want to sign with Jericho Promotions, I'll make sure that Chicago is one of the cities on the tour."

"Why Chicago?" I asked, even though I already knew the answer.

"It would give Kenya a chance to come watch you guys perform."

"Paul, I appreciate what you're trying to do, but I'm putting all of that emotional baggage behind me. I'm sure Angela and Kenya have moved on with their lives and I need to do the same."

"Okay, it was worth a try. Anyway, I've got to finish some paper work at the law office, but before I go, I wanted to give you something."

Paul opened his briefcase and pulled out a small bottle of champagne. "Here you go," he said, handing me the bottle.

"What's this, an early Christmas gift?"

"No, this is a small gesture on my part to say congratulations on a very successful year for you and Infinite Noise."

"I'm glad it's not a bottle of Moet," I said, laughing to myself. Paul looked at me with a puzzled look on his face. "Never mind, it's a private joke. Anyway, thank you for the champagne," I said, reaching over the desk and shaking his hand.

"You're welcome. Now, please go home and get some sleep," he said, getting up to leave.

"Okay, I will. Have a good weekend." I said, as Paul walked out of the office.

I waited a few minutes to make sure Paul had left the office building and I turned on my computer. "Go home and get some sleep. He must be crazy. I've got too many important things to do," I muttered to myself. As I tried to update the Infinite Noise website, the computer screen became very blurry. I leaned back in my chair and closed my eyes. "Okay, maybe he's not so crazy," I said to myself. I opened my eyes and began to smile when I saw the bottle of champagne on my desk. Paul was absolutely right. This was a very successful year for Infinite Noise. Earlier this year, Infinite Noise started performing again after a two year break. Then we won the Battle of the Bands a few months ago. One month later, we recorded our first CD in over two years. The CD went gold in six weeks, selling over one million copies and each band member received a very nice payment. Reggie formed a new, young rap group called the Xtreme Team, which he is now managing. Damon and Gail moved into a beautiful home in Decatur with a big back yard for Darius to play in. Warren and Layla got engaged and have planned their wedding for next June. Other than Angela running back to Chicago to get back with Preston, it had been a very good year. My thoughts were interrupted by the ringing of the office telephone. I really didn't feel like talking to anyone, so I waited for the answering machine to get the call. "Hello, Terry," a man's voice said from the answering machine speaker. "This is Jack Murphy with Skyline Properties. I know your building lease doesn't expire until the end of this month, but I was wondering if you've made a decision about doing the two year extension we talked about. I'm going to be flying out of town tomorrow morning for Christmas vacation and won't be returning for two weeks. If you could call me back before I leave, I would really appreciate it." After hearing the message, I realized that Paul might be right. With the recent success of the band and doing numerous radio and television appearances, I really didn't have the time to open a youth center. I needed to call Jack Murphy and cancel the building rental lease. I didn't think it was very smart to pay Murphy another $1,500 if I wasn't going to be here next month. I reached into my jacket, pulled out my wallet, and began searching for Jack Murphy's business card. I looked through every part of my wallet, but couldn't find his business card anywhere. I tossed my wallet on top of the desk and began searching through the pockets of my jacket. I suddenly remembered that Paul had Murphy's number. I quickly grabbed my cell phone and dialed Paul's number. After the first ring, Paul's voice mail came on. He must be talking on his phone, I thought to myself. I quickly jump out of my seat and ran out of the building in an attempt to catch up with Paul before he left. As I ran outside into the cold, night air, I saw Paul's car driving away in the distance. "Damn, I just missed him," I muttered to myself, trying to catch my breath. I figured I would just call him later and get the number. As I walked back to the office building, I was so engrossed in my thoughts that I barely noticed the two guys approaching me. As I reached the entrance of the building, one of the guys walked up behind me. I quickly turned around and noticed a teenager around seventeen-years old, with a cigarette dangling between his lips. The other teen, standing a few feet away, appeared to be about fourteen-years old.

"Hey, homey, you got a light?"

"No, sorry, I don't smoke."

Suddenly, the teen standing next to me reached into his jacket and pulled out a small 9 mm handgun.

"Yo, nigga, give me your wallet!" he said, nervously looking around.

"Are you serious?" I asked, feeling more shocked than frightened.

"Nigga, give me your damn wallet or I'll shoot yo' ass!" he said, angrily.

"Okay, calm down," I said, reaching into my jacket. A sense of dread came over me as I realized I left my wallet inside on the office desk.

"I don't have my wallet on me," I said, staring at the gun in the teen's trembling hand.

"Look, nigga, don't fuck with me! I will blast yo' ass right here!"

"Hurry up, C-Dog! What's the problem?" the other teen said, walking up.

"This lying nigga sayin' he ain't got no wallet on him."

"I'm not lying. Here, see for yourself," I said, taking off my jacket and handing it to the teen.

The teenager snatched the jacket from me and quickly searched through all the pockets.

"There ain't shit in here," he said, angrily. "Empty your pockets, nigga!"

I reached into my pockets and pulled them inside out, showing the teen I had nothing in them.

"I oughtta shoot yo' broke ass for wastin' my fuckin' time," he said, pointing the handgun mere inches from my face.

I tried to speak, but I was overcome with fear. Not fear from this young punk shooting me, but from the fear of my mother having to go through this painful ordeal again. As I stared at the barrel of the gun in my face, I wondered if this was how my father felt in that dark parking lot two years ago. I looked into the teen's eyes and saw his nervousness and fear. I wondered if there was a chance I could reason with the teen.

"Hey, don't do this," I said calmly. "I have a little girl at home."

"I don't give a fuck about yo' little girl. If you don't come up with some money, I'm gonna shoot yo' ass," he said, jabbing the gun in my face.

It became very obvious to me that this little punk was going to shoot me if I didn't give him something of value.

"C-Dog, you need to hurry up before somebody comes," the younger teen yelled.

"Shut the fuck up and keep a look-out. I got this handled," he yelled back at the younger teen. "Gimme that ring!" the teen said, jabbing the gun at me.

I looked at my hand and realized the ring that the teen wanted was a gift my mother and father gave me on my twenty first birthday. Even though I didn't want to give him my ring, I realized I really didn't have a choice. I tried to take the ring off, but it wouldn't slide off my finger.

"Hurry up, nigga!"

"I'm trying, but it won't come off," I said, still tugging and twisting the ring.

"Don't fuck wit me, nigga! Gimme that damn ring or I'll blow yo' fuckin' head off!"

Suddenly, a beam of light came shining toward us from down the street.

"Yo, C-Dog! Somebody's coming!" the younger teen yelled, as a car came down the street.

I quickly realized that the distraction was my only chance to get out of the situation alive, so I decided to make my move. The on-coming car distracted the older teen long enough for me to lunge at him and grab the hand that was holding the gun. I could feel the teen's hand tense, as he pulled on the trigger, but instead of hearing the explosive sound of gun fire, I heard a soft metallic click. Thank God, the gun misfired, I thought to myself. The surprised teen swung at me with his other hand, hitting me above my right eye. I immediately felt a stream of blood trickle down the side of my face. In anger and desperation, I twisted and bent the teen's wrist backwards until I heard a muffled pop. The teen screamed out in agony as the gun fell to the ground. With my heart racing and my adrenaline flowing, I swung at the teen's face and landed a solid blow to his jaw, sending him sprawling to the cold, hard pavement. The other teen saw the handgun on the ground, a few feet away from me. He tried to run over and retrieve the gun, but the car coming down the street, blocked him off. I quickly ran over and picked the gun up from the street. As the car passed and continued up the street, the younger teen saw the gun in my hand. With a look of fear on his face, he quickly turned and ran down the dimly lit street. I turned my attention to C-Dog, who was lying on the street, still dazed from my punch. As I walked over to him, I used my shirt sleeve to wipe the blood dripping down my face. C-Dog began crawling on the cold street, trying his best to stand up. He looked up and saw me standing over him, holding the gun in my hand.

"Don't hit me no more, man. I think you broke my jaw," he said, spitting a mouthful of blood on the pavement. "Hey, man. I'm sorry. Please don't shoot me," he said as he began to cry.

As I looked down at the young teen sobbing and pleading in front of me, I almost felt sorry for him. "What's your name, kid?"

"They call me C-Dog." he replied, grimacing in pain.

"What's your real name, boy?!" I asked, raising my voice.

"Cory," he said, softly.

"How old are you?

"Fifteen," he said with tears streaming down his face.

This kid was only fifteen-years old, I thought to myself. He should have been at home watching TV, playing video games, or talking to his friends on the phone. Instead, this young punk was out on the streets, trying to rob people. Suddenly, the teen tried to stand up.

"Stay down!" I yelled, pointing the gun at the teen.

"Okay, man. I'll stay down. Just don't shoot me," he pleaded as he flopped back down on the cold pavement, holding his wrist. "Oh, God, it hurts. I think you broke my wrist," he said, gritting his teeth in pain. "Hey, man, I swear to God, I wasn't gonna hurt you. I was just tryin' to scare you, that's all."

"Shut up!" I said, tired of hearing his whining.

For several seconds, I looked down at the scared teen who was shivering on the cold street, contemplating my next move. If I called the police, I'm sure the fifteen-year-old boy would be sent to a youth detention center or possibly to jail. Either way, after he got out, I knew he would be right back on the streets looking for a new person to rob or possibly kill.

"Cory, do you believe in God?"

"What?" Cory asked, looking confused.

"You keep swearing to God. Do you truly believe in God?"

"Yeah, I guess I do."

I looked at the teen with a hard piercing stare.

"Cory, you've got three options. Option one, I can call the police and you'll be arrested and charged with attempted armed robbery. Option two, I can go ahead and blow your head off and tell the police I was defending myself," I said, raising the gun and pointing it at Cory's face. "Option three, you can swear to God that you'll stay out of trouble and never rob anyone else again and maybe I'll let you go."

"I swear to God, I'll never rob anyone else again. I swear I won't," he said, getting on his knees, pleading.

"It doesn't feel so good having a gun in your face, does it?" The teen dropped his head down and didn't answer. "Answer me!" I yelled.

"No, it doesn't feel good!" he said, sobbing.

"God is smiling on you tonight, Cory. This is your chance to get your life together. No more robbing!" I said, firmly.

"Yeah, I swear to God, no more robbing!"

"Get up, Cory. Get out of here before I change my mind."

Cory staggered to his feet and cautiously walked backwards, still facing me, probably worried that I would shoot him in the back. Once he was at a safe distance, Cory turned and ran down the darkened street. As I walked back to the office building, I could feel my heart racing and my body trembling. I entered the building and quickly locked the door behind me. I walked into the office, staring at my wallet, cell phone and car keys I had left on the desk. As I took a few deep breaths to calm myself down, I realized that I still had the teenager's gun in my hand. I took the magazine clip out of the gun and found that it was fully loaded. That young punk was serious about shooting someone tonight, I thought to myself. I knew the logical thing to do was to call the police and report the attempted robbery, but I wasn't feeling very logical at that time. If I called the police, there would be numerous questions, statements to be made, paperwork to fill out and a loaded gun with my fingerprints all over it. I came up with a better idea. On my drive home, I would throw the gun out of my window as I crossed the bridge over the Chattahoochee River. I figured the gun could never be used to harm anyone again if it was resting at the bottom of the river. I gently placed the gun on the desk and sat down. I leaned back in the chair and covered my face with my hands as the realization of almost losing my life began to sink into my head. "Thank you, Jesus," I whispered to myself. If not for the pain from the gash above my eye and the blood stains on my shirt, I would have almost believed I had just awakened from a bad dream. As I sat there staring at the gun on the desk, I began to realize that I was wasting my time trying to open a youth center. Who was I fooling? A lot of these young kids don't care about staying out of trouble or going to school and getting an education. All they cared about was hanging out on the streets with their friends, getting drunk or getting high. They could care less about finding a good job and supporting themselves. All they cared about was finding a quick way to make money which usually involved selling illegal drugs or robbing someone. What the hell was I doing here? After all the years of practicing and performing all over the country with my band, I was finally in a position to reach my goal of signing Infinite Noise to a major record deal. So, why was I wasting my time trying to open a youth center in one of the most crime- infested areas in the city? I wasn't a social worker or a guidance counselor. I was just a hard-working musician trying to make it to the top. Instead of sitting in an old, drafty, office building, I should have been at home wrapping Christmas gifts or writing some new songs for our next concert. I should have been focusing all of my time and energy on Infinite Noise. I needed to go swallow my pride and sign that contract with Rise Up Records. I knew that would mean our band wouldn't have control over our music, but it was time for me to accept the fact that the music industry was in control. Our band was just a little fish in a huge ocean. If Infinite Noise was going to be successful, I would have to play by their rules. It was pretty obvious what I needed to do. I needed to call Jack Murphy, cancel the lease for the building, sign with Rise Up Records, and finally make some real money. I didn't even know why I made it such a difficult decision. I almost lost my life trying to open a youth center, but through the grace of God, I was still alive. "Through the grace of God," I said to myself, smiling. I probably should be dead right now, but God was with me. Suddenly, it became clear to me. I knew what I needed to do. I reached for my cell phone, pulled up Paul's number and tried to call him again. He answered.

"Hey, Paul. I've made my decision. I want to keep looking until we get a contract offer that will allow our band to be in control of our music and image. I also need you to contact Jericho Promotions and let them know we're very interested in doing the tour, but it will have to wait until next summer. If they agree, make sure Chicago will be one of the cities on the tour. One last thing. Please call Jack Murphy of Skyline Properties. Let him know I want to sign that two-year lease extension on this office building.

Yes, I'm sure that's what I want to do. I'm moving forward with the youth center. Thanks, Paul. I'll be in touch with you."

As I put my cell phone down on the desk, I leaned back in my chair and smiled. I felt a sense of happiness and inner peace, knowing that I had made the right decision. It was the only decision I could have made. After all, it's what my father would have wanted me to do.